Waterfall

WATERFALL

DAVID ZINI

LANGDON STREET PRESS

Copyright © 2011 by David Zini.

Langdon Street Press
212 3rd Avenue North, Suite 290
Minneapolis, MN 55401
612.455.2293
www.langdonstreetpress.com

All rights reserved. No part of this publication may be reproduced, stored in a retrieval system, or transmitted, in any form or by any means, electronic, mechanical, photocopying, recording, or otherwise, without the prior written permission of the author.

All characters appearing in this work are fictitious. Any resemblance to real persons, living or dead, is purely coincidental.

ISBN-13: 978-1-936782-56-7
LCCN: 2011939141

Distributed by Itasca Books

Edited by Marly Cornell
Cover Design and Typeset by Nate Meyers

Printed in the United States of America

CONTENTS

Prologue vii

PART 1: Tunes, Goons, and Swoons 1

PART 2: Shiv.. 99

PART 3: Say Who? 187

PART 4: Double Take 237

PART 5: Twilight Zone 317

Epilogue 361

PROLOGUE

The African sun seared the back of Chiamaka's neck, as it did most every morning. Dreams of answered prayers for rain evaporated along with the sparse dew. Finding the creek bed to be every bit as dry as it had appeared in the distance, Chiamaka moved on. Finally, after two hours of fighting off unbearable heat and depression, she spotted the smallest of springs, a barely perceptible rivulet of water bubbling out of the ground, mercifully providing nourishment to a few miserable tufts of wool grass. Chiamaka bent down, tipping her ladle to catch little more than a few spoonfuls, carefully transferring them to her bucket. An hour's worth of repetition would result in a day's supply of the precious liquid.

Thousands of miles away in a wealthy suburb of Denver, Colorado, a computer screen displayed a graph depicting Chiamaka's dismal existence and forecasting an even more abysmal future for her and her family.

"You see, Jeremy, where these two lines intersect? The tipping point. After that, it's game over."

"I get the picture, Ross. The singularity where world population growth outstrips the earth's ability to sustain those numbers."

"Exactly. And, of course, one can only imagine the nightmare to follow: war, famine, utter chaos. Mankind—those who survive, that is—will be catapulted back centuries. Subsistence living will be the new luxury."

Ross donned a wry smile. "Obviously, we cannot allow that to happen. Quite simply, some will have to exit."

"And the Council? I assume they are aware of the gravity of the situation. Are they still good with the plans to mitigate this whole ugly scenario?"

"Oh, yes, they're quite satisfied—except for Margaret. She would welcome an *immediate* mass extinction if only, in her words, to keep 'the loathsome beggars' out of her flower garden. I mean, I like her enthusiasm but her technicals could use refining."

"Well, Ross, my guess is that we have little choice but to forge ahead. Count me in."

"That's good, Jeremy, that's very good."

PART ONE

Tunes, Goons, and Swoons

Chapter 1

Michael Carpenter stared deeply into the glass of water held by a hand barely in control, his body resonating with waves of surreal thoughts surfacing in tandem with gut-wrenching emotions. Suddenly, it all focused on a single theme. What would his family, his friends, think? What conclusions would they come to?

In his mind's eye he could see his two children, Emily and Jacob, running through the sprinkler in the front yard, their laughing faces frozen in a cell phone picture. The scene overloaded his mental circuit breakers, his thoughts rerouted to the dreary blackness of the here and now.

The inevitable could be put off no longer. The time had come; there was no other way. Michael Carpenter gave a little sigh, hesitated slightly, and returned the somber stares of the pills. First the pills, then the water. He lifted the glass to his lips—and drank.

In a few minutes it was over.

The lazy July morning found Sergeant Mark Truitt of the Minneapolis Metropolitan Police Department completing the paperwork on yet another murder case. After a trend of declining homicides, this year had been brutal for the Twin Cities. A sudden upsurge in violence had stretched the department razor thin, engaging its personnel with the sole task of keeping the peace rather than the preferred option of promoting it. Sergeant Truitt, a twenty-five-year veteran, was not even making "baby steps" of progress in most of his assigned cases. Doing his best to ignore the effects of a more-than-less unreliable air conditioning system, Truitt concentrated on the task at hand.

As he was about to open a file on the latest unsolved murder, Truitt heard footsteps closing in from behind. One shoe spanked the floor with a little less intensity than the other; he knew the gait well. The slight limp was the result of an old bullet wound and belonged to his supervisor, Lieutenant Guy Lompello.

Lompello was not only Truitt's superior; he was also his mentor and friend. From the onset of Mark's law enforcement career, Guy had taken him under his wing, teaching him the finer points of the profession while demanding from Mark the highest of standards. Both their professional and personal relationships blossomed to the point where Mark came to regard Guy as part of his family. Lompello was grateful for this as he had no family of his own.

Though at the doorstep of full retirement age, Lompello harbored no thoughts of terminating his career. An impeccable record, dedication to duty, and type-A personality drove him on. Police work was his life, as it had been his father's and grandfather's before him. Waiting around to die, as Lompello referred to retirement, wasn't an option.

Though Lompello's interaction with others generally resembled all the finesse of an elephant stepping on an ant hill, most everyone understood Guy's earthy temperament—crusty on the outside, soft but explosive on the inside.

"Mark, got a minute?" Lompello called out as he approached Truitt's desk. Accordingly, his definition of "Got a minute?" translated to: "Drop whatever you're doing and focus on me."

Because their mutual show of affection routinely required a complementary dose of bantering, Truitt attempted a feigned resistance at Lompello's request.

"Actually, Guy, I was...."

"Good." Lompello maneuvered a cutoff. "We just got a call from the Terrace Inn. A body was found in one of their rooms. The motel registrar shows that the deceased checked in last evening. Better take a ride over there and see what's going on."

Truitt let out a purposeful sigh and lifted himself out of his chair. "I may be wrong, but I believe that in spite of the recent budget constraints there may be a detective or two still on the payroll...but, it's okay, I'm here to serve. Just give me a couple of minutes to tape up my shoes and I'll set course for the Terrace Inn."

"Your loyalty brings me to tears," Lompello blankly responded. "Now get moving. And, by the way, speaking of detectives isn't your partner due back from vacation pretty soon?"

"Yup," Truitt quipped as he made his exit, "he should be making his way back from God's great north woods in a couple of days."

"I hope so. Maybe he has an extra pair of shoes you can borrow. Let me know what you find out."

Chapter 2

Truitt pulled out of the precinct parking lot and onto the street. As he adjusted the rear view mirror he glanced upon his image for an instant. *Wait a minute.* He looked again.

Why did there appear to be more salt and less pepper in his hair than he had been noticing lately? Hopefully, it was just an illusion caused by the sunlight reflecting off the car windows. *Oh well, denial won't change anything, and at least it's all there—for now, anyway.*

The years had not been unkind physically to Mark Truitt. Mark supplemented nature's generosity by maintaining an ongoing exercise regimen that kept him on the fit and trim side of a man in his early fifties. Mark believed in the attributes of a strong body and clear mind, especially when one's "clients" often hailed from the darker side of society.

As Truitt turned into the entrance of the Terrace Inn he could see activity already underway. A couple of squad cars and an ambulance along with the county medical examiner's car were parked in front of one of the motel rooms.

A dense haze and the acrid smell of cigar smoke greeted Truitt as he approached the room, the telltale sign that Dr. Jim Carmody, the county medical examiner was close by. While Truitt admired Carmody's dedication to his work, he could not fathom a profession dealing exclusively in death. Carmody brushed that aside with, "The secrets for longevity in this job include a good cigar, a sense of humor (although sometimes it bordered on the perverse), and the *occasional* libation."

Once inside the room Truitt sidled up to Carmody, who was standing over the body and writing on a notepad. The ever-present cigar, though now unlit, protruded from under his bushy, Stalinesque moustache.

"Hi, Doc. So, what's up?" Truitt greeted, while placing his hand on Carmody's shoulder. "You know, Jim, not that I don't like you, but lately we've been congregating around too many dead bodies." Truitt exhaled a puff of air. "Looks like today's no exception."

Carmody frowned, assumed his usual grumpy posture, and pointed to the body lying on the floor. "Right now all that's 'up' are this man's toes. And, by the way, what's with this 'What's up, Doc' business? Who am I, Elmer Fudd? I admonish you, my Kojakian comrade; please show a little respect for the profession, if not the person."

Truitt cleared his throat. "I stand corrected, Dr. Quincy. Please accept my most humble apology."

"Apology accepted." Carmody tugged at his sport coat in feigned justification.

"So, what's up, Doc?"

"Thanks for asking."

Carmody pointed to two pinkish pills lying on top of a dresser. "I would strongly speculate that these pilules contain a substance of a deadly nature, companions of which I am sure we will find in generous quantities within the deceased. I further speculate that this empty glass lying on the floor held the contents which provided the means to transport the lethal potion from mouth to stomach."

Truitt shrugged. "Well, that's a mouthful. If you're right, there will be a quick conclusion to this case. I can't argue with your theory; but I guess maybe, as long as I am here, I'll poke around a bit, see what I can find."

Carmody smiled, pulled out a lighter. "Always looking for the long ball, aren't you? Well, have at it, Sherlock. I'll get out of your way. At the moment I've got a stogie that needs a little stroking."

Truitt went right to work. His meticulous and methodical approach when sweeping a crime scene usually left no clue unnoticed. Complementing this expertise was his ability to comfortably interact with people. While possessing the professionalism and directness of a Joe Friday, Truitt also displayed the humility and down-to-earth style reminiscent of Columbo.

Mark put on a pair of disposable gloves. He gingerly reached into the deceased's back pocket and carefully removed his wallet. The driver's license identified the man as Michael Carpenter and the birth date showed him to be forty-three years old.

Next, Mark removed a company identification card with Carpenter's picture on it. The card belonged to a company by the name of Midwest Research Laboratories. He was familiar with the name but didn't know a lot about the company. Truitt completed his search of the deceased man, finding no further clues.

Mark took a last good look at Carpenter. He had been a very handsome man. Standing out among his physical features were perfectly trimmed brown curly hair and a skin color implying at least a partial Mediterranean heritage. His suit coat, now lying limply on a chair, was Armani. *Class all the way.* A sadness momentarily overwhelmed Truitt as it did every time he investigated a death. To see anyone leave this world in an untimely fashion is sobering.

The detective next proceeded to the bathroom. The room offered only a tub and stool. A close inspection turned up no clues. Just outside the bathroom was a sink and dressing area. A purplish smudge on the edge of the sink caught his eye. Truitt took a closer look. The smudge appeared to be lipstick. Mark took a small sample, leaving the bulk of the smear for the forensic crew.

An examination of the bedsheets produced stains that would be analyzed. The room provided no further clues. As Truitt passed through the entrance door, he noticed an unused toothpick on the ground. Although it was most likely meaningless, he placed the toothpick in an evidence bag. He next visited the motel office, hoping to interview anyone who may have come into contact with Michael Carpenter.

Fortunately, the clerk on duty had also manned the front desk the previous evening. Spencer Trelow was a twenty-year-old college student who normally worked evenings but had switched schedules for this day.

After identifying himself, Truitt asked to look at the registry in order to see what time Carpenter checked in. "Here's the registry, Sergeant; but as you can see, Mr.

Carpenter didn't check into room 109 last night, Mrs. Carpenter did."

Truitt raised his head and looked directly at Trelow. "Say what? Mrs. Carpenter?"

Trelow leaned over the counter. In a voice not much above a whisper he said, "Um, if you want my opinion, I don't think she really was 'Mrs. Carpenter.' Happens around here all the time...if you know what I mean. Definitely fit the category."

Mark was all ears. "Would you please describe her for me?"

"That'll be easy, she was real looker. About five-foot-eight, blonde, dark eyes, long eyelashes, light-purple lipstick."

Truitt produced the smudge sample he had found by the sink. "Was the lipstick this color?"

"Yeah, I would say."

"Do you remember what she was wearing?"

"A dark, um, I think it was gray v-neck low cut sweater and a tight black skirt cut just above the knees. And black silk stockings."

"Anything else?" Truitt asked.

"That's it," Trelow responded.

"Thanks. Your detailed description of 'Mrs. Carpenter' was helpful."

"Well, I took the time to get a good look, if you know what I mean," Trelow winked.

The forensic team arrived by the time Truitt completed his interview with the motel clerk. Hopefully they would come across something he had overlooked, because at the moment there wasn't a whole lot to tell about the death of Michael Carpenter.

An apparent suicide, a questionable registration, stained bedsheets, a smudge of lipstick. *An indiscreet romantic liaison?—possibly. A toothpick? Well, probably forget the toothpick.* Another death with more questions than answers. However, this passing should be resolved quickly, as it had all the trappings of being self-induced.

Chapter 3

Truitt set the Michael Carpenter home as his new destination. He strongly suspected the soon-to-meet Mrs. Carpenter would not fit the motel clerk's description. He dreaded the unpleasant task of informing most probably the *real* Mrs. Carpenter that her husband was dead.

For Mark Truitt, informing the next of kin was by far the least desirable of his duties. The task served up a memory that left an indelible mark on his life.

The year was 1969. Mark was ten years old and his brother and only sibling, Phillip, was nearing completion of basic training, and following a short leave was to be deployed to Vietnam.

Mark's father, Alden Truitt, a WWII Army veteran, had followed General Patton from Normandy through the Battle of the Bulge. War hardened and battle-scarred he was yet a kind and gentle father.

Alden was also a devoted husband, and he and his wife Theresa seldom argued. That is why it was so unusual when young Mark awoke late one night to raised voices emanating from the kitchen. He would never forget the conversation he overheard.

"Theresa, I'm telling you, I don't like this Vietnam situation. It's not right what they're making our soldiers go through. I'm afraid for Phillip."

"Alden, don't fret like this. They're negotiating a peaceful end to the war. You know, the Paris Peace Talks. It will be over soon and Phillip will be home safe."

"*Peace?*" Alden countered. "I'll tell you when you get peace. I know. I've been through it. You get peace when you pound your enemy into the ground, when their body counts rival the blades of grass on the battlefield. When Hanoi looks like Hiroshima or Nagasaki or Berlin did in 1945; then and only then will you have peace. Don't any of these morons in Washington understand what war is? War is the last defense, the final option, and once decided upon its architects are obligated to throw every weapon in their arsenal at the enemy so our soldiers have the best chance possible. And if our politicians are not willing to go down that road then don't start a war. Either give Abrams the 200,000 troops Westmoreland's looking for and the firepower he needs…or bring everyone home. NOW!"

"But, Alden, I heard the president say…look I even wrote it down so I could show Phillip: 'The greatest honor history can bestow is the title of peacemaker. This honor now beckons America.'"

"Theresa, you're too naive. Nixon is really saying, 'How do I get out of this mess and look good doing it?' And while the politicians are playing their games, the casualties are piling up. I guarantee you, if Nixon had to man a foxhole in Da Nang Provence until peace was achieved, all the boats and planes this government owns wouldn't be able to pull our troops out of 'Nam fast enough."

Soon after, Phillip came home on leave, which ended way too soon for everyone.

The drive to the Minneapolis-St. Paul International/ Wold-Chamberlain Field was a somber one for the Truitt family. Phillip was to board a plane and then meet up with his unit for deployment to Vietnam.

As the Truitts pulled into the parking lot at the airport Phillip's favorite song "Fortunate Son" was playing on the radio. Phillip asked his dad if he could finish listening to the song.

When the song was over Phillip gave each of them a long hug. It would have to endure forever as it was the last time they would embrace.

Five months later the soldiers came.

All Alden Truitt could offer was, "For what? For what?"

From then on, as a tribute to his brother, Mark stopped whatever he was doing and listened to Phillip's song whenever it played on the radio.

Chapter 4

"Are you Mrs. Carpenter?" Truitt asked the petite brunette woman who slowly opened the door. *Definitely not the "Mrs." Carpenter that signed the motel registry last night,* he noted.

This was the moment Mark had hoped to avoid, not only informing the real Mrs. Carpenter that her husband was dead but relating the sordid details. He softened the scene somewhat, telling her as much as he felt she could handle.

Truitt's account of her husband's death appeared to put Denise Carpenter into a trance. Staring blankly for a few moments, she finally responded. "He...Michael, called me last night and said he and Brewster had an emergency at the Houston facility, and they had to go there right away. He told me he would call in the morning...and now you say he's dead?"

Truitt knew that any questioning would have to be delicate. "I'm so sorry for your loss, Mrs. Carpenter, but I have to ask, who is Brewster?"

"Brewster Pallidin. You know, they own the company."

"Midwest Research Laboratories?"

"Yes."

As this was the time for grieving, and given Denise Carpenter's emotional state, Truitt did not press for more information. There would be time for that. Mrs. Carpenter would have to identify the body, but for now he resisted from pressing her further.

After seeing to it that Mrs. Carpenter and her children were not alone, Truitt prepared to leave. As he opened the door, Denise grabbed his arm.

"Detective, this is wrong. This is very wrong. I know my husband. He would not voluntarily put himself in the situation you described, and he would most certainly not kill himself. You must find the truth. Please, promise me you will."

"I'll do my best, Mrs. Carpenter. I promise."

Maybe not as open and shut as I thought, Truitt reassessed as he left the Carpenter home.

Chapter 5

The young convenience store clerk glanced at her watch: 9:52 p.m. *Thank god,* she thought. *Another hour and I can get out of here.*

It had been a slow, boring night and she was anxious to see her boyfriend. The night was still young enough to go out and get a pizza and...*whatever.*

The entrance door opened and a customer walked in.

Oh no. Not her. Not "Chatty Cathy." My worst nightmare, the clerk bemoaned.

The customer was a woman in her mid-twenties. The "Chatty Cathy" handle was well deserved. The woman talked constantly to anything and anyone, animate or inanimate. Tonight, dressed in a pair of lime-green too-short and tight shorts and a pink tank top, Cathy wasted no time in entering into an extended conversation with a bottle of Mrs. Butterworth's pancake syrup on various recipe options for batter. Soon after, she addressed a can of chicken noodle soup followed by a stop at the frozen foods case with only a minor acknowledgment to a quart of ice cream.

Oh, boy, here she comes. The clerk braced herself for the verbal avalanche about to engulf her.

The clerk really did feel empathy for the woman, because obviously she mentally existed in a universe where most humans do not assume occupancy. *But, darn, she is SOOOO...irritating.*

The only other person in the store at the time was an older gentleman, who approached the counter in unison with Cathy. In stark contrast, he was as quiet as she was vocal. He was also a regular, generally purchasing the same items: a quart of milk, a loaf of bread, and two packs of cigarettes. He seemed lonely so the clerk usually tried to strike up a conversation. He was pleasant, although somewhat distant.

As the clerk rang up the woman's purchases, seemingly out of nowhere appeared a man wearing a ski mask and brandishing a handgun.

The gunman ordered the two customers to get down on their knees. He then directed his attention to the clerk. "Empty the till and don't set off any alarms or I'll blow you away. Now *move!*" The robber appeared to be nervous.

The clerk, crying uncontrollably, was somewhere between fainting and doing as she was ordered. Gathering herself together, she succeeded. The till was open.

The robber suddenly stepped back. "YOU HIT THE ALARM. DIDN'T YOU? DIDN'T YOU?" he shouted.

The clerk screamed. "NO! NO! I DIDN'T TOUCH ANYTHING!"

CRACK.

A bullet slammed into the clerk, knocking her backward into the cigarette storage case.

Blood gushed from her chest as she slid to the floor, her eyes fixated on the gunman. *I didn't set off the alarm—* she mouthed with her final breath.

The young clerk would not meet her boyfriend tonight, or any other night.

A second bullet was discharged, hitting Chatty Cathy in the left thigh. She would live to talk another day.

A third shot lodged harmlessly in the counter.

The fourth round caught the older man behind the left ear. He was dead before he hit the floor.

Chapter 6

The alarm sounded as usual at 5:45 a.m.

Mark Truitt's left index finger automatically hit the shutoff button. Now the battle with gravity began. The ritual typically included three attempts to separate body from bed. Finally, the body succeeded and Mark reluctantly set course for the bathroom.

As Mark was completing his preparation for the day there was a knock on the door. "What are you doing up this early?" Mark asked as he opened the door to his son, Brian.

"I gotta test at 8:30. Gotta study," Brian responded.

"Well, good luck. Say, how about catching a Twins game tomorrow night?"

"Ah, I don't think so. I promised to help Travis work on his car."

"Okay," Mark pushed out a breath, "but I think we need to sit down and talk about a few things."

"Dad, not now! I told you, I have a test. Let me know when you're done." The bathroom door closed, hard.

Brian, the younger of the two Truitt children was a freshman in college. He should have been farther along but a waning interest in higher learning had set up roadblocks to his advancement.

Mark's apprehension concerning his son's future and well-being had intensified in recent months. A tall, thin boy, Brian had always been on the fragile side, leaving him rather vulnerable. His gentle demeanor and reserved personality kept him on the fringes of conventional interaction not only with his peers but with life in general.

Mark anticipated that Brian would come into his own as he approached manhood but it appeared that quite the opposite was evolving. Brian was, in fact, more elusive, more aloof. Communication between father and son degenerated to an almost non-existent state. The idea that his son might be experimenting with drugs was attaining more credibility. Mark could not ignore the signs in Brian that he had been trained to see in others. There had been confrontations and denials. Many an argument and conversation went unfinished.

Truitt stared into the mirror as he wiped the last bit of shaving cream from his face. *Maybe tonight we'll talk,* he hoped, even though he knew the chances of that were slim.

Mark stepped into the kitchen just as Liz, his wife of twenty-eight years, was setting a plate of freshly cooked waffles on the table. Hovering with fork in hand and ready to pounce was Maggie, the older Truitt offspring. In contrast to Brian, Maggie was self-assured and independent. Recently graduated from college, Maggie was starting a career, having accepted a position with a fast growing software company.

Thankfully, Maggie has her head screwed on straight, Mark thought as he took his place at the table. "Morning, ladies! Well, this sure is a good start to the day." Mark grinned as he stabbed a waffle, putting his concerns with Brian on the back burner for now.

"How many more should I make?" Liz asked as she poured batter into the waffle iron.

Truitt gazed upon his wife. *No doubt about it, Liz is the anchor of this family. Never a complaint about my schedule. All the late nights, extra shifts, weekends. Only support.*

Liz knew Mark's decision to leave teaching and enter law enforcement would be a strain on their marriage. Her acceptance of his decision had been unwavering, but recently there appeared to be a few cracks in her armor. She was more irritable and argumentative. Mark sensed that her anxiety over Brian's erratic behavior might be the cause. At any rate, he promised himself to make a better effort to address the issue.

After the morning goodbyes were said, Truitt set course for precinct headquarters.

Mark backed out of the driveway, at the same time turning on the radio. Instantly a voice blared out from the dashboard, *"HEY DERE, MUDDA..."* *Oops.*

Truitt hit the "off" button and shoved the car in park. Pushing several more buttons finally produced a disk. Following a quick search, the floor under the passenger's seat gave up a case with a couple of tough-looking guys on it and the title..."D. FUNKED."

Oh, that's right, Truitt remembered. *I let Brian use the car last night. Looks like we have another item up for discussion.*

Truitt hit the "on" button and searched for his oldies rock and roll station. *Let's see, it's 1…0…ah, got it.*

The music was Mark's companion, functioning as a time machine, serving up memories of the past, and offering solace when the chips were down, and even inspiration when a situation became challenging. He cranked up the volume.

Chapter 7

Precinct headquarters was bustling as usual as Truitt settled in his chair and prepared to dig into the pile of papers on his desk. Also, as usual, Truitt's supervisor, Lt. Guy Lompello, was blowing off about something of no earth-shaking consequence to an unfortunate detective he had cornered. When Lompello spotted Truitt, and much to the captive investigator's relief, Guy did an about-face and charged. "Mark, I have one of the lab reports back in the Carpenter case, the one concerning the stains on the sheets."

Truitt felt a wave of anticipation.

"A portion of the stain was semen from Carpenter. The rest was vaginal fluid. Looks like our Mr. Carpenter partied one last time and then capped himself. Nice guy, huh? I think he did his family a favor. They're better off without him."

Mark stared at his desk. Though he wasn't surprised at the report, he knew from experience that things aren't always the way they appear. No, he wasn't going to let this die. He had promised Mrs. Carpenter.

Lompello tapped Truitt on the shoulder. "Hey, are you in there? Look, forget about Carpenter for now. I think the stars are lining up for a quick conclusion in that case. Besides, there's more pressing business. There was a convenience store robbery last night. Two dead, one injured. I've got Moller and Hogan working the case but I'd like you to help, too. Take a look at the surveillance tape. Give it your eagle eye."

Truitt frowned. "Okay, but let me chase Carpenter's death a bit longer. I want to look into a few things before I close it. In fact, I was about to line up an interview with the head of Midwest Research Laboratories, Brewster Pallidin."

Lompello thought for a moment, and then relented. "All right, I won't reel you in just yet. But take a look at that tape. Let me know if anything jumps out at you."

Mark honored his supervisor's wishes and reviewed the surveillance tape. Although nothing really jumped out at him, there was this one little item....

Chapter 8

Lunch for Mark Truitt usually necessitated a short walk from his office to a little deli that served up, in his opinion, probably the world's best Reuben sandwich. As he ambled down the sidewalk, his thoughts turned to days' past. Mark found himself recalling his decision to leave teaching and go into law enforcement. He had enjoyed a comfortable life as a high school teacher. However, he could not ignore the restlessness within, which increasingly became more pronounced. Ultimately he decided, along with Liz's blessing, to pursue a career in police work. And, yes, over the years Mark helped many offenders put their lives back on track. At the same time he did his part to get the bad guys off the street. It had been the right choice; a decision with few regrets.

As he entered the deli, Truitt jolted back to the here and now. *Call Jamie. He should be back from vacation tomorrow and I want to fill him in on the Carpenter case.*

Jamie was Jamie Littlebird, Mark's Native American partner. Littlebird was a full-blooded Ojibwa Indian. He grew up on a reservation located on one of the beautiful lakes that adorn the northern part of the state and this is where he had been recharging his batteries the past several days. Littlebird would never pass up an opportunity to return to his birthplace to "wash off" the encumbering drawbacks of city life and inhale the freshness and serenity that defined northern Minnesota.

The two detectives' relationship fairly paralleled Mark's experience with Guy Lompello years before. Truitt's professionalism and expertise held the keys to a promising career for the younger apprentice.

Littlebird eagerly soaked up all his mentor had to offer. Complementing that with his own tenacity and prowess, Jamie rapidly became one of the top investigators in the department. When Littlebird got on the trail of a suspect, he was relentless. More than one criminal who thought they had eluded the long arm of the law would be surprised to have the young detective knocking on their door in the wee hours of the morning. Fortunately for Jamie, he had been a good student, as his training would soon be tested to the hilt.

Not surprisingly, Truitt's call to Jamie Littlebird went unanswered. He still had one more day of vacation and probably wanted to enjoy it undisturbed.

Chapter 9

Mark Truitt was able to schedule an interview later that afternoon with Brewster Pallidin, who, along with his father, A.M. Pallidin, founder of Midwest Research Laboratories, had built their business into a large, multifaceted enterprise. As he approached the address, Truitt was immediately impressed with the size of the complex. The seven-story building consumed more than a square city block. Behind that was a slightly smaller structure of similar architecture.

Mark parked his car and walked to the building's entrance. Two large glass doors opened to a cathedral-style, open and airy lobby boasting a large, circular reception counter in the center. The cordial receptionist directed Truitt to the third floor. Once there he was seated in a small but elegant waiting room. Soon an attractive blonde woman motioned him to follow. "Mr. Pallidin will see you now. This way, please."

"Good afternoon, Sergeant Truitt, how may I help you?" Brewster Pallidin extended a hand. A tall man in his early forties, Pallidin had the looks, polish, and swagger of a person in charge.

"Nice to meet you, Mr. Pallidin," Truitt responded. "I would like to ask you a few questions concerning Michael Carpenter."

"Yes, I assume that's why you came." Pallidin rubbed his chin. "I cannot believe Michael's gone. I don't know the details, but I understand it may have been a suicide. I say impossible. Michael was the most stable person I knew."

Truitt continued, "You have my condolences certainly, Mr. Pallidin. I know this is a hard time for you but I'm looking for some insight into Mr. Carpenter's responsibilities with Midwest Research Laboratories and your relationship with him."

"Well, Michael was the president and chief operating officer of Midwest Research Labs. He was in charge of our research and development activities. He was very good at what he did. Paid attention to every detail. As for myself, I am responsible for the financial end of our business. We made a good team, Michael and I. He will be terribly missed."

"Had you and Mr. Carpenter made any plans to go to Houston the night he died?"

Pallidin looked surprised. "We do have a small satellite business in Houston but we had no plans to go there."

Truitt questioned further, "Did Mr. Carpenter give you any indication that he was having problems of either a personal or professional nature?"

Pallidin answered firmly, "Oh no, not at all. Michael was totally dedicated to his family. As far as work was concerned, Michael mentioned to me last week that he was most pleased with the progress of one of our more important projects."

"And what project is that?"

"You have probably heard about the recent strain of bird flu virus that's come out of Asia. It is potentially quite deadly. We are working on a preventative vaccine and I believe we're close to succeeding."

"So that is what Midwest Research Labs is all about?" Truitt asked.

"Well, that's only part of what we do here," Pallidin responded, "albeit a very important part."

Truitt pressed further, "Is there anyone else in your business that Carpenter was closely associated with?"

Pallidin thought for a second. "Well, yes. There's Peter Malik. He has duties on both the research and financial ends. Peter has been with us for about four years, came with excellent credentials. He is a Serbian who left his country during the Croatian war. Couldn't stand all the fighting and killing."

Soon Peter Malik stood before Truitt, offering his hand. Malik's jet-black hair, thick eyebrows, and definitive Eastern European accent pinpointed his origins.

Dark piercing eyes fit well with Peter's straight, self-assured posture. "It is nice to meet you, Sergeant Truitt." Malik went on to describe his business association with Carpenter and his admiration for him as a person of intelligence and integrity.

After asking Malik a few questions concerning Michael Carpenter, Truitt decided to end the interview.

"Thank you for your cooperation gentlemen," Truitt stated. "I'm sure this must be a difficult time for you, so I'll be moving along. I may have more questions in the future."

Pallidin retorted, "We will be happy to do whatever we can to help shed light on what really happened with Michael and, by the way, this is a doubly hard day for us."

"Why is that?" Truitt looked puzzled.

"We lost one of our top research scientists last night—George Thurber. He was shot and killed in a convenience store robbery."

Truitt was suddenly in a hurry to leave. "I'm sorry to hear that. Thanks again for your time."

As he was pulling out of Midwest Research Labs parking lot, Mark Truitt's thoughts were spinning around faster than his hubcaps.

Chapter 10

Truitt returned to precinct headquarters after the Pallidin interview to find Jamie Littlebird digging in his desk.

"Hey man, good to see you back." Truitt looked surprised.

"Good to see me because you missed me or because you need my invaluable services?" Littlebird quipped.

"Well, it's mostly A, but maybe a little B also. Anyway, you're back early." Truitt placed his hand over his chest. "You know, it's heartening to be associated with such a conscientious public servant."

"I don't want to ruin your golden moment," Littlebird unemotionally retorted, "but actually I came for my apartment keys. I left them locked up in my desk."

"As long as you're here, I may as well fill you in on the latest happenings. We have an interesting case to dig into. Hope you're rested up and ready to go."

"Not exactly, got a sore wrist, see?" Jamie held out his right forearm, wrist dangling limply.

"What happened?" Truitt's tone was suspicious.

"Too many fish. Reel 'em in, throw 'em back. Reel 'em in, throw 'em back. Know what I mean? But, fortunately, it wasn't all hard work. I took in some beautiful sunsets and was even treated to a few northern lights displays."

"Well, I'm surprised you don't have a stiff neck too," Truitt deadpanned as he walked over to the first aid cabinet. He grabbed an Ace bandage and tossed it to Littlebird.

"Is this meant for my wrist or my neck?"

"Take your pick."

A quick fling via the "sore" arm sent the bandage back at Truitt. "You have piqued my curiosity." Jamie settled into his chair. "Tell me what's happening."

Truitt reviewed the Michael Carpenter case with his partner, including the interview with the motel clerk and the lab findings. "But most compelling was my encounter with Mrs. Carpenter.

Not for one moment did she hesitate dismissing the possibility of her husband committing suicide or being with another woman. The determination in her voice, the look in her eyes, the body language. I'm really thinking that the obvious may not be so obvious."

"Was it a case of deception to cover a murder?"

"Possibly. I don't have a stitch of anything to go on; well, except maybe..."

"Maybe what?" Jamie probed.

"There was a convenience store robbery last night. I want you to take a look at the surveillance tape."

"Show time. I'll get us a cup and we'll watch the tape."

"Good idea. I could use some coffee." Truitt was glad to have his partner back.

The tape was reviewed several times. Finally, Littlebird asked, "How much did the creep get?"

"Thirty-five and some change."

"Two people dead and for thirty-five lousy dollars? I would like to get this assignment myself."

"Well, if my improbable theory pans out, that may happen. Look at the shooter. Concentrate on his mouth. See anything?"

Littlebird put on his cheaters. "Hmm, there might be a toothpick or something sticking out of his mouth, but it's hard to tell."

"Exactly. A toothpick," Truitt retorted. "That might be a connection. I found a toothpick on the ground outside of Michael Carpenter's motel room."

Jamie whirled around, his ponytail brushing across his shoulder blades. "That's your connection? If I didn't know you better, I would immediately ask to be reassigned."

"Don't write this off yet. The toothpicks and the fact that Michael Carpenter and the man killed in the convenience store robbery, George Thurber, both worked for Midwest Research Labs may be more than just coincidence. We have two toothpicks and two deceased employees of the same company."

Littlebird put his head in his hand. "I'm going to look into it, but I think everyone is partnered up. So…I guess I'm in. What's next?"

"Well," Truitt responded, "I think we should pay a visit to the founder of Midwest Research Labs, one Armondo Pallidin."

Chapter 11

Tom Moore stared blankly out the of his motel room window at an approaching storm. Slumping in his chair with his feet propped up on the bed Moore welcomed the cool pre-storm breezes blowing across his oversized body. Dressed only in a pair of boxer shorts and a sleeveless undershirt, which, at the moment did not totally cover his protruding, hairy belly, Moore appeared to be a rather hapless character.

Adding to this slovenly image was a crop of greasy black hair, combed straight back. Thick, black-rimmed glasses rested on a reddish-purple nose attached to a slightly puffy face that had long ago lost the acne wars. As for the rest of his body, well, it was prone to missing regular bathing appointments. Although the snapshot may have cast a pitiful image, in reality nothing could have been further from the truth. Moore's unbecoming appearance only helped to hide his true identity.

All six-foot-two-inches of his sixty-year-old body were pure venom. Moreover, the soul that dwelled within drifted aimlessly on a sea comprised of souls of the dead, those who chose a path where streetlamps emitted only beams of darkness and surfaces were paved with evil.

Although Moore had no reservations about taking another life, the thought of his own death terrified him. This paradox had its humble beginnings in a country church Tom and his family attended. The fiery preacher never tired of reminding his flock of the consequences of man's sinful desires and the resulting roadblocks to the path to glory. The minister often referred to a place called Hell, where men "wept and gnashed their teeth," the concept of which simultaneously scared and piqued Tom Moore's interest.

The other spiritual home, Heaven, was portrayed as a place which could be reached only by the "ladder of righteousness," with rungs that were placed few and far between so only those with legs that were extended by the grace of a harsh and judgmental God could reach the top. Young Tom subsequently determined that if any of *his* extremities were to be supernaturally extended, the story of Pinocchio more accurately defined his fate than the Holy Bible did.

Although Tom feared the less attractive alternative to Heaven, even had nightmares about it, he couldn't help but "peek over the fence." Every look brought further enticement, every stare, a beckoning. As Tom's life progressed, he one day came to the juncture which all humans must at some point face, the decision to climb to good or slide to evil. Moore's decision was immediate, his slide absolute; for, on that day, Tom Moore offered his soul to those who stoke the fires of Hell. Having made his decision he attempted to shut the door on the matter, dismiss the horrible concept of *eternity*. However, over the years his demons would persist in regurgitating the whole, fearful subject.

The general public had little to fear from Tom Moore, save for the occasional prostitute who chastised him for his vulgar demands or his lack of personal hygiene, or the barfly who demeaned his frumpy physical features. Those unfortunate souls would be stuck and bled out much as a hog being prepared for processing. For the most part Moore's skills were reserved for clients requesting the permanent silencing of an antagonist.

While Moore generally performed the generic *quick hit*, he was also a master at *graphic arts*. If a client's pleasure was to send a message, Tom was more than capable of granting that request. A victim may have had a personal demonstration on the finer points of operating a circular saw. Or the departed may have been the recipient of an internal body cleansing via a high pressure washer. "The ultimate enema" as Moore proudly referred to his handiwork.

A further clue into Moore's persona could be found in his cultural and familial background. Tom grew up in Southeastern Missouri to a family that expressed neither love nor emotion of any kind. The ever-present expressionless faces and minimal communication emphasized the perpetual isolation in which the Moore family dwelled, save for their church visits.

Young Tom translated this into a valueless image of human life, which in later years provided him with the justification for the expertise that proved deadly for many a victim.

Moore did not fare any better at school than he did at home with human contact. His homely looks, slouching stature, and loner personality fueled recurring unkind remarks, occasionally accompanied with physical abuse by classmates.

Two of those classmates that left an indelible mark were Brick Statler and Joanie Arkle. They were always the center of attention, the most popular twosome at school. Joanie and her girlfriends frequently walked by Moore, pinching their noses or hiding their eyes. Brick and his buddies would lie in wait for Tom, ready to pounce at the right moment. On good days he was just shoved around. Generally, however, Brick delighted in wailing on Moore's face. Tom never struck back, not once. What would have been the point? They would have beat on him all the more.

Bide your time, Tom, Moore thought to himself. *Your day will come.*

The lightning was very close now and the rain started. Moore closed the window. It was getting late. There would be no call tonight. He turned off the light and went to bed.

Chapter 12

Armondo Mattia Pallidin, the seventy-seven-year-old patriarch of the Pallidin family, and founder of Midwest Research Labs, was a lifelong resident of the Twin Cities. Armondo's father immigrated to America from Italy following the end of World War I. Although his surname was Pallidini, a scribing error at Ellis Island during registration resulted in the omission of the final letter of his last name. Thus Pallidin was created. The more American-sounding name stuck. After establishing himself in St. Paul, the elder Pallidin married a young woman of the same nationality through an arrangement, which was not uncommon for that time.

At first the Pallidins were prosperous and life was good. When the Great Depression struck, the family fell on hard times. Little Armondo was brought into the world during this period of hardship. Armondo's middle name "Mattia" translates into "gift from God." However, that was a stretch as there was so little to go around.

Armondo's father died when Armondo was only eight years old and so an already meager life became even more difficult. Armondo was forced to grow up smart, tough, and opportunistic. As he came of age, Armondo developed a keen business prowess that gained the respect of his peers. Though his early successes did not always stem from entirely legitimate enterprises, Armondo reasoned that, "You have to start somewhere."

The engagement in activities in this period of his life forged deep-rooted bitterness between Armondo Pallidin and Guy Lompello. An incident took place one evening, involving a relative very close to Lompello. The relative, an uncle, was an undercover cop who on this particular night coordinated a raid on a warehouse thought to contain stolen items. A shoot-out ensued and Lompello's uncle was killed. Although completely untrue, rumors persisted of Pallidin's connection to the thieves. The Lompello family fell victim to the rumors and so, for a young Guy Lompello, Armondo Pallidin would forever be an antagonist to be pursued.

Years passed and Guy Lompello joined his father as a police officer with the Minneapolis Police Department. The quest to avenge his uncle's death remained. But, try as he might, Guy would never be able to tie Pallidin to any illegal activities.

Lompello's futile but pesky attempts to associate Pallidin with criminal involvement did not go unnoticed; and, over the years, mutual dislike—no, hatred—grew exponentially between the two men. This scenario was a ticking time bomb, and neither man realized how few "ticks" were left before one, final explosion.

Chapter 13

The morning following the Brewster Pallidin interview found Sergeants' Mark Truitt and Jamie Littlebird at precinct headquarters discussing their plans for the day, which included a visit to the A.M. Pallidin estate. The several-acre property was remotely located in one of the far western suburbs of Minneapolis.

"I contacted Armondo Pallidin last evening," Truitt explained. "He said if we can get there by 10:00 a.m. he would be able to see us."

"Do you think he will give up any more information than you got from his son?" Jamie asked, tapping a pencil on his desk.

"We'll see. Brewster Pallidin appeared truly saddened at Michael Carpenter's loss and appeared shocked by George Thurber's death. However, he became markedly more stiff and reserved when Peter Malik entered the room. There was body language by both men that made me speculate there may not be a real high comfort level between them."

Littlebird stood. "Well, let's go chat with the big guy."

"Not so fast, you two!"

Unfortunately for the detectives, Guy Lompello's well-honed eavesdropping abilities allowed him to catch every word of their conversation.

"Wait for me. I want to be in on this."

Mark cringed. *Oh boy, just what we need.*

Truitt gamely tried to convince Lompello that this was not one of his better ideas. Littlebird stared at the ceiling.

"Ah, Guy, are you sure you want to do this? I mean you know how you two dislike each other; and, well, you wouldn't want any personal animosities to disrupt the interview."

Lompello stared Truitt down. "Look here, sonny, I hope that after all these years of working together, you would be of the understanding that my professional integrity will not be compromised when it comes to conducting business."

Littlebird took his eyes off the ceiling. "Does that mean you're coming with?"

Truitt mentally checked his options, the possibilities displayed on an empty page. He knew he was playing a dead hand. After all, Lompello was their boss.

Mark was actually a little concerned about his mentor as he had noticed for past several months that Guy seemed, ever so slightly, to be losing his edge. He was a little slower, slightly more forgetful, and a little less feisty. This led Truitt to become more protective of his friend. Though Mark couldn't stop Guy from coming along, he took a shot at laying down some definite ground rules before they left for the Pallidin interview.

"Okay, you win. But you have to promise, and I mean promise, you will not refer to anything that's happened in the past. You will only address the issue at hand. Can you do that?"

Lompello played down the request. "Yeah, I guess. Whatever."

"No, it's not *whatever*! You have to promise or you're not coming, period."

"All right, I promise."

"You're sure?" Truitt winked at Littlebird.

"I said, *OKAY*! What do you want, I should write it on my forehead in blood?"

Truitt didn't answer, but a small upward curl came to his lips. He had gotten his point across.

Littlebird mumbled an assessment to himself that was mostly incoherent, although Truitt was sure he heard the term "palefaces" surface.

Punks, Lompello thought, but did not say it out loud.

The threesome proceeded to their destination without much further conversation.

Chapter 14

A wrought-iron gate ringed with a granite stone arch guarded the entrance to the A.M. Pallidin estate. Built into the arch was an intercom. After the proper introductions had been made the gate opened and the trio started up the long drive. The road began to curve into a teardrop shape as it approached the residence. In the middle of the teardrop stood a fountain, at the center of which a concrete swan spewed blue water from its mouth.

The front entrance to the home was accessed by four cement steps. The entrance itself was constructed of inlaid tile and sheltered with an overhang supported by two concrete pillars. The architectural style rather impressed Truitt. To Jamie Littlebird it was an example of unnecessary indulgence.

Guy Lompello just grunted and said, "Ring the bell."

"Please, come in, gentlemen," greeted Armondo Pallidin as a butler led the men through large, double doors into a generously sized room boasting a vaulted ceiling. This was Armondo's study/meeting room.

To the left of the double red oak doors sat a leather couch. To the right were two plain but highly polished oak chairs. An outside wall supported a complement of windows that consumed most of the available wall space.

The far wall was evenly divided between a floor-to-ceiling bookcase and a bar/kitchen area. All of the components, including the bar itself, were crafted in red oak. Two leather chairs, one on either side of an oak coffee table occupied the space in front of the remaining wall.

Truitt extended a hand. "I'm Sergeant Mark Truitt. This is Sergeant Jamie Littlebird, and this...." Pallidin's hand found only air.

"Sergeant Truitt, you don't have to introduce me to this man. We go back a long way." Pallidin's frown turned to a sarcastic charm. "Why, Guy Lompello. How many years has it been? You've come to visit me? Ah, it's good to renew old friendships, isn't it?"

Lompello glared at Pallidin, verbal lava speeding to the surface, a vocal eruption close on its heels. "Pallidin, I don't care how long it takes; the day will come...."

Littlebird looked at Truitt. "I think this is going well, don't you?" he said blankly. "Obviously he took your cautionary remarks to heart."

Jamie was well known around the department for his dry sense of humor. In this case, however, Truitt was not amused. He hastily positioned himself between the two adversaries.

"I think the lieutenant should wait outside." Truitt grabbed Lompello's arm and quickly ushered him out of the study.

Once outside, Truitt opened the back door of the car and pointed. "Wait in the car. Do not even THINK about coming back in. This is it. The last time...stay put!"

When Mark returned to Pallidin's study he was quite red-faced. "I apologize for the lieutenant, Mr. Pallidin, you know he's..."

Pallidin waved his hand, cutting Truitt off. "Forget it. He'll never change. Anyway, let's get to the reason for this visit."

"Mr. Pallidin," Truitt began, "we would like to ask you a few questions concerning the deaths of Michael Carpenter and George Thurber."

"I am, of course, very distressed and puzzled over Michael's death but I don't understand about Thurber. He was killed in a convenience store robbery, wasn't he?"

Truitt continued. "I, too, am puzzled by Carpenter's death and at this point I am not at all sure I buy the suicide theory. As for Thurber, well, I think his murder merits further investigation. It's purely speculation on my part, but the two deaths may be connected."

Pallidin slowly walked around his massive oak desk, quietly sinking into a leather chair that threatened to swallow his diminutive frame.

"Michael and my son ran our business like a Swiss watch. They worked together extremely well and had the highest respect for one another. Michael was as solid as a rock, always upbeat. Even in the most difficult of circumstances Michael could find a solution. Brewster is more the one to get discouraged and lose his cool when things don't go right. Michael was always there to get him back on course."

"What can you tell us about Thurber?" Littlebird asked.

"George had been with Midwest Research Labs for the past fourteen years. He was currently working on a vaccine to counteract the most recent strain of bird flu virus that has been spreading throughout Southeast Asia. George was a very intelligent man. Kind of a loner, though. He didn't mix well with people. Actually, there is only one person he interacted with to any degree."

"And who is that person?" Littlebird interjected.

Pallidin rose from his chair. "The employee's name is Amy Weldon. She has been Thurber's cohort on the bird flu research project. Amy is about the only person who could work through Thurber's crankiness."

Truitt thought for a moment. "I guess that's all the questions we have for you right now. However, I would like to interview Ms. Weldon."

"That should be no problem," Pallidin answered. "Just call ahead."

As Truitt and Littlebird turned to go, Pallidin stopped them. "Hold on a second. Something just struck me that may be of interest. Brewster mentioned recently that one of our receptionists complained to him about receiving phone calls the past several weeks from people requesting to speak with Thurber."

"Did she know who the phone calls were from?" Littlebird asked.

"She suspected they might be from credit card companies or bill collectors. They were very adamant about speaking to him."

"Thanks. We'll check into that," Truitt responded.

Just then a snappy brunette walked into the study.

"Oh, Chelsea," Pallidin placed a hand on the young lady's back. "I would like you to meet Sergeants Truitt and Littlebird. They are police investigators."

Chelsea's look quickly turned from placid to quizzical. "Ah, hello. Nice to meet you...I think?"

Littlebird smiled. "Don't worry. We just came to ask your father a few questions. And he has been very cooperative."

Looking relieved, Chelsea replied, "Well, I'm glad to hear that and 'for the record' he's always been my hero."

"Uh-oh, she must need something," Pallidin laughed and patted her backside. "Get outta here."

"Nice to meet you," Chelsea grinned and continued on her way.

When Chelsea disappeared through another doorway, Pallidin remarked, "You have met my shining light, gentlemen. I don't know what I would do without her. She is so full of energy and she transfers some of that to me. Chelsea is definitely the best medicine there is for this old man."

"Does she work for Midwest Research Labs, also?" Truitt inquired.

"Yes, Chelsea works in the accounting department. I know she's being a good soldier, doesn't want to disappoint me. Unfortunately, I realize her heart's not really in the business. If she hangs in there, okay; but if not, that's all right too. Brewster minds the store well enough for all of us."

"Are there other children in your family?" Truitt continued.

"No, only Brewster and Chelsea. Of course, there are my three grandchildren and my daughter-in-law, Ann. Ann is the head of our Human Resources department. She and Brewster met when she was just a young trainee. I like Ann, but she never seems to have much time for me."

"Unless you have anything more to offer we'll be on our way," Littlebird concluded. "Thanks for your cooperation."

"Yeah, fine," Pallidin responded, followed by a hand quickly placed on Truitt's shoulder. "Oh, say, as long as I'm giving you my family circle, I probably should mention Vincent."

"Vincent?" Littlebird repeated.

"Vincent Ponce, Chelsea's fiancé. She met him at a night class at the 'U' a couple of years ago. He's followed her around like a buck in heat ever since. They're planning to get married next year. I guess I can live with that. Like I have a choice, if that's what she wants."

"Does he work for you, also?" Truitt asked.

Pallidin shrugged. "Yeah, but only because of Chelsea. She talked me into it. What could I do? She's my little girl. I keep him busy, but not with anything too important."

"Thanks again for your time, Mr. Pallidin," Littlebird said. "We'll let ourselves out."

A lone, dejected figure sitting in the backseat greeted the detectives as they returned to their car.

Truitt climbed in the front seat and glanced back towards Lompello. "And thank you for your cooperation."

No response.

Other than the radio playing oldies but goodies, the ride back to the office was spent in silence.

Chapter 15

After (barely) finishing high school, Tom Moore enlisted in the Army. Being the lone wolf that he was, the thought of becoming part of any group was repugnant to him. However, the Vietnam War was in full stride and he would have been drafted anyway. Besides, he mused, it would provide a good opportunity to pick up some survival skills.

Moore was pleasantly surprised to find that he loved the rigors of basic training. As the intensity of the training increased, his darker side responded in kind. By the time the preparation for war was completed Tom was tougher and meaner, and very anxious to get to the killing fields. In his mind he had already killed a hundred gooks. However, there was one piece of unfinished business. A short leave provided Tom with the opportunity to address that issue.

"Thanks for picking me up. I see you got the 'ol '55 Merc running pretty good," Moore said to his brother, Liam.

"Yeah, runs okay. Hey, why did you have me pick you up thirty-five miles away in Parkersburg when you could've taken the bus right to town?"

"Cuz I don't want no one knowing I'm around. So don't say nothing. I'll let you know when to take me back."

A pretty safe bet, for a Moore not to talk. The rest of the ride was spent mostly in silence.

Saturday night. The local armory was hopping with the usual weekend dance. *Good place to look for Brick and sweet little Joanie.*

Sure enough, there was Brick's '57 Chevy, all spiffed up and polished. Moore would wait. He pretty much anticipated their next move.

The wait wasn't a long one. The love-struck couple soon headed to their favorite parking spot, the Lake Wappapello boat landing.

Moore followed at a safe distance. As expected, they turned into the landing. Moore tucked his car in a turnoff a short way up the road.

Brick's car was rocking back and forth rhythmically when Tom and his baseball bat approached. He looked in the backseat and saw Brick's bare butt staring back at him.

A swing of the bat shattered the left rear window, spewing glass everywhere. An instant later the door opened.

Before Brick could turn around, Moore had a grip on his pants belt which, along with his pants, was down around his knees. Moore yanked him backwards. The next swing of the bat caught Brick between the shoulder blades, shattering several vertebrae. Joanie screamed but a stiff backhand put her into a semi-conscious state.

Moore addressed his now-helpless victim.

"You know, Brick, I said to myself during all those whuppings you gave me, 'Be patient, Tom, your chance will come.' Well, Brick, my chance has come." With that, Tom Moore proceeded with batting practice.

When Moore was done with Brick he turned his attention to Joanie. He took her not so much because he wanted her, but because it was the ultimate insult. Then he slit her throat. In a few violent moments Tom Moore reigned judgment over his tormenters and in doing so destroyed an ugly bridge to the past. Sadly, his road to the future would also be founded upon the blood of others. The small town of Wempler, Missouri, would never remember Tom Moore, nor would its residents ever forget what happened to Brick Statler and Joanie Arkle.

Chapter 16

Guy Lompello slowly ascended the worn, telltale creaky stairs to his second-floor apartment. Normally the climb offered little resistance, but tonight it was as if cement blocks were tied to his legs. When Guy reached the top he gave out a sigh and ambled down the dimly lit hallway. Arriving at his door he halfheartedly pushed his key into the lock.

Once inside, Lompello walked by the vintage 1950-era embroidered couch and past the antique coffee table that displayed his parents' wedding picture. He continued past the wall adorned with various awards, commendations, medals from three generations that proudly testified to brilliant careers in police work.

He made his way into his bedroom where he emptied the contents of his pockets onto a varnished, well-worn maple dresser that had originally been owned by his grandfather. Then he removed his service revolver and carefully placed it in a drawer.

After staring at the dresser for a few moments he rubbed his fingers lightly along its top edge. It made him think of his dad. Many a night he had watched his father follow the same routine.

Guy's dad had always been his hero. *What would he think of me?* Lompello sat on the edge of his bed and rested his elbows on his knees. *What I did today was inexcusable. I interfered with an investigation. I acted like a child. I lost my professionalism. Worst of all, I lost my dignity in front of two of the people who mean the most to me. I may as well admit it. I'm getting too old for this. It's time to get out while I still have a shred of respect left.*

Lompello decided, since he wasn't one for parties or fanfare, to work until early fall, secretly deciding when to end his service. He would allow himself a brief vacation followed by a new career, one of community service. He certainly knew of many wounds that needed to be healed. With many overlapping thoughts sifting through his head, sleep did not come easily that night.

Chapter 17

Mark Truitt was at Midwest Research Labs by 9:00 a.m. the morning after the Pallidin interview. The cheerful and smartly dressed receptionist in the main lobby gave him directions to the research lab. Truitt entered an elevator and quickly made the two-floor decent.

The doors opened to a long hallway. There were windows on one side that looked into a large room containing rows of counters supporting various types of lab equipment. The far end of the room held several small offices. Truitt walked towards the offices, stopping at the one which had the names THURBER-WELDON posted above the entrance.

As he was about to pass through the open door, a voice from behind asked, "May I help you?" Amy Weldon was a strikingly attractive "fortyish" woman. Her shoulder-length black hair and intense sky-blue eyes, which rivaled his Scandinavian blues, were complemented by her stylish Claiborne glasses. Her figure, which on a scale of 1–10 was a solid 11.5, suddenly induced a youthful shyness in Truitt.

After his brain processed an internal *WOW*, Mark rather clumsily introduced himself and immediately dove into the interview. "Ms. Weldon," Truitt began, "I understand you were George Thurber's colleague. I would like to ask you a few questions concerning your research work."

Weldon did not answer. Instead, she slowly retrieved a piece of paper from her purse. After a protracted silence, she spoke. "I...I have a note that George mailed to me. I really don't know what to make of it." She handed the piece of paper to Truitt.

Amy, regrettably this will be our last contact. I'm afraid I have done something terrible and I cannot make it right. My life is in danger. I cannot explain any further or your life will be in danger also. All I can tell you is how much I will miss you. I am so sorry that I have failed you—and myself. Goodbye, George.

Truitt folded the note. "I would like to hold on to this if I could, Ms. Weldon."

"Sure, Sergeant, but I don't understand. George was killed in a robbery, right? And now, this note."

Truitt's sweat glands were popping. This woman was making him uncomfortable. "Well, robbery appeared to be the motive...but, I don't know. Did you notice anything out of the ordinary about Mr. Thurber lately?"

Weldon thought for a moment. "George was always a little on the cranky side. However, he seemed more agitated than usual the days prior to and especially on the day of his death. George was in and out of the lab I don't know how many times. It was almost like he was fighting with himself about something. I was actually relieved when he decided to call an early end to his day. What was really out of character for George was that the entire shift he went out of his way not to talk to me or anyone else."

Truitt scratched his head. "Now, if I understand correctly, you and Thurber were working on a bird flu vaccine project. Was anyone else involved in your research?"

"No, George and I were the whole team. However, we were required to have weekly briefing meetings with Peter Malik."

Truitt was thinking hard, and it was getting harder to think. This woman was not only strikingly good-looking, she was wearing a tantalizing perfume.

Weldon let him off the hook by continuing, "There is something else that maybe I should share with you. When George didn't come to work on Wednesday morning I got concerned. He *always* lets me know when he's not going to be here. He hadn't said anything about taking the day off, and then with his strange behavior and all that… well, since there was nothing from him on my email, I looked at his email, just in case…Don't take this wrong, Sergeant. Our computers are open books to each other. We were a team in every sense and constantly shared data. Anyway, there was an email George had received at 2:20 a.m. Wednesday that was rather puzzling. The message read, *Gyg-h7 received, awaiting next package, remittance forthcoming.* The address from which it was sent was—jinxuexiang@seasiapharm.com."

Truitt's professional self was back in charge. "Do you have any idea what the message meant or who may have sent it?"

"I know that *seasiapharm* is the email address for Southeast Asia Pharmaceuticals. They are partnered with us in our bird flu research program. Jinxuexiang doesn't ring a bell with me and I don't understand about the remittance part of the message. Neither George nor I have ever had anything to do with finances. As far as the Gyg-h7, I think I might know what it means, but I'll have to do a little probing."

"Look, Ms. Weldon, I don't want to get you into any trouble, but...."

Weldon stopped Truitt in mid-sentence. "Don't worry. I have a lot of latitude in my job. I want to help in any way possible. George and I were pretty close; he was my main confidant. A strange bedfellow in that respect, but we did have one thing in common, both loners for the most part. George, because that's the way he chose to live, and me, well, that's not important. And, by the way, just call me Amy."

Truitt smiled and did everything in his power to keep from melting into a pile of Jell-O.

"Thanks for your cooperation, ah, Amy. Now, would you please give me that email address again?"

Chapter 18

The dark aura that defined Tom Moore only intensified as he settled into his tour of Vietnam. He increasingly relished the thought of putting his fighting skills to the test against another human being. The adrenalin flowed, and for once in his life Moore began to feel some emotion. In this bloody land of war and death Tom concluded that this was what he was born to do—kill and conquer.

A day in particular that exemplified Moore's total disregard for the sanctity of life began in the usual manner. Go on patrol, seek out the enemy, secure the area. After a few hours of walking, the soldiers found themselves on the outskirts of a small village. They were soon spotted by the enemy and an intense firefight began. The Americans quickly gained ground and began pushing through the village.

After raking one particular hut with gunfire, Moore burst inside. Huddled in a corner were a woman and a boy. Moore impassively raised his rifle and fired. He genuinely enjoyed watching the bodies flinch as they were being hit.

Suddenly, hearing voices from behind, Moore whirled around. His beady eyes focused on two of his comrades standing in the doorway. He knew they had witnessed the killings. Already pumped, he made a split-second decision.

WHAM. WHAM. Both soldiers were dead.

Moore shut off the DVD player, stood, stretched, and shuffled to the refrigerator for another beer. He had just finished watching the movie *Predator* for, well, more times than he could count. It was the only movie he liked. He couldn't help but feel camaraderie with this warrior from outer space. After all, the similarities were startling; vicious, precise, relentless. No conscience.

Yup, that's me all right. Tom Moore, the human predator...right down to the ugly looks.

And the way the movie ended? With the character Arnold played besting the Predator? *Hollywood garbage. It should have ended with Predator having wish-boned that piece of human bacteria.*

With the aid of fourteen beers, Moore's thoughts expanded. *What if Predator were president? There would be only one lobbyist in Washington. How about Predator as Santa Claus? No doubt, ALL the children would be good!*

The ringing of Moore's cell phone jolted him back to the present. He looked at his watch. 10:03 p.m. That would be X, his handler. The ten o'clock hour was the appointed time for X to call if Tom's services were required. Since Moore did not know this person's true identity, his tag of X was as good as any for Tom's purposes.

"I'm here," Moore answered. "Yeah, okay. I can do that. I'll need to set up a few things and wait for an opportunity. It shouldn't be more than a few days."

Moore closed the cover on his cell phone. He liked this contract. X wanted to send a message. That always made it more interesting.

There was one overriding problem, however.

Flipping the phone over and over in his hand, Moore considered his situation. It didn't bother him that he didn't know X's superiors. In fact, he preferred it that way. He reasoned that if he was ever caught carrying out a contract, his life wouldn't be in danger because he couldn't identify anyone. On the other hand, if *they* surmised that he did hold any damaging information there would be no facility secure enough to prevent his erasure.

Now X was another story. As a matter of self-preservation Moore needed to be able to identify the person to which he reported. He concluded that his handler was fairly low-level and, if caught, Moore could give up X in a bargaining agreement and (hopefully) the larger organization would set their sights on that person and not pursue his elimination.

The number that appeared on his phone when this person called would be sure to trace back to a false identity. Also, X used a voice transformer when talking. The transformer produced a child's voice so Moore couldn't determine if it was male or female. He didn't even dare ask any questions that varied in the slightest from the task at hand as it might be construed as "fishing," which may result in his swimming with the same.

Moore did have a shot at it, however.

An old Army acquaintance might be of some help. The risk was worth it.

DAVID ZINI

Chapter 19

Minnesotans love their lakes, and in this state there are a lot of lakes to love. The shorelines created by all of the lakes and rivers within the Minnesota border totals more than the shorelines for California, Florida, and Hawaii combined. The slogan on Minnesota license plates boasts the "Land of 10,000 Lakes." Actually there are 11,842 lakes larger than ten acres in size.

The Truitt family was heading to their cabin on one of these beautiful lakes this warm and muggy summer morning. Spirits were high and the two-and-a-half-hour drive north from the Twin Cities seemed to take no time at all.

Far from being fancy, the Truitt cabin was rustic but comfortable. Mark hoped the opportunity to enjoy the tranquility and beauty of the setting would lend itself to a renewal of openness among the four of them. Yes, this mini-vacation may be just the prescription their family needed right now.

The extended weekend started out well. The morning after arriving, Mark and Brian tried their luck at fishing. There is no better way to relax than sitting in a boat on a bright, warm summer day with fishing rod in hand. Rocking back and forth in rhythm with the waves, father and son took full advantage of nature's offering.

Eventually the subject of chemical abuse was brought up and even though Brian skirted the issue, the dialogue between them was not uncomfortable. By the time the boat pulled up to the dock Mark felt that, if nothing else, a small gap had been bridged. They had talked and the conversation ended in a genial manner. A minor victory maybe, but a start nonetheless.

The ensuing days were spent with everyone relaxing and enjoying the good weather. Maggie missed her boyfriend, but there would be plenty of time to make that up. Overall, things were looking very good to end the vacation on a positive note.

Unfortunately, on the last morning Liz's mood took a u-turn. She once again drifted towards being distant and uncommunicative.

"Liz, you seem to be in another world today. What's going on?" Mark asked.

"Oh, I don't know, Mark," she answered. "It's just that you seem to think that...well, because we've had a few quiet days together everything's going to be all right. I'm sorry; I'm not of the same opinion. Brian isn't even close to the Brian we've known for the last twenty years. Now we'll go home and you'll be back to working all hours of the day and night and leave me alone to worry not only about Brian but about you. I never know if you're coming home or if I'm going to get a call." Indicating she had no further interest in continuing the conversation, Liz stood and made her way down to the lake.

Mark watched his wife standing on the beach, arms folded, one foot aimlessly digging at the sand. In front of Liz, flashes of sunlight reflected off the tips of small waves, which ended their lives quietly as they rolled up on shore. From the opposite side of the lake, a loon beckoned his mate with an unmistakable call. The scene would have been very serene had it not been for their exchange.

Mark wondered if Liz's words were truly heartfelt or more a result of frustration. Her support for his profession had always been uncompromising. Until now they had been on the same page as far as the kids were concerned. The Liz Mark knew and loved was upbeat and positive.

What could be the problem? What was happening to them?

Mark was determined that they would work this out. Their family would stay intact, no matter what. Then, out of the blue his thoughts drifted to Amy Weldon—just for a moment.

Chapter 20

The trip back from the Truitt cabin was filled mostly with small talk. Mark's red cheeks were compliments of a sunburn caused more by secondary sunlight reflected from the lake's surface than directly from 'ol Sol himself. A snapshot look at the Truitt family would confirm that the sun and fresh air had taken their toll. In the final count it was Minnesota summer weather: 4, Truitt family: 0. The Truitts would be retiring early tonight.

Mark was in an REM sleep mode when he was awakened by the ringing of his cell phone. A rather faint "Hello" stumbled out as he got the phone to his ear.

"Mark, it's Jamie," a subdued and somewhat shaken voice responded.

"Jamie?" Truitt was quickly becoming alert. "What's going on? It's 3:20 a.m."

Littlebird avoided a direct answer. "Mark, meet me at County road 17 and Forest Lawn Drive. You know where that is, don't you?"

Truitt was already half-dressed. "Yeah, but...."

Jamie cut him off. "Just get here as soon as you can."

Truitt jumped in his car and took off...fast. He was getting more anxious with every mile he peeled off. The unsettling tone in Jamie's voice forewarned Mark that something was terribly wrong.

As he approached the intersection, Truitt could see bright lights flashing from emergency vehicles. He parked his car a short distance away and walked towards the lights. Littlebird spotted him and quickly positioned himself between Mark, several law enforcement officers, and emergency personnel who were huddled over a body bag.

Before he could speak, Jamie grabbed Truitt by the shoulders.

"Mark, I'm...sorry. It's Guy. He's dead. Now, before you go over there, I have to warn you. It's not a pretty sight. He died hard. He was stripped naked, rolled up in poultry netting and dragged down this dirt road. There is not much of him left to recognize. We only know for sure it was Guy because his wallet was stuffed in his mouth... and there was a note attached to what was left of the netting—'packaged for your convenience.'"

Truitt stared at Littlebird. "Poultry netting? You mean, *chicken wire?* Guy was wrapped in *chicken wire?*"

Jamie looked down. "Yes."

Mark turned and vomited.

When he had regained his composure, Truitt walked over to the body bag. He slowly unzipped the bag and peered inside. Jamie was right. There were few features left to recognize.

What kind of monster would do this? And why? Obviously, there was planning and purpose to this. *But, why Guy Lompello?...Wait a minute.*

Suddenly, things were starting to jell for Truitt.

Observing Mark's stride as he approached, Littlebird mumbled a faint "Oh, boy."

With electricity in his voice, Truitt blurted out, "It's Pallidin! It's got to be Pallidin! I mean, Jamie, they weren't together thirty seconds and we had to separate them. You were there. You saw it. And...he had Carpenter and Thurber murdered to cover up who knows what? Well, he's not getting away with it! I'm dragging him down to the station TONIGHT, and if I don't beat him to death on the way there, which I may well do, I'm booking him for murder."

Littlebird held tight onto Truitt. "Mark, stop and think...*you* are not going after Pallidin. You're in shock. We both are. Guy was a mentor to me just as he was to you. We loved him, but he's gone now. We can't do anything about that. What we can do is properly grieve for him. There will be plenty of time to catch his killer and we will do that, in the professional manner he taught us. Now c'mon, let's cry a bit and then we'll call it a night."

Chapter 21

Mark Truitt was gaining a new understanding of the term "blue mood" as he shuffled around the office. The time to grieve had been taken. Guy Lompello was properly laid to rest. And, as usual, Jamie Littlebird's calming wisdom had put things into perspective. Mark took Jamie's advice and avoided Armondo Pallidin.

"Morning, partner." Truitt's mood instantly brightened as Littlebird strode into the office and headed towards the coffeepot. "Can I get you a cup?" Jamie offered.

"Why, yes. I think I will," Truitt replied.

The two investigators comforted each other one more time, then got down to the business at hand, which included three dead people: Michael Carpenter, George Thurber, and Guy Lompello. Totally unrelated. Or were they? Truitt just had this feeling.

Jamie Littlebird was struggling to harvest the same field of thoughts.

The only new piece of information gleaned involved George Thurber's financial woes. Thurber had accumulated a substantial amount of debt, both in the form of loans and also money owed to credit card companies. A probe into Thurber's life had revealed a man with few possessions and fewer friends. He lived alone and apparently the only person he had any frequent contact with was Amy Weldon.

Sooo..., Truitt reasoned, *unless Ms. Amy Weldon has anything to do with Thurber's financial problems, my guess is that Mr. Thurber was a gambler.* Mark had decided not pursue the foreign address Amy had pointed out on George Thurber's email until he spoke with her again, an appointment he admittedly was anxious to keep.

With little to go on, the detectives decided to employ their "high road/low road" tactic. Truitt would keep a high profile, staying close to the main players, while Littlebird would do some poking around on the other end of the food chain.

Jamie had developed an impressive network of informants that often reaped abundant fruits. Also, he was familiar with a variety of bars, nightclubs, and other gathering places frequented by solid citizens as well as those that fit the definition of the non-taxpaying public. If a killer dwelt among them, chances were that Littlebird would find him.

Chapter 22

Truitt was considering an interview with A.M. Pallidin when his cell phone rang. It was Amy Weldon. She sounded apprehensive and wanted to meet him as soon as possible. A small restaurant near Midwest Research Labs was decided upon. Truitt immediately headed for the destination.

Amy arrived first and was seated next to a window at the far end of the room. Truitt felt tiny pangs of anticipation as he approached her booth. Although a combination of concern and sadness dominated her expression, it took nothing away from her attractiveness. Mark untwisted his tongue and greeted her. After exchanging pleasantries and ordering coffee for two, Weldon got to the matter at hand.

"I've deciphered *Gyg-h7,* you know, the code on George's email? And...well, I think I know what George was up to, although I don't want to believe it. I'll try to explain it in layman's terms."

Truitt was all ears.

"Midwest Research Labs is partnered with a company by the name of Southeast Asia Pharmaceuticals, located in Hong Kong. As partners we develop and distribute anti-flu virus serums. Now, this game can get very dicey. Chasing a strain of virus that has a sustained transmission, one that is already wreaking havoc is kind of like trying to put out a forest fire that is being pushed by forty-mile-per-hour winds. Ideally, we strive to stay ahead of the next strain of virus that would enter the human population and be of a lethal nature."

"You mean you try to anticipate what the next strain of flu is going to be?" Truitt asked.

"Well, in a manner of speaking. The majority of this type of work is done at the Center for Disease Control in Atlanta and also by flu researchers overseas, mainly in the Netherlands. Through genetic engineering they artificially breed new viruses in high-containment labs from viruses that already exist in the animal and human populations. Hopefully from this research those combinations that might prove harmful to humans will be discovered. Our lab at MRL delves into this arena, but on a smaller scale. And this brings me to the reason I called you."

Amy took a sip of coffee and continued, "Now, the email message. *Gyg* stands for Guiyang, a city in South-Central China. A strain of avian-flu virus was discovered there last year. Fortunately, only two people are known to have died from it. It appears to have been contained. The *h7* is the troubling part of the equation; *h* stands for hybrid, and *7* refers to its pathogenic potential. Level 7 has a fairly high potential for causing widespread harm to humans. I dug deep into George's research data. Sergeant, George had artificially bred a strain of virus at this level.

We were not sanctioned to be working on this type of a project. This was clandestine."

Truitt cocked his head. "So, what are you saying?"

"I'm saying that George artificially engineered a deadly strain of flu virus and, going by the contents of the email, sent the formula to their partner lab in Hong Kong. Also, he had completed the development of the serum to counteract the virus. That's probably what 'awaiting the next package' meant."

"What about the name on the email—ah, jing...or something?"

"Jin Xuexiang. I called one of the researchers I correspond with at Southeast Asia Pharm. Jin works in the research department but is fairly low level."

"Okay, Amy, let me get this straight. George Thurber developed a potent strain of flu virus, sent the process to, or through, this Jin guy, brewed up the antidote, and was preparing to provide that information also. I hate to think of what the ultimate purpose for this was but I'm speculating a pretty dark explanation...They were going to infect a populace somewhere, start an epidemic, and then provide a cure, the sales from which would bring a very healthy profit. Am I anywhere close to what your thoughts are?"

"That's pretty much the way I take it, Sergeant." Weldon looked down, staring at her cup of coffee. Obviously this was hard for her.

"I mean, think of the consequences. How many people could die because of this?"

"I know. I know," Amy cradled her head in her hands.

Truitt backed off. "Look, um, Amy. Drop the 'Sergeant.' Mark is fine."

Amy raised her head. Tears were sliding down her cheeks.

As if it were acting on its own, Truitt's hand moved across the table and folded around hers.

Weldon quickly drew her hand back.

"I'm sorry." Mark silently prayed for invisibility.

"No, please, don't be sorry," Amy admonished. "I truly appreciate your kindness. It's just that...."

"Just that what?" Truitt pursued.

Weldon locked eyes with Mark. "Other than George, who was more like a father than anything, you are the first man I have actually had a real conversation with outside of a business setting in a long while." Having said that, Amy quickly looked away. "Forget it. I'm sorry. I didn't mean to bring up my personal life."

Truitt was more than happy to seize the moment. "No, please, go on."

"Well, all right, but you'll be sorry. It's not a happy story." Weldon raised a half smile above her tears. "I got married when I was twenty-four to a handsome, macho, athletic type. Fell head over heels. But I soon found out that his favorite exercise to stay in shape was beating on me. It took me six years, but I finally escaped the creep. I swore I would never fall for anyone again—that is, until I met Nathan. Nathan was not the most handsome man in the world, but he ultimately turned out to be the man of my dreams. He was the sweetest, kindest, most gentile man I have ever met. After three years of getting to know each other, I felt comfortable enough to marry a second time. Two weeks before the wedding, Nathan was killed in a sky-diving accident. And now, George. Of course our relationship was totally platonic. So you see, Mark. I guess I'm just not meant to interact with men." As she was saying this, Amy's smile ratcheted up a notch and she reached out and grabbed Truitt's hand, just for an instant.

An instant, a few nanoseconds; that's all it took. Skin on skin. The surge that flashed through Mark's being nearly shorted out his self-restraint mechanisms. This was suddenly the height of puberty revisited and he was "pubing" from top to bottom, half expecting acne to break out on his hot, red cheeks.

"Mark? Hey, what are you thinking about so intently?"

"Oh...ahhh, excuse me. I was just, um, thinking about what you said," Truitt embarrassingly blurted out.

After clearing his throat (and his thoughts), Mark continued. "I'm sorry for your losses. But you know, as they say, time heals all wounds. And don't worry, Amy, your time will come again."

"Well, my policy has always been never to argue with the police, sooo...I guess I'll have to take you at your word." Amy grinned.

"Good policy. Now let's get back to the business at hand," Truitt stated rather authoritatively, having gained back a measure of self-control.

"Being that Southeast Asia Pharmaceuticals is out of country, the FBI will have be involved. I'll contact the local office. Hopefully, something concrete will come out of the information you gave me."

"I guess we're...done here, then?" Weldon questioned, somewhat hesitantly. "I don't know if I can be of any further help, but if I come across anything I think might be important I will let you know, Mark. And, thanks for listening to my personal tale of woe."

"Hey, no problem. But be careful. I don't want you to get yourself in any danger. Keep a low profile. If you need me, you have my number."

Truitt walked Amy to her car. As she drove away, he silently prayed to the Gods of Trouble, Need, and for good measure, Loneliness, that Amy would require his services in the near future.

After she was out of sight, Mark pulled out of the parking lot and flipped on the radio.

Although Mark and Amy weren't in Baltimore,
Nor was she from "Ole Miss."
Mark and moon were all too ready for a wet kiss,
to make the tide rise again.
Thanks, Starbuck.

Chapter 23

A call to the local FBI office initiated an investigation into Southeast Asia Pharmaceuticals, and one Jin Xuexiang. Mark spent the evening contemplating a possible connection between Michael Carpenter and George Thurber—that is, between thoughts of a possible connection between Amy Weldon and himself.

If there's truth in the saying that a picture's worth a thousand words, then a snapshot of Mark's fellow detectives as he entered the office the next morning would have implied a scenario of impending doom or, at the very least, that the Twins lost again.

"Why all the gloomy expressions?" Mark asked a passing colleague.

"Guess you haven't heard," answered a sullen detective. "Say hello to your new boss." The detective pointed to Guy Lompello's old office.

Truitt tentatively ambled in that direction. When he got close enough to glance in the window he saw none other than Laverne Hathaway sitting in Guy Lompello's chair.

Laverne Hathaway was in the last half of his forties decade. His slim, six-foot frame featured a balding hairline with a neatly trimmed amount of hair showing around the edges. At times he wore glasses, though mainly for effect. Hathaway had come up through the ranks, a few years junior to Truitt. Aloof by choice, he shunned all but the necessary contact with his fellow detectives. Although opportunities came and went to establish relationships, Hathaway remained unabashedly self-centered. As far as Truitt was concerned, Laverne Hathaway was motivated by one overriding consideration; the bottom line—that is, *his* bottom line.

Looks like he achieved his goal, Truitt mused.

Hathaway noticed Mark passing by his office. "Come on in a minute, Mark," he hailed. "As I'm sure you know by now I've been promoted to Guy's position," Hathaway beamed. "I know how close you and Guy were, and I certainly can understand if this transition may not be easy for you; but I sincerely hope we will gain each other's trust and be able to work well together. Of course, that goes for Jamie, too. By the way, where is he?"

Truitt measured his response. "Well, he's following up on a few leads concerning Guy's murder."

"And how about you? Tell me about the deaths surrounding the Pallidin family."

Mark didn't have a choice. Hathaway was his supervisor. He had no alternative but to fill him in on the latest developments pertaining to the Midwest Research Labs case. He finished with—"and I have the FBI following up with a possible Hong Kong connection."

Hathaway clasped his hands behind his back, paced in front of his desk. Truitt suspected the show was for effect. "The public and media are not exercising much patience with Lompello's death. They are soon going to want answers. You may have to back off on the Pallidins for now. It's good that Jamie's out there hunting the killer, but I need you out there, too."

It's starting already, Mark thought to himself. *What he's saying is: "This is high profile. I need to look good and you're going to help me do it."*

Not desiring a confrontation at this early juncture in their new relationship, Truitt politely made an attempt at compromise. "I want to find Guy's killer more than anyone. However, we are the only investigators working the Midwest Research Labs case. I feel confident that Jamie and I can work both cases without doing injustice to either one."

Hathaway cleared his throat, a slight shade of pink welling up on his cheekbones. He would like to have exerted his newly-acquired authority and set this investigator straight right then and there. However, there were more important things to consider. "Okay, Mark. But let's do this. I'm going to get Spargo and Duchenne working on the Midwest Research Labs case, too. They can keep in touch with the FBI and start digging for leads on this end. Fill them in on what you've come up with so far."

Hathaway definitely failed at his first attempt at making a positive connection as he had just taken a proverbial sixteen-pound sledge hammer and planted a very precise blow directly in Truitt's gut.

Being that Mark was armed, and at this moment dangerous, he thought it best to leave—with haste. "I'll look them up and fill them in. And, um, congratulations on your promotion."

If Hathaway had only realized the hidden sarcastic intent of that congratulatory offering... Then, again, maybe he did.

Lenny Spargo and Charles Duchenne. Now there was a pair to draw to. Lenny Spargo, at six-foot-three, whitish-blond hair combed straight back, and a surfer's build was a real ladies' man (just ask him). For Lenny, there was no bribe too small, no trick too cheap, no hustle too meager. Labeling him as a dirty cop would be paying him a compliment. Flies would postpone hibernating just so they could hang around him. The only attribute that could be paid to Lenny was that he was smart. If he wasn't he would have been off the force and probably in jail long ago.

In total contrast to Spargo was Charles Duchenne. A chunky man oozing a total lack of self-confidence and misplaced priorities, Charles sealed his shaky image with a baby face and skin slick as frozen rain on a sidewalk. Shaving for him might well have been an annual event. Charles could much more appropriately be envisioned having sprouted wings, flitting around draped in one of those white robe "thingies," and wielding a bow and arrow. In all the annals of copdom there may never have been a person more unsuited to be a law enforcement officer than poor Charles. The only reason he got into the Department at all was due to his uncle having been a police commissioner. The only reason he stayed in the Department was because of Lenny Spargo. Charles was Spargo's gopher. His minion. Without Charles realizing it, probably because he admired Spargo and wanted to emulate him, Lenny was holding him hostage just in case one of his shady deals went sour. There was no question but that Spargo would kick him out of the plane if he couldn't maintain altitude.

There was one more oddity concerning Charles Duchenne, especially in light of his position. Charles was afraid—of just about everything. His normally pink, porky cheeks were enhanced to various shades on the red end of the spectrum at the very thought of a confrontation. He survived only by hanging onto Lenny's coattails.

Stranger yet, for reasons known only to Charles, one of his greatest discomforts was being up close and personal with Jamie Littlebird. Jamie was well aware of this and played it to the hilt, only because of the dishonor that Dushenne and Spargo brought to the profession.

Truitt recalled a recent conversation between Jamie and Duchenne. Jamie had seen Charles coming out of the bathroom and soon had him cornered. After some small talk, Littlebird got down to business. "Ever skin a beaver, Chuck?"

"Uh, no." Duchenne's face was already heating up.

"Well, it's not really too hard." Jamie got in close. "Kind of fun, actually. You see, what you do is lay him on his back, then you take your knife, make a cut, and then...wait a second." Jamie lifted his right foot onto a chair seat and pulled up a pant leg. Strapped to his calf was a Paragon boot knife. The 4 and 3/8-inch blade was sharp as a razor. Jamie unstrapped the knife from its case and removed it. "Like I said, take your knife and kind of scrape it between hide and flesh. You know, sort of a shaving motion." Littlebird scraped the knife across his hand, while pulling in close to Duchenne.

That was enough for Charles. He feigned a call from nature and beelined back to the bathroom. For the next several weeks Duchenne gave Jamie even a wider berth than normal.

Chapter 24

Jamie Littlebird parked as close as possible, covering the remainder of the distance on foot. His destination was 8th Street and Nicollet Mall, in downtown Minneapolis. There he hoped to find his most productive informant, Bernard "Binky" Shepard.

Binky was a slightly mentally handicapped man in his early thirties. The handle "Binky" was of his own choice and not in the least bit demeaning. His parents had bestowed the nickname on him when he was very young. He liked it and so it stuck.

Bernard grew up in Golden Valley, not far from downtown Minneapolis. Binky's childhood was not an easy one, save for the unconditional love given to him by his parents. As can happen with handicapped young people, whether it be mental or physical disabilities, Bernard was subjected to bullying and taunting by his peers. Bernard and his parents often anguished over the question as to why in God's world the "stronger" feel the need to bully the more vulnerable rather than protect them.

Bernard often came home in tears, asking his mother, "Why are kids mean to me? Why do they tease me?"

"Because they don't understand you, Binky," his mom answered, "...because they want to be popular. They want to be accepted by their classmates...and because, well, their parents might not give them a loving, caring home like ours. I know it's hard, honey. But try not to feel bad. The other kids that tease you...well, they're lacking self-confidence. They're unhappy. You, on the other hand, you have love in your heart. That's what really counts in this world. You, my young man are one of God's angels on earth. Hold your head high and be proud of who you are."

Bernard did not forget his mother's words, nor did he betray them. Forever upbeat, always affable, Binky's destiny was to become the well-loved "unofficial" ambassador of downtown Minneapolis. His "office" was usually the corner of 8th Street and Nicollet in front of Barnes and Noble, although depending on the direction of a cold winter wind he might be found in front of Macy's.

Dressed in a Minnesota Twins jacket and baseball cap (courtesy of the organization), Binky also sported a San Francisco Giants emblem sewed to his jacket. When asked to explain the significance of the patch, he answered, "Willie Mays. The greatest ballplayer ever. My team in the other league. But don't worry. Joe Mauer's gonna catch him."

Binky greeted every passerby. Many he knew, many he didn't. It didn't matter. They would all get the same friendly smile and greeting, "Have a great day!"

Beyond being an "ambassador" Bernard was an excellent resource for information on just about anything going on in the downtown area.

Jamie found Binky on this warm, but gray summer morning, holding down his usual spot in front of Barnes and Noble. "Hey, it's the Binkster! How're you doing, my friend?" Jamie greeted as they knocked fists together.

"Chief Jamie," Binky answered, sporting a wide grin and shaking an index finger, "I bet I know why you're here."

"I'm not a 'chief' yet, and how do you know why I'm here?"

Binky raised his finger towards the sky. "Because Lieutenant Guy is dead and you want to find who did it."

"Well, Bink, I guess I can't fool you. You're pretty much right about that, and right now I don't have any leads. I sure could use your help. Have you seen anyone new hanging around or have you heard of any trouble going on lately?"

"I loved Lieutenant Guy. I miss him. He would always stop and say 'Hi' to me when he was around."

"We all miss him, Bink. So do you think you can help me? Anything bad been happening?"

Analytical thought was not an option for Binky. A piece of information was either readily available for dispensing or it wasn't there at all.

"Only Marsha. She lost her boyfriend. He's been missing for a while."

"Who's Marsha?"

"She's a waitress. She works at...," Binky hesitated for a moment. "...at H. Kitchen."

"You mean Hell's Kitchen, the restaurant around the corner?" Littlebird thought for a second. "Why did you call it H. Kitchen?"

"Because it's a swear word. I don't like swear words."

Jamie attempted to explain. "Well, you know, Bink, they don't mean anything bad by it. It's like, for effect, so people will remember the name. And it's also the way it's decorated inside. It's what we call 'theme.' Okay?"

Binky was not to be placated. "Why can't their theme be Heaven, instead? Their food is very good. I help them sometimes and I eat there. The people who work there are nice to me. I think it should be called Heaven's Kitchen."

Littlebird could see that this was hitting a dead end. "Yeah, I guess you're right, Bink. Maybe you can bring it up to them. Now, why don't we take a walk down to H. Kitchen. Maybe you can point out Marsha to me."

"No, I can't."

Littlebird looked puzzled. "Why not?"

"It's Thursday. Marsha doesn't work on Thursday."

"Oh, okay. Well, I guess I'll walk down there anyway. Someone may be able to tell me where she lives."

"Why can't I?"

"Why can't you what, Bink?"

"Tell you where she lives. I've been there. I helped her move furniture once."

Jamie shook his head. "Binky Shepard, you never fail to amaze me. I love you, man."

"I love you, too."

As always, Jamie attempted to pay Binky for his help. And as always Binky refused the offering with the answer, "It's my civic duty."

The apartment building where "Marsha" lived turned out to be only a short distance away. After returning Binky to his corner, Littlebird went back to the building and was soon scanning names alongside the intercom located just inside the entrance.

Binky didn't know the apartment number but he knew it was on the second floor. Also, he knew Marsha's last name. A match was easily found: M. Porter–204. Jamie pushed the call button.

"Who is it?" a raspy voice answered.

"Sergeant Jamie Littlebird. I would like to ask you a few questions regarding a missing person." No response. Finally, after several seconds the security door unlocked.

Marsha Porter projected an image that, at least this morning, appeared worse for the wear. Her glossy eyes were red and swollen. Both she and her apartment looked as though they had survived a category-four hurricane. The mounds of debris, including clothes, bags, blankets, papers, and other objects unidentified were not inviting anyone to sit on whatever might be beneath them. Jamie quickly decided to conduct the interview standing just inside the door. "Ms. Porter, I understand you may have some information concerning a missing person."

Porter stared at Jamie for a few moments and then slowly put a hand to her face and leaned against the wall behind her. "Okay, yeah, I do. My boyfriend, Rollie. I haven't seen him in a couple of weeks."

"Why haven't you reported him missing?" Jamie asked.

Porter looked away. "Because I thought he may have gotten caught up in something bad and didn't want to be found. Now, I'm sure he's dead. He would have contacted me by now if he was all right."

"Please tell what you know. Maybe we can find him for you."

"Well, Rollie loved photography. And he had big ideas, Rollie did. Always big ideas. We were going to go to Hollywood and he was going to work in the movie business. He entered every photo or film contest there was. Anyway, the day he disappeared he came home late in the afternoon all excited. A guy he had met at Pinkey's Pub about a week before called Rollie about a job. I guess Rollie must have told him about his expertise and given him his ad card. He needed some camera work done early that evening so Rollie rushed home to pick up a few things."

"Did he give you any idea what the job was about, where it was, or who this guy was?"

"I asked him all those questions. He said the guy didn't give him any details except where to meet him. Rollie offered to bring his equipment but the guy told him that all he would need was a cell phone. Rollie also said the guy told him not to breathe a word about this to anyone. Rollie seemed a little apprehensive. I think he was a bit scared. But if there was a risk, it was worth it to Rollie. I mean two grand for fifteen minutes work—you know, hard to resist."

"Did Rollie tell you anything else that might be helpful?" Jamie pressed.

Porter coughed up a small laugh. "Oh, yeah. Keeping his mouth shut was not one of Rollie's stronger points. The guy told Rollie to meet him in the McDonald's parking lot on 23rd and Heartstone Lane in Plymouth at 5:30 p.m. When Rollie didn't come home that evening, I drove over there but his car was nowhere in sight."

"By any chance did Rollie describe this guy?"

Porter lit a cigarette. "No, but Rollie drinks mostly at Pinkey's so I asked around there. One of the bartenders remembers seeing him talking to some big dude a couple weeks back. The bartender thinks he had thick glasses and was wearing a baseball cap. But he said he only remembered him because of his hands."

"What about his hands?" Jamie asked.

"The bartender said that his hands were huge."

After providing Jamie with Rollie's full name (Roland Albert Caramesian), a photo of him, and his vehicle license renewal card, Littlebird completed the interview. "Thank you for the information, Ms. Porter. Oh, one more question. What was the date of your boyfriend's disappearance?"

July 26th.

July 26th. The same night that Michael Carpenter died.

I really do love you, Binky, Littlebird thought to himself as he left the apartment building.

PART TWO

Shiv

Chapter 25

Although a second interview with A.M. Pallidin had been delayed, Mark Truitt now stood not only before the father, but also Brewster Pallidin. He had decided not to bring up Southeast Asia Pharmaceuticals until more information had been gathered on that matter. He didn't want to tip off anyone who might be involved in criminal activity.

"What can we do for you this morning, Sergeant?" the elder Pallidin asked as he leaned against his massive oak desk, sending cigar smoke swirling into the air. "Oh, and you may doubt my sincerity, but I *am* sorry about Guy Lompello. A terrible way to die."

Truitt replied tersely. "I am not questioning your sincerity, *and* I assure you I will bring the guilty party to justice." Taking a step closer to the elder Pallidin, Mark continued, "I asked to see you because we have new information on the deaths of Michael Carpenter and George Thurber."

Truitt was trumping this up in order to evoke a response.

"This information leads me to believe your company may be in some trouble. Now, the only way for me to properly sort and solve is for you two gentlemen to be completely transparent concerning any problems surrounding your business, and I don't believe that has happened so far."

Father and son looked at each other. After a long moment Armondo lifted himself out of his chair and walked over to the minibar. He swung open a round brass cover built into the bar's surface and dropped his cigar in the opening. A soft, whirring noise from within signaled the cigar's disposal.

At the same time, Brewster stood, walked over to a window, and stared outside. "You're right, Sergeant," he admitted. "You haven't been told the whole story. Although it's true that our business deals with human disease research, we do have a whole other branch that is, well, futuristic looking. At the present time..."

A.M. raised a hand, interrupting his son. "What does clean, fresh, drinkable water mean to you, Detective Truitt?"

"What do you mean?" Truitt asked.

Pallidin continued, "We don't think that much about it, do we? Especially in the land of 10,000 and...whatever, lakes. Water for us is a minor consideration. Well, that's not the case in many corners of the planet. The world's population is increasing by the day and along with it the demand for fresh water. Mankind is not actually running out of fresh water as it is constantly being recycled naturally. However, only a small fraction of that water is *both* accessible and fresh, and growing populations as well as ever-encroaching pollution increase the pressure on it by the day. Add to that the fact that close to forty per cent of the earth's ice-free land is devoted to agriculture. This land needs fresh water, and lots of it. In fact, two-thirds of our fresh water is used to grow the food that feeds a world population that is growing by over eighty million people a year, eight billion souls by 2025. By 2050, the rate of food production will have to double to keep up. Ain't gonna happen without new, abundant sources of fresh water."

Introducing a flame to a new cigar, Pallidin continued. "And then, of course, there is the issue of changing climate cycles as well as human-inspired climate change. The southwestern part of our country is a good example. The twentieth century was one of the wettest centuries in the last one thousand years in the Southwest. That is now reversing and vast quantities of water will eventually have to be transported to that region if the present burgeoning population is to be maintained. And how is climate change affecting the planet on a worldwide basis? Well, for one thing, monitoring stations indicate that the soil is slowly drying out just about everywhere. This phenomenon will mean lower crop yields. More people and less food—not a good combination."

Brewster turned away from the window and took over the conversation. "Lack of fresh water is taking a terrible toll in the form of disease and death. Women in some African countries spend up to eight hours a day searching for fresh, clean water. And the crowded cities in India? People have been beaten to death trying to cut in line where limited amounts of clean water are dispensed. So, what does all that have to do with Midwest Research Labs? Well, Sergeant, for several years we have been working on a cheap, fast, and efficient method to desalinate sea water. I mean pennies per gallon, not dollars, as it is now...and with the ability to desalinate huge quantities in a short amount of time. Our goal is to accomplish this not only with permanent facilities but also portable units."

He went on, "I understand that this must sound like science fiction but I assure you, we are so, so close. Water, water everywhere, Sergeant, and all you want to drink, and bath in, and water your crops. A cascade, no, better yet a waterfall of fresh, clean water quenching the thirst of an increasingly desperate world. We are even working on an environmentally friendly method to dispense the salt byproduct. The potential is enormous, the benefits incalculable, the urgency is, well, imperative."

Brewster took a long breath and looked in his father's direction. Armondo nodded, giving him the signal to continue. "Now, please understand: we are not seeking personal gain from our efforts. That was decided early on. The terrible consequences of the approaching fresh water shortage transcends any attempt to personally profit from this process. The future of the civilized world is at stake. Our plan is to use the proceeds from building desalinization plants in rich countries to subsidize similar facilities in poor countries. We want the world to share equally in what rightfully belongs to all humanity."

Truitt interrupted, "Admittedly, I don't know much about the subject, but how are you presumably so far ahead of present day methods of desalinization?"

A.M. took up the conversation. "Several companies are presently working on different types of innovative processes, including a procedure involving a forward osmosis process, a technology utilizing carbon nanotubes, and also a biomimetics process, all of which their developers hope to bring online in the next few years. Our offering, well, let's just say that sometimes in order to think big, you have to think small, very small. Add that concept to some already proven techniques, throw in a bit of luck, as in when by accident part A is mixed with part Y. Finally, never allow negativity to undermine your vision."

"Now, I'll tell you the dark side to all this." The voice came from behind. Chelsea Pallidin was standing in the doorway. "The financial burden from years of research and experimentation on this project has taken a terrible toll on our company to the extent that four years ago Midwest Research Laboratories was facing bankruptcy. We sought every option for the necessary funding to stay afloat, unfortunately to no avail. Finally, and quite out of the blue a company by the name of Paramount Investment Partners approached us. After quite intense negotiating we reached an agreement. What they really wanted was a full partnership in all aspects of our business, including the desalinization project. We did manage to derail that demand by offering royalties derived from income received from the process, but only for a limited time. As Brewster said, our vision of the desalinization process is not meant to be for profit, but we were forced to bend a little. Anyway, we wound up with the necessary finances to continue our research. We also inherited an onsite representative from Paramount."

"And that person is?" Truitt asked.

"Peter Malik," Brewster Pallidin answered. "We agreed to let him coordinate our disease prevention and research division, as well as including him in our financial decisions. However, and over his protests, we have not allowed him to get close to our desalinization research. This has greatly frustrated Peter and until a couple of months ago he had become increasingly belligerent. Paramount even threatened to pull their support."

Armondo walked behind the bar, setting his forearms on its smooth, shiny top. "Quite suddenly the threats from Paramount stopped entirely. Even Malik toned his protestations down to almost nothing. This aroused our suspicions, so I contacted an old friend who is well-connected in many circles. I asked him to find out what he could about Paramount Investment Partners. A few days later he got back to me. His first words were 'The snake must have your head in his mouth.' His inquiries suggested that even though on the surface everything appears to be legitimate with Paramount, the rumor is that it is actually one of several concerns owned by a covert union of extremely powerful people, at least some of whom believe it is their destiny to maintain order in an increasingly chaotic world. And, Truitt, think about it: How better to accomplish that than to control a basic life source that all humanity requires? I asked him about his 'snake' comment. He said that once they determine their objective, the game is all but over. They get what they want, always. And one more thing, Truitt; I've known this man for over forty years and this is the first time I have detected fear in his voice. He made me promise that he and I didn't even have the conversation, lest 'they' find out that he inquired about them. He left me with a final warning, 'Let it go, Armondo, if you want your family to be safe. They will get what they want. Human life is of little value to them.'"

Brewster broke in. "And I'm afraid that if you also don't heed that warning, you and those around you could be in danger. The hunter could become the hunted."

Truitt doubled down on his gaze at the Pallidins. Who were these people, and what were they really about? He half expected one of them to claim they had been contacted by alien beings with an offer to defend them against this horrible, covert "snake," or whatever.

"Mr. Pallidin, your story would more easily be corroborated if I could interview your friend. If you refuse to reveal him, that is, if he *is* real, well, that's only going to make your story harder to prove. And as far as Paramount Investment Partners, I will look into them."

Truitt pointed a finger in their general direction. "Now, let me give you some advice. There have been strange and deadly happenings surrounding Midwest Research Laboratories lately. Add to that the rather unbelievable story about a phantom covert organization trying to steal an equally phantom invention. This sounds like something right out of the *X Files*. I strongly suggest that you folks do everything you can to help me help you, because I foresee strong headwinds bearing down on the Pallidin family."

Armondo Pallidin displayed a look of disgust at being lectured. Brewster sensed this and cut his father off as he was about to speak. "Look, Sergeant, I promise we will not interfere with any investigation into Midwest Research Labs." Brewster turned to Chelsea. "Speaking of headwinds, are you ready for Paramount's audit later this week?"

Chelsea put a hand on his arm. "Oh, yes. And don't worry, bro, we'll get through it."

Truitt ended the interview with only a minor attempt at closing pleasantries. As he turned to leave the study, a younger man with an athletic build, ruggedly handsome face, and short-cropped black hair approached the small gathering.

"Am I interrupting anything?" the man asked. "I just needed to speak with Chelsea a moment."

Chelsea placed her arm around the man's waist. "No, not at all. We were just wrapping things up. Vincent, I would like you to meet Sergeant Truitt. Sergeant, this is my fiancé, Vincent Ponce."

"I've heard your name mentioned around here quite a bit lately," Ponce noted as the two men shook hands.

Vincent impressed Truitt as a person who appeared polished, but with a tinge of roughness around the edges.

Truitt left the Pallidin residence and made his way down the long driveway and out onto the highway. He mused that every time he interviewed a Pallidin he came away with more questions than answers. Mystery seemed to surround this family. He decided that they were either telling the truth...or they were nuts.

Chapter 26

Tom Moore stood at the sink in the kitchenette of his present motel room. Every few days he moved to a new location. He did not want to become a familiar face.

Moore looked down, staring for a moment at the roll of stomach and undershirt hanging over his belt buckle. Thoughts of trimming down were quickly dismissed as he unwrapped slices of processed cheese and set them on a plate. He ripped open a package of soda crackers, crumbs flying, and set them alongside the cheese. Next, he opened a beer.

Before delving into his snack, Tom dismissed his wad of chew, spitting it into the sink with the force of a dart being propelled out of a blowgun. Some of the discharge landed in the sink, some hit the splashboard, while other particles of the fine cut attached themselves to the wall above the sink. There were even a few specks left over to decorate the front of his undershirt.

The force of the launching action caused Moore's nose to twitch, which in turn induced a gigantic sneeze. When the blowout erupted, microscopic droplets of mucus were hurled in every direction, many of which came to rest on the cheese and crackers. He wiped his nose with his forearm, gathering up most of the residue but still leaving a telltale remnant on his moustache. Tom was now ready for his snack.

Moore's cell phone came to life as he bit into his third cheese single. "Yeah," Moore answered with his standard introduction.

Not one for small talk, X got right to the point. "There are two men arriving from Atlanta on Thursday to audit Midwest Research Labs. We want them to go back in a box. It's imperative that the blame gets properly placed. Here's what I want you to do..."

Following those orders, X had one more item. "There are two cops of particular interest to us. They're part of the reason you took out the old guy. Pictures of them will be sent to your post office box. Get to know what they look like."

When the conversation ended, Moore clicked his phone shut and thought to himself, *the next time you call I should be ready and, with any luck, soon after that the playing field will be level.* He took comfort in the fact that his handler's identity should soon be revealed.

As for now, back to those cheese slices.

Chapter 27

A few days had passed since Mark and Jamie split up. The one conversation between them included Truitt recalling the "strange" Pallidin interview and Jamie cautiously offering a possible lead. An inquiry into Paramount Investment Partners turned up a completely legitimate corporation. This made Mark wonder all the more what the Pallidins were really up to. Hopefully, the FBI would soon be able to shed some light on this whole, confusing cluster…however, the Pallidin fiasco wasn't the only reason for Mark being rather out of sorts this morning.

Mark's angst was also focused on his son. Brian had barely passed his recent college summer session and was becoming more unapproachable than ever. At least until recently Maggie had been able to extract some form of conversation from him, but even now that door had been closed. Worse yet, Brian announced that he was moving in with some friends, which set off an horrendous confrontation between Brian, Mark, and Liz. The battle ended with Brian leaving, and Mark and Liz not talking.

As Mark drove to work he prayed for some positive news of any nature. He also really wanted to see Amy Weldon, although, he admitted to himself, not for the right reasons. He was about to be granted his wish on both counts.

Truitt no sooner plunked down at his desk when his supervisor, Laverne Hathaway, waved him into his office. Already in attendance were detectives Lenny Spargo, irritatingly chomping on a wad of gum, and pinky-cheeked Charles Duchenne.

A meeting of the minds, Truitt thought as he entered the office.

Hathaway grabbed a piece of paper from on top of his desk. "The FBI has some information for us regarding Southeast Asia Pharmaceuticals. The Hong Kong authorities arrested this, ah, Jin Xuexiang, the guy George Thurber was in contact with? According to the report, at first Xuexiang feigned ignorance, but they have their ways and he quickly folded."

Hathaway continued. "The story he gave them was that he and one of the company vice-presidents, a guy by the name of Wu Zhong, conspired with Thurber and one other person at Midwest Research Labs to spread a mutated bird flu virus, which was to be followed up with a cure developed by MRL. Midwest Research Labs would make a hefty profit from the sale of the anti-flu serum and Zhong would get a nice kickback. Xuexiang and Thurber were to be given a one-time payoff and then disappear. He swore that was the extent of his involvement. Lenny, take the next part."

Spargo temporarily banished his gum to a remote corner of his mouth. "An inquiry into MRL's account didn't turn up any unusual financial transactions with Southeast Asia Pharmaceuticals." Spargo returned the gum to an active status. Charles Duchenne sported a blank look.

Hathaway continued, "The Hong Kong authorities noted that 150,000 dollars showed up in Zhong's personal financial account a couple of days before Thurber's death. I'm guessing it was about to take an electronic trip across the ocean."

"What about this Wu Zhong? What's his story?" Truitt asked.

Hathaway frowned. "He hasn't got one."

"Why not?"

"Because he's dead. The coward committed suicide. I guess he left behind a wife and six kids."

Truitt grimaced. "Why am I not surprised? Shades of Michael Carpenter. Okay then, did Xuexing finger the other conspirator at Midwest Research Labs?"

Hathaway answered the question with sweet authority in his voice. "He named Mr. Brewster Pallidin as the other conspirator involved. And to back this up there were two different emails discovered by the authorities in Zhong's email trash bin from Brewster Pallidin's email address, referring to the mutant virus and the amount of money to be sent. Now, I think it's time we introduce Mr. Pallidin to our cozy little quarters. Lenny, Chuck, go pick up Pallidin and bring him down for a little chat. Mark, good job on the information you provided. Keep your source active. See what else you can dig up."

I'd like to keep my source active all right, just not in the way you meant, Truitt reflected as he left Hathaway's office and headed outside. Once in his car, Mark contemplated all he had just heard and tried to match it to what he knew so far. Soon his brain was playing host to a "thoughts and questions pinball extravaganza." One thing that was not in question, however, was Laverne Hathaway's thinly masked elation at being in the middle of a rapidly developing high-profile case, and Truitt had no doubt he would make the most of it. Look out, Pallidins!

Once he processed the information, Mark realized this was the moment of truth for him concerning the Pallidins. Their world was about to cave in and either he was going to be part of the destruction or he would take on the role of Big John and hold up the supporting timber.

Chapter 28

Truitt ultimately let his conscience be his guide and decided to throw his weight with the Pallidins. He wasn't sure why. Maybe it was because their story was so implausible that it was plausible. At any rate, when the appropriate amount of solid evidence was lacking in a case, Mark often relied on his ability to read into people, and his inclination in this circumstance leaned towards the Pallidin family as the victims and not the aggressors. Now he would have to try to prove their innocence.

Mark shared his decision with Jamie Littlebird, who was always supportive, and Jamie declared, "You're crazy."

Mark returned his support in kind by wishing him well in his continuing search for Guy Lompello's and maybe Michael Carpenter's and maybe George Thurber's killer, followed by, "I thought you would have made better progress by now."

Truitt now focused his attention on Amy Weldon. She may well hold the key to Brewster Pallidin's future. A call set up a meeting at the same restaurant where they had met earlier.

Mark arrived before Amy this time and was settled into a booth when she walked in. As soon as he saw her, Mark had that youthful feeling of "flirtility," a contrived word coined by a college buddy, the definition of same open to interpretation.

"Hello, Sergeant, ah, excuse me, Mark," greeted Amy with a half smile, partially exposing a set of perfectly placed teeth enveloped by a layer of cocoa brown lipstick. Truitt struggled at pushing away dark thoughts as he began the conversation.

"Amy, I want you to know that because of the information you gave me regarding Southeast Asia Pharmaceuticals, we have a substantial lead which may involve Brewster Palldin."

Amy sat up straight, looking surprised. "Brewster Palldin? I can't believe he would be involved in anything criminal. I mean, he's tough and all business, but he's always been fair and supportive to all of us who work for him. There must be some mistake."

Truitt kept his voice low. "I didn't say that Brewster Palldin is guilty of anything. However, he has been brought in for questioning. For now I'm in his corner and, admittedly, I am fairly desperate for any information that would benefit him. Is there anything you can think of that might help his cause?"

As Amy started to speak, a waitress came to take their orders. Coffee for Mark, tea for Amy.

"As I was about to say," Weldon continued as the waitress left to fill the orders, "I've been trying to fill in some of the blanks leading up to George's death. Really, the only thing I can think of is that George, you know, reported to Peter Malik. They had weekly progress meetings in Peter's office. Well, one day late last winter George came back from one of those meetings in a real foul mood. Very agitated. Pounded on his computer keys, shuffled papers, grumbled to himself. After that, I don't know, but when I think about it now he seemed different. He was very sullen, like he was carrying a weight around." Weldon let out a deep breath, "I know that's not much of a help but that's about all I can think of."

"Every piece of a puzzle, no matter how small, helps to complete it. If you think of anything else, you have my number."

Mark and Amy lingered over their drinks long enough for the situation to plainly suggest that neither of them wanted to leave. Finally, Mark broke the stalemate. "Well, I guess we should be on our way."

"Yes, unfortunately," Amy said with an apparent hint of disappointment.

Truitt hoped that "unfortunately" meant what he wanted it to mean.

Mark and Amy continued their small talk as he walked her to her car. As Mark reached to open Amy's car door, she gripped his arm, rather tightly. "I so hope you can help Brewster. He's a nice man."

Truitt placed his free hand behind Amy's shoulder, pretending the gesture was necessary to make a point. He looked straight into her eyes; Amy returned the stare. They stood motionless for a few seconds, then each leaned a little closer to the other. For Mark Truitt this was it...THE moment of truth. In this timeless instant all that Mark had ever known, had ever seen, had ever felt, was placed in a vault of distant memories. In this moment there was only Amy.

They were now close enough that his breath drifted into hers, the two tiny masses of exhaled air floating together as one entity—swirling, dancing into the atmosphere. The point of no return was upon them...and then... and then...Mark's cell phone rang. It was Jamie.

"Hi, partner. Anything going on?"

Amy sank back against the car, smiled, and whispered, "We'll talk soon."

Mark started for his car, let out a big puff of air as he answered Jamie, "Looks like the cavalry got here just in time."

"Cavalry? Gee, thanks," Littlebird admonished. "You might guess they're high on *my* sentimentality list."

"Ah, sorry, poor choice of words. Having any luck finding our boy?"

"I've been passing around the vague description I have of him. Surprisingly, I've received a few nods so I'm hopeful that we may cross paths sooner than later. I'll call in a few days unless something comes up. See ya."

As Truitt put the phone in his pocket, he couldn't help but smile to himself. Once again Jamie had protected his backside, only this time he didn't know it.

Chapter 29

Brewster Pallidin was questioned and released. The ever-vigilant news media promptly dispersed the story throughout the Twin Cities and surrounding area—"PROMINENT TWIN CITIES BUSINESSMAN QUESTIONED IN MUTANT FLU VIRUS CASE."

The story held most everyone's attention and one thing was for sure; it certainly had not promoted a favorable opinion of the Pallidin family. In addition, an anonymous rumor surfaced that the Pallidins were somehow attached to the Guy Lompello murder.

Mark Truitt did not let on to his supervisor, Laverne Hathaway, about the Pallidins' suspicions concerning Paramount Investment Partners. Without proof, their speculation concerning the company's true identity would not serve to promote their cause. What Truitt needed right now was evidence of involvement in this case coming from a direction other than the Pallidins. A smoking gun, so to speak.

There about to be one. Unfortunately, it would be pointed directly at Brewster Pallidin.

There are few better ways to relax and temporarily banish one's problems to the back burner than to spend time in the family garden. This was exactly what Mark Truitt planned to do on his day off. He arose early and was about to start tying tomato plants when his supervisor called.

Hathaway said, "Mark, I know it's your day off, but I would like you to ride over to the Royal Suites. Two men were found this morning shot to death in a rental car in the hotel's parking lot. Spargo and Duchenne are on their way there now, but I think you'll want to be involved, too."

"Why is that?" Truitt asked.

"Because the victims were auditors employed by a company by the name of Paramount Investment Partners. They were here yesterday to audit Midwest Research Labs. A guy by the name of Peter Malik is on the way here to give a statement."

"I'm on my way," Truitt responded. A double half-hitch in his stomach would make the trip uncomfortable.

Jim Carmody, cigar in hand, was at the scene when Truitt arrived. "I love these outdoor gatherings. I can smoke."

"I'm glad you're having such a good day." Truitt rolled his eyes. "Not to ruin your merriment, but could you fill me in on what you've got so far?"

"Two deceased white males. One, early-thirties, the other, mid-forties. Estimated time of death, eight to eleven hours ago. Cause of death in both cases is attributed to small caliber bullets fired from very close range and penetrating the victims' skulls from the rear." Carmody added, "a particularly grisly scene for what appears to be a robbery. Maybe more than meets the eye here?"

Truitt shook his head. "As much as I would like to say it ain't so, I'm afraid my current case just got a little more complicated."

While Spargo and Duchenne were in the motel, interviewing employees and checking out the victims' room, Truitt waited as the paramedics removed the bodies. When the ambulance crew left, he began an inspection of the car in which the victims were found. On the surface the motive appeared to have been robbery. The victims' wallets were missing and their pockets had been turned inside out. If there were other items such as planners, briefcases, or whatever else auditors possess, they had either been taken or were in their motel room. The one item Truitt did find was a pair of glasses lying partially under the front seat. Mark picked them up with his pen and dropped them into an evidence bag. Having completed his search, and not desiring contact with Lenny or Chucky he left the parking lot and drove to precinct headquarters.

Peter Malik was sitting in Hathaway's office when Truitt arrived. "Mr. Malik, have you met Sergeant Truitt?" Hathaway gestured towards Mark as he entered.

"Yes, we have met," Malik replied somewhat curtly. "Good. Ah, Mark, Mr. Malik is aware of the deaths of the auditors from Paramount Investment Partners. He was with them yesterday when they were conducting their audit."

"Who else was at the meeting?" Truitt asked.

"Besides me, Brewster and Chelsea Pallidin."

"Please tell us all you can about what transpired yesterday," Hathaway urged.

"Well, the audit meeting started at 9:00 a.m. From the beginning it did not go well. The auditors produced one set of figures, Brewster and Chelsea had another. Now, please understand, I am not an accountant. I was brought in by Paramount to coordinate with research and development. However, as Paramount's representative onsite, I was required attend the meeting.

Anyway, after two hours of mostly arguing, we took a break. When we reconvened, Chelsea was not present. Brewster did not elaborate. After another hour of mostly finger pointing we broke for lunch.

Unfortunately, the afternoon session proved even less productive. The auditors told Brewster that Midwest Research Labs was headed for insolvency and that they were going to recommend to Paramount they should strongly consider pulling their support."

"How did Pallidin react to that?" Hathaway asked.

"He said he was being set up. Paramount wasn't going to live up to its end of the bargain—that they were trying to force him out. Then he stood, picked up his papers, announced that the meeting was over and stormed out."

"Were you with the auditors at all after the meeting?" Truitt asked.

"Oh, yes," Malik answered. "We were done early so I gave them a tour of the part of our facility where I have my privileges. That took a couple of hours and then we went downtown to Roggio's. We had drinks, ate, listened to a live band, had a few more drinks. We left the restaurant at approximately 10:00 p.m. They said they were going back to their motel. They had an early flight to Atlanta."

Truitt pressed on. "I assume they must have had papers, laptops, briefcases, things like that with them?"

"Of course," Malik answered. "They had all of their equipment and paperwork with them because we went right from the meeting to the restaurant. All of that should have been in their car."

"Do you recognize these?" Truitt set the evidence bag containing the pair of glasses on Hathaway's desk.

Malik stared at them a moment and then gave Truitt a puzzled look. "Yes, they look familiar. Where did you get them?"

"Who do they belong to?" Truitt had an ominous feeling.

"They look very much like the glasses Brewster wears for reading."

Hathaway was clearly getting excited. "Where did you get these?"

"They were under the front seat of the rental car," Mark somewhat reluctantly offered.

Hathaway extended a hand to Peter Malik, "That's all for now. Thank you for your cooperation. We'll call you if we need you."

As Malik was leaving, Hathaway's two aces wandered in. He quickly flagged them over to his office. "What did you find at the motel?"

Spargo spread his jacket and placed his hands on his hips as if he was about to make a great revelation. "Nothing. Absolutely nothing. No employees saw or heard anything. The victims' clothes and personal items were in their rooms, but that was it."

"No laptops, briefcases, nothing like that?" Truitt asked.

"Nope," Spargo answered, not looking at Truitt.

Hathaway shoved his hands in his pockets, jumbled his change around, and walked slowly around his desk, becoming increasingly consumed with his good fortune, as well as himself. After a few moments he laid out *the* plan. "All right, here's what we're going to do. I'll arrange for a search warrant for the Brewster Pallidin residence. Spargo, Duchenne, pick up Pallidin and bring him to his house. Then I want the three of you and Littlebird to turn that place upside down and inside out. Also, I'll have Moeller and Hogan search his office. Brewster Pallidin is connected to these murders and I want the proof."

Truitt contacted Jamie and arranged to meet him on the way to the Pallidin residence. As Mark was driving to meet Jamie he contemplated the recent events. His years of experience at sensing and sorting people convinced him of two things. One, Brewster Pallidin did not murder the two auditors, nor did he contract for their deaths.

Two, Peter Malik knew more, a lot more than he was letting on to. And if that was the case, what about Paramount Investment Partners? Was Armondo Pallidin right about them? Truitt shuddered at the thought.

Chapter 30

"Why did Hathaway have to send those knuckleheads to Pallidin's, too?" a very annoyed Jamie Littlebird barked at Truitt, referring to Lenny Spargo and Charles Duchenne. "I mean, honestly, there's a better chance of a blizzard in Belize than them finding anything. Am I right? Don't you agree?"

"I'll vote for the blizzard," Truitt calmly answered. "But I'm thinking there may be an ulterior motive. I know this is way out there and I hate to even think it; but I'm getting bad vibes from Hathaway. I don't trust him and I wouldn't put it past him to have those two around just to keep an eye on us. And another thing: this Peter Malik. I don't think he is who he says he is." Truitt hesitated for an instant, then continued. "I think it's time, my friend, we start taking care of ourselves. We're going rogue."

"Wow, a rogue Indian cop. I like the sound of that," Jamie said with a devilish grin.

Spargo and Duchenne were inside the Pallidin residence when Mark and Jamie arrived. There were two other cars in the driveway. Mark assumed that one of them belonged to Brewster Pallidin.

Although Brewster's home didn't advertise excessive wealth as did his father's, it definitely reflected a well-to-do owner. The two-story home was capped with multiple high-pitched roofs. The entire structure was encased with earth-tone shades of brick. Huge windows looked out onto a rolling meadow on one side and an hourglass-shaped lake on the other.

Littlebird rang the doorbell. Almost immediately the door was opened by a very distraught Brewster Pallidin. Behind him stood another man dressed in a business suit. Truitt assumed that was the owner of the other car.

"Would you mind telling me what is going on, Truitt? These cops (pointing to Spargo and Duchenne) show up at my office, drag me home, and serve me with a search warrant. What's this about?"

"Mr. Pallidin, we are going to conduct a search of your property," Truitt answered. "We may have some questions for you."

"Any questions should be directed at my lawyer," Pallidin gestured to the man in the business suit.

It was decided that Spargo and Duchenne would conduct a search of the house and Truitt and Littlebird would cover the garage and outside grounds.

"If there is evidence in the house, it's safe unless one of them trips over it," Littlebird speculated.

"They couldn't spot a whale in a swimming pool," Truitt added.

Truitt combed through the contents of the garage while Jamie covered the outside grounds, including the outbuildings.

It wasn't long before Mark heard his name being called. He stuck his head out of the side door of the garage but didn't see anyone.

"Mark, bring a shovel and come behind the storage shed," Jamie beckoned as he appeared from behind the shed.

Truitt retreated to a corner of the garage where the hand tools were stored. He found a shovel amid several other yard implements. As he removed the shovel he noticed fresh dirt on the blade. He scraped off some of the dirt, put it in an evidence bag, set the shovel aside, and grabbed another.

The storage shed was surrounded on three sides by a flower garden. Though summer was still at high tide, many of the flowers were in the first stages of an exit strategy, most likely due to a lack of water. Truitt found Littlebird behind the shed, crouching down, focusing on a patch of dirt in the flowerbed.

"What have you got?" Truitt asked.

"Looks like somebody's been doing some digging. Look at how the dirt's been turned over. There's even a little fresh dirt on the grass here."

Truitt held out the shovel. "Do you want the honors, or should I?"

Littlebird grabbed the shovel. He dug down about a foot when his shovel hit something hard. A few more shovelfuls exposed a brown briefcase. Under that briefcase was a second one.

Jamie put the shovel down and brushed the remaining dirt aside with his hand. "I guess this is what they call paydirt. Pun intended."

Truitt tried his best not to look disappointed. "Let's look inside."

The first briefcase contained a laptop, papers, a wallet, and change. The wallet produced a driver's license which bore the name of Sidney Fulton. A quick scan of the papers produced the name of Midwest Research Laboratories. Truitt didn't look further.

The second briefcase also contained papers, a laptop, change, and a wallet. A driver's license belonged to James Wristo.

The second briefcase contained one other item. A Walther PPK .32 caliber handgun. Truitt whistled. "Shades of James Bond."

Jamie gave Mark a puzzled look. "What do you mean?"

"Sean Connery used to flash one of these around in his movies."

The flowerbed held one further clue. A footprint.

When Mark and Jamie returned to the house, Brewster, his lawyer, along with Spargo and Duchenne, were gathered in the living room. "Did you find anything outside?" Spargo asked with unappointed authority.

Truitt ignored the question and asked directions to Pallidin's bedroom. Once there, he and Jamie rummaged through the closet.

"Found 'em." Jamie said, holding up a pair of jogging shoes. He put them in a bag and then he and Mark headed downstairs.

Brewster Pallidin and his lawyer were alone in the kitchen when Truitt caught up with them. Littlebird rounded up the Hardy boys and brought them along. Pallidin was arrested, read his rights, and brought downtown.

The case against Brewster Pallidin was solidifying with each piece of evidence recovered. Pallidin claimed that the reading glasses found in the rental car had been missing for a couple of days previous to the murders. The auditors' briefcases, papers, wallets, and the gun, which was registered to Brewster Pallidin (later proved to be the murder weapon and with partial fingerprints on the barrel matching Brewster's), were all recovered on the Pallidin property. Added to that, Brewster Pallidin had no alibi for his whereabouts around the time of the murders. His family was out of town for the week and he claimed he had spent the evening home alone unwinding with a few drinks after the tense day he had endured with the auditors.

The news media had a field day. Brewster Pallidin was literally the talk of the town. Hardly a day passed when the Pallidins' name wasn't mentioned either on television or popped up in a newspaper. Popular opinion had his fate signed, sealed, and soon to be delivered.

The "delivered" part would have to wait for the New Year, as the trial date was set for the following January. In the meantime Brewster Pallidin was in seclusion at his home, having been granted bail.

As for Laverne Hathaway, he seized every opportunity to be seen as well as heard. This was his day in the sun and he made the most of it. He managed to sprinkle some credit on Lenny Spargo and Charles Duchenne, and would have liked to have brought Truitt and Littlebird into the fold also, but they did their best to stay on the sidelines.

Chapter 31

Tom Moore dug the ringing cell phone out of his pocket with one hand and flicked a toothpick towards the garbage can with the other. 10:12 p.m. Did his handler have another assignment for him? He hoped so, it had been several days since taking out the auditors and Moore was getting bored. Before he answered the phone he flipped the switch on the sound analysis equipment he had borrowed from his old Army acquaintance. *This better work,* he thought to himself.

Moore answered with his standard "Yeah, I'm here."

"Good job with the auditors. The 'evidence' produced from our handiwork, along with the road grading episode courtesy of their lieutenant, should swing this Truitt and Littlebird in our direction for good. But listen, this is why I called. Keep on the ready because I may yet need your services. If these cops waver, even a little, we'll have to hit this Mark Truitt right between the eyes. It's not an option for either one of them not to be in our corner."

"That important, huh?" Moore wanted to keep X talking in order to get as many sound bites as possible for the decoder.

"Look, they are two of the most respected cops in the community. Pitting them against Pallidin puts a big nail in his coffin. I mean, we have all the players exactly where we want them right now. If they think Pallidin is innocent, they could screw up everything. If it got to the point where we had to take them out, even if it looked like an accident, red flags would go up everywhere. No, it's easier all around if they believe Pallidin is guilty."

X had heated up the air waves long enough to satisfy Moore. "Okay, that's it, then?"

"Goodbye."

Moore turned to the computer and started the decoding program. This wasn't a sure bet by any means. X was obviously using one of the more hi-tech transformers, which meant that analysis and reversal would be more difficult. Standard voice changers are merely "pitch shifters," resulting in higher pitched voices sounding like chipmunks and lower pitched voices sounding like giants.

Transformers independently control pitch and harmonics so that an altered voice can sound completely normal. Tom kept his fingers crossed. For what seemed like an eternity a whole lot of things he didn't understand flashed on and off the screen.

Suddenly "PROGRAM COMPLETE" appeared. Moore pushed the "run" icon. A voice came across loud and clear. Tom Moore had his voice. Now he needed a face and a name. He was ready to put the second part of his plan in motion.

It had been a good night. Why not go out and celebrate? Maybe even find a whore.

Chapter 32

Sooner or later everyone comes to a point in life when events overpower one's ability to function in a normal manner. At this juncture one needs to separate oneself from the confrontations and challenges of human interaction and, well, take a time out.

This is exactly what Mark Truitt found himself doing this night. Having the house to himself he decided to partake in a one-on-one therapy session. One of the ones in the one-on-one was himself; the other resided in his liquor cabinet.

Having removed the good "Doctor of Liquid Libations" from the cabinet, the two strode bottle-in-arm to the sacred sanctuary—where else? The garage. Now, there is an old saying that a man's home is his castle. Not true. It's the garage. And here is where Mark prepared to make his stand, to sort out all that had happened in his life the past several weeks, and to make a plan to bring normalcy back into it again. Mark set the bottle on top of his workbench and pulled up a stool. Just as he began to unscrew the cap, he remembered that, preceding a "therapy" session, ground rules best be reviewed.

Rule number one: If the little woman happens upon the scene when the session is in progress, say as little as possible. Remember, everything you say and do *will* be held against you the next day. Try to get away with smiling and nodding (It never works).

Rule number two: Operation of any power tools or associated equipment is prohibited. This includes the riding lawn mower, even if you're convinced that setting a new world record time for cutting your lawn is within grasp.

With the ground rules established, Truitt was ready to begin. The cap was removed and out came two fingers of inspiration. The first order of business was, well, the first thing on his mind; Amy Weldon. Much background work had gone into finding a solution to this problem. Mark had wrestled with it for days. The conclusion was that there was but one answer. Mark had always been, and would always be, faithful to his wife. Sure they were having problems right now, but that could be worked out. What kind of a husband would he be if he abandoned her in a time of such distress?

Amy was a desire, an illusion of sorts, a nice person who possibly was fantasizing much as he. He would talk to her and that would be the end of it.

Problem solved. Next item.

Mark poured another two fingers. No, make it three. Liz. She had been so hostile and remote lately. Mark decided that whatever it took, he would leave no stone unturned to get their marriage back on solid footing.

Problem solved. Next item.

Another round of two up. No, make it three. Brian. Mark admitted to himself that he did not relish confronting Brian. It was easier, much easier, to avoid what had become the obvious. With Brian now living away from home, his issues were even more "out of sight, out of mind." This had to stop. Mark promised himself to bring the situation to a head.

Problem...solved? No, addressed. Next item.

Mark poured himself another two fingers. *No, make it..., ah, keep it at two.* Brewster Pallidin. The effects of Doctor Inspiration had not altered his convictions about this person. Brewster was not guilty of any crime. Mark knew it, but how could he prove it? And again, if he was innocent then quite simply Paramount Investment Partners was guilty. If that was true and if Armondo Pallidin was right about them, then it's a whole new ball game.

This frightening possibility put the whole therapy session on hold. No way was he or Jamie prepared to go against sinister, powerful, wealthy people. They were just regular cops trying to do their jobs. To say that they were in over their heads may have been an understatement. There was only one action to be taken at this point—*raid the kitchen!*

A few minutes later Mark returned to the garage armed with barbequed potato chips and venison jerky. Nothing to clear the mind like wholesome food.

Several chips and two jerky sticks later, Mark felt the urge. On his way to the bathroom he passed by the washer and dryer. A thought surfaced that would have to be expanded upon with the return trip.

On his way back to the garage, Mark looked at the dryer. There were three unmatched crew socks lying on top of it. Why? At one time three matched pair of socks had been sent to the washer for cleaning. One half of those pairs had gone AWOL. Where did they go? Why did they leave? And why won't they come back? *A matter for further contemplation!*

Then again, maybe not so much. Socks had not been on the agenda. *Guess I should have used pinky finger measurements,* Mark determined as he trudged back to his sanctuary.

Realizing the night was getting long in the tooth and all the dragons had been tamed, it was time to put the genie back in the bottle, and hope that tomorrow morning would take a couple of days to arrive.

Garage lights off. Bathroom light on. Bathroom light off. Bedroom light on. Bedroom light off.

Bathroom light on.

Chapter 33

While Mark Truitt was in his "therapy" session, Tom Moore sat on a bar stool, stripping pull tabs and nursing a beer. His elbows rested on the bar, propping him up but not entirely relieving him of a hunched position. The baseball cap riding low on his eyes discouraged a good look at his face. Tonight, contact lenses replaced his thick glasses.

The bar was crowded with patrons at the height of their merriment, their conversations competing with the country-western music playing on the turned-up amplifiers.

Eventually, a tall, thin, quite inebriated man zeroed in on Moore. Staggering, he nearly landed in Tom's lap. "Whaddya say, Rudolph, gonna to buy me a drink?" the drunk leaned in close to Moore, bellowing in his ear.

The "Rudolf" comment was a poke at Moore's red, bulbous, nose.

Moore didn't look up. "Get lost."

"Stringbean" didn't take the hint. "Hey, Ugly Butt, you got two choices, buy me a drink or I'm going to make you even uglier." Then, almost falling into Moore, he pushed a long, skinny finger into Tom's chest. "By the way, you know, your mother should have kept the afterbirth and thrown you away. I'm sure it was prettier."

Tom Moore quietly stood up, threw fifty dollars on the bar and walked out. Stringbean grinned, scooped up the money, ordered a drink. Moore got in his car—and waited.

Stringbean celebrated all fifty bucks into the bar's cash register, buying drinks for himself and showing off with rounds for other customers. When the money was gone, he decided to call it a night. The now extremely drunk man was most pleased with himself as he staggered to his car. He had paid for tonight's good time with someone else's money. *What a deal!*

Stringbean opened his car door and flopped into the driver's seat. Just then something grabbed his left wrist and yanked his arm backward. About all he got out was, "What the...." Suddenly, searing pain was shooting up his arm, well overpowering the numbing sensation of the alcohol in his system.

The car door moved and a wad of paper towels was shoved in his mouth. Stringbean realized his arm had been slammed in the car door. Before he could react, the door slammed again. Stringbean looked down. The lower half of his forearm was at a right angle to the upper half. Then he looked up, and stared into the face of Tom Moore.

Moore headlocked Stringbean with his right arm. Then, a switchblade opened in his left hand. Stringbean was feeling nauseous, residue of the night's partying gathering in his throat.

"You know what?" Moore said in a low, sadistic voice, "You really need to speak with more respect to strangers. Too bad you won't have the chance to improve on your manners."

With that, Moore thrust the knife into Stringbean's throat, in line with his collarbone, slowly pulling it up to his chin. The razor-sharp weapon made a surgical cut, neatly slicing Stringbean's throat in two, the blade tip gliding along his neck bones. The knife continued through the epiglottis and beyond, giving this miserable drunk a truly forked tongue, right up to the front of the jawbone. Stringbean half-chortled, half-gurgled, simultaneously suffocating and bleeding to death.

Moore cursed himself as soon as he removed his knife. He had lost his temper and that could bring complications. Now he really needed to secure X's identity.

Chapter 34

For Mark Truitt this was one of those "never again" mornings. The "good doctor" had become a witch doctor intent on revenge. It was going to be a long day. Truitt hoped it would be a quiet one.

Mark's cell phone rang immediately following his silent prayer for a quiet morning. *So much for hoping.* It was Jamie. "Come down to the Lost Oasis Bar and Grill. I'll meet you there."

When Mark arrived, Jamie was standing in the parking lot with Jim Carmody. Alongside them a stretcher supported a body bag. A cloud of cigar smoke encircled Carmody.

"Man, you ought to be ticketed for an air quality violation," Truitt quipped as he brushed at the air with his hand.

"Sorry, my environmental steward," Carmody apologized. "This is purely medicinal. The fresh air hurts my lungs."

Truitt turned his attention to the body bag. He hesitantly unzipped the bag as his stomach was in no mood to observe a dead body. Mark didn't have much unzipping to do before the organ cried foul.

"What's the story?" Truitt turned to Jamie as he re-zipped the bag.

"His name was Donald Borchart," Jamie answered. "The reason I got you down here is that I can connect this level of violence with Guy's death. Wallet was on his person. There's cash inside the wallet. He was found in his car."

"Robbery apparently was not the motive, then," Truitt contemplated. "So, maybe either kicks or revenge?"

"Could be either one," Littlebird agreed. "The bar owners are on their way down. Should be here shortly."

As the bar owners drove in, Carmody and the ambulance left the scene. Mark and Jamie followed the owners inside.

Dushan Paklovich was a large, husky, brooding man, the perfect specimen for keeping order in a liquor dispensing establishment. In contrast, Leroy "Lam" Olson, stood barely a head and a pint above the bar. A real Mutt and Jeff duo. Olson was by far the more talkative of the two.

After explaining what had transpired in the parking lot, Littlebird began the questioning. "What can you tell us about Donald Borchart and any trouble you may have had here last night?"

Olson was quick to answer. "I tell ya, Officer, I'm not surprised this happened to Donnie. He was always pushing on people. You know, panhandling for drinks, threatening them if they didn't produce." He turned to Paklovich, "Right, Dewey, right?"

Before Paklovich could answer, Olson continued. "We've thrown him out of here I don't know how many times. I mean he needed his butt kicked, but...geez, this was a little harsh."

Littlebird turned to the big man. "Do you remember if Borchart was with or talking to anyone?"

Paklovich rubbed his chin. "The only reason I remember this is because I keep an eye on Borchart in case he hassles my customers. Pointing to the opposite end of the bar, Paklovich continued. "There was a guy sitting over there, minding his own business. Pretty soon I seen Donnie talking to him. Not long after, the guy gets up and leaves. Well, I go over there, ready to toss the creep, and he hands me a fifty and says, 'Gimmie the usual, and a round for my friends.' What could I do?...and here I thought he really scared that guy."

Fending off pitchforks tipped with ample doses of the revenge of Doctor Inspiration, and taking dead aim at his digestive system, Truitt pressed on. "Can you give us a description of the fellow Borchart hit on?"

Palkovich thought. Olson answered. "I remember, Officer. I gave him a couple of beers. He was wearing a green army jacket and a baseball cap. Dark brown it was, I think. He had the cap pulled down over his eyes. I remember his nose, big, reddish-purple. And, oh yeah, when he paid me I couldn't help but notice his hands, I mean they were like bear paws."

The bar owners were thanked for their cooperation. As Truitt and Littlebird headed to their cars, Mark's phone rang. It was a quick conversation. "Hathaway wants to see us...now."

"The day just keeps getting better," Jamie quipped.

"My headache's getting worse."

Chapter 35

Truitt resigned himself to the fact that this was not destined to be one of his better days. His stomach and head were retaliating for the previous night's transgressions. The sight of a body relieved of its earthly status in a most heinous manner further added to his rather droll disposition. As luck would have it, the morning was about to degenerate even further.

"Well, well, if it ain't the Wit brothers," Truitt remarked as the detectives exited their car at precinct headquarters.

"Wit brothers?" Jamie queried.

Truitt pointed to the building entrance where Lenny Spargo and Charles Duchenne were positioned on the steps. "Yeah, Half and Dim." Spargo was enjoying a Marlboro while Duchenne patiently awaited his next command.

"Just walk by them, don't say anything. I'm not in the mood," Truitt pleaded with his partner. Unfortunately

Mark's self-induced "condition" this morning, Jamie decided, did not justify a whole lot of sympathy.

"Hey, Lenny," Littlebird pointed to the cigarette. "Don't you know those things can kill you?" Jamie always knew how to light the fire.

Lenny blew an "O" ring of smoke into the air and flicked ashes onto the steps. "Put your mind at ease, Littlebird. Our wonderful elected officials are working on that problem. They think they can tax cigarettes out of existence. You know, if cigarettes cost too much, surely smokers will crush their packs and throw them into the nearest trash can. Yeah, right. Do you know what that tax is, Littlebird? A coward's tax, that's what. Smokers are a tax-producing 'whipping boy.' Whenever there's a shortfall in the state's coffers it's pretty non-controversial for these self-righteous politicians to pick on a relatively small segment of the voters. It's a win-win for them. They don't upset the majority, they bring in more money, and they perform a 'morally' just act at the same time. And how many of these legislative 'heroes' have been picked up for DUI's?"

Lenny was up to full speed. There was no stopping him now.

"You want to be fair? Then I say, let's tax obesity, too. I mean less than a quarter of us smoke, but close to a third are considered obese. How much do *they* add to the cost of medical care? And you know what? I know how to do it. Put a certified scale in every courthouse in the country. At the beginning of each year, everyone gets weighed and those who are porked up pay a 'Fat' tax."

Truitt was looking for a garbage can. Littlebird was pretending to be entranced.

Spargo pointed a finger at Jamie. "Of course, that will never happen. And do you know why it won't happen? Because obesity affects too many voters and it's big business. I mean look at all the money people spend on food then turn around and throw more money at trimming down. An obese person shells out about six thousand more bucks a year on average than the rest of us. Votes and bucks, Littlebird. That's what it's all about. You know what I say? Forget these excessive sin taxes. Everybody's got their own deals. Leave people alone. I mean, who wants to be addicted to something? It's supposed to be a free country, so let people work out their problems on their own terms. One thing that won't work, for sure, is trying to tax an addiction away."

Satisfied with his rant, Spargo lit another cigarette.

Mark cast an evil eye at Jamie, "I'll get even, I promise."

"You're looking a little better, by the way."

One person not sporting a pleasant disposition this morning was Lieutenant Laverne Hathaway. In fact he was not looking very happy, not very happy at all, as Mark and Jamie entered his office.

"Where have you two been this morning?"

Littlebird took the initiative. "We were at the Lost Oasis Bar and Grille. You know, where that homicide occurred last night."

Hathaway slapped a handful of papers onto his desk "Why were you there? Nobody assigned you to that case. You two are not the only investigators in this department."

"Hold on, you don't...." Truitt tried to explain.

"No, you hold on a minute," Hathaway pointed his finger at Truitt. "Right now, you have two assignments. One is to find Guy Lompello's killer, regarding which, I don't see any progress being made. The other is to complete what probably amounts to a mountain of reports for the DA in the Pallidin case. Also, he wants to meet with you guys; *that is*, if you can spare the time. We need to be properly prepared when Pallidin's trial starts and I expect you two to do your part to make sure that happens."

Truitt's face radiated a full flush, which didn't go unnoticed by Littlebird. "We're on it, Lieutenant," Jamie said, yanking Truitt out of Hathaway's office.

As they headed towards the stairway, Hathaway called after them. "Oh, and by the way, the FBI called yesterday. Remember that Jin Xuexiang, Thurber's contact in Hong Kong? Seems like he couldn't take the heat either. He was found hanged in his cell." Hathaway shrugged his shoulders and stepped back in his office.

Once outside the building, Mark expounded his feelings. "You see what I mean, Jaim? Hathaway's trying to keep us contained and if he thinks that he can bully us... well, we can work around that. Somebody's whispering in his ear; I'm sure of it."

"You mean he's on the take?" Jamie asked.

"Wouldn't surprise me, and because of that possibility we have to be extra cautious. How about if we do this? We'll both have to meet with the DA, but other than that, you keep with the crowd and continue searching for our boy. I have a feeling that catching up with him may be Brewster Pallidin's only chance at redemption and maybe our ticket out from under Hathaway's thumb. I'll poke around and see if I can come up with anything on Hathaway."

"Good plan. What do you think about Xuexiang? Looks like the Hong Kong connection is a dead end."

"Our phantom organization appears to be very efficient at tying up loose ends. And, if you noticed, Hathaway didn't seem to be all that disappointed."

As the two detectives were about to part ways, Jamie produced a final thought, along with a wink, "We're still rogue cops, right?"

Truitt put a finger up to his lips and grinned, "Yeah, but we're gonna keep it a secret."

Chapter 36

The neatly dressed gentleman smiled politely at all those with which he made eye contact as he entered the main lobby at Midwest Research Labs. Looking rather lost he slowly ambled over to the reception counter. Once there, he tipped his Belfry fedora to the receptionist and bid her good morning.

"Excuse me, my name is Edward Higgins. I represent the Canby Vessel Company. We are a lab equipment supplier. Would you be so kind as to tell me whom I may speak with concerning my products?"

The receptionist pointed to a clock on the wall behind her. "I'm sorry, sir, our business hours are from 8:00 a.m. to 4:00 p.m. As you can see it's only 7:45. Also, our purchasing manager, Jeffery Granover, is seen by appointment only. I will be happy to give you his number and you can call for an appointment."

While the receptionist was talking, the gentleman scanned the area around the reception island. Behind her, were rows of identification badges. This was just what he wanted to see: a perfect scenario.

"Thank you, young lady. I appreciate your help. I will arrange an appointment with Mr. Granover." The gentleman again tipped his hat with his right hand, while at the same time, sticking a small device to the underside of the counter with his left hand.

Once outside, Tom Moore rubbed his hands together. What luck! It looked like many, if not all, of the employees at Midwest Research Labs were required to wear identification badges. That meant they would have to stand at the counter and use their voice, at least a little. The bug Moore planted under the counter was very sensitive. It could pick up a near-whisper. The conversations would be relayed to decoding equipment Moore had in a van in the parking lot.

Why had Tom Moore chosen Midwest Research Labs to seek out his handler? Quite simply, he had little choice. Moore had nowhere else to look and if good fortune was with him, by the end of the day X would have a face.

Moore climbed into the van and turned on the receiver, which was programmed to alert him when the exact pitch of X's voice came through the transmitter. Now all he could do was wait.

Sitting in his van, listening for the sweet sound of the matching voice required Moore to live the phrase, "all dressed up and nowhere to go." Finally, the four o'clock hour rolled around. Employees were turning in their badges and exiting the building. Voice after voice flowed into the receiver, but no matches were made.

When the flow of people leaving the building trickled down to one or two at a time, Moore became frustrated. He needed this to work. Suddenly the receiver came to life.

The machine emitted several beeps, then—MATCH—flashed across the screen. Moore peered through his windshield. Only one person passed through the doors to the outside.

Tom Moore got his first look at X. From here it would be easy to come up with a name.

Chapter 37

The six o'clock hour had come and gone leaving a tired Mark Truitt in its wake. He had spent most of the day either meeting with the DA or pouring through the mountains of paperwork associated with the Pallidin case.

Jamie Littlebird somewhat begrudgingly also participated in meeting with the DA and, according to plan, exited when the paperwork rolled around. Because of the vicious and unusual nature in which Donald Borchart was murdered, Jamie calculated that their killer most likely had held the murder weapon. If that were the case, Jamie speculated that their man would move his social life out of the downtown area, where the murder had been committed. Littlebird took a guess, deciding to check the nightclubs in the western and southern Twin Cities suburbs.

Even though he really wanted to call it a day, Truitt had one more thing that needed to be done and he couldn't put it off any longer.

"Amy, this is Mark. I know it's late but is there someplace I can meet you?"

Weldon sounded surprised. "Well, sure, um, I just got home. Why don't you come here?"

After getting directions, Mark drove to Amy's apartment. His hands were clammy on the steering wheel. He really wasn't sure what he would say or how he was going to say it.

Upon reaching Amy's door, Mark took a moment to collect his thoughts.

"Come on in," Amy beckoned as she opened the door.

Maybe it was the perfume. Maybe it was her new hairstyle. Maybe it was the formfitting dress that outlined her perfectly shaped figure. Most probably it was all of the above that consorted to nearly lock Truitt's lower jaw in place.

With all dignity abandoned, Mark managed to force out a loosely structured sentence. "Amy, uh, I need to talk to you and it's, well, not about the Pallidin case."

Amy's alluring smile turned to one of concern. "Well, then, come and sit down," she said, pointing to the couch.

Mark placed himself on one end. Amy sat also, about in the middle. Mark's heart was pounding so hard he was sure that any moment it would fly out of his chest and land in her lap.

Alone with a beautiful woman. No one knows that you're there. And worst of all, Mark knew—he just knew that if he grabbed her right now, she would not resist. Her body language exuded passion. *Okay, Truitt, this is it.* Mark swallowed, hard.

"Amy, I have a confession to make. I don't know how to say this any better than...I want to be with you. I'm afraid I've fallen for you. I think about you all the time and it's driving me crazy."

Weldon stared downward, saying nothing.

Truitt continued. "Look, I know I'm being foolish. Fantasizing on my part, yes, I'm sure. I mean someone as attractive as you chasing around with the likes of me? What am I thinking? I'm sorry. This must be awkward for you. I'll just say goodbye. I won't bother you again."

Amy's eyes welled up. She put her hand on his forearm. "I'm sorry, too, Mark. I'd be lying if I said I didn't feel the same way. Don't blame yourself. I led you on because I wanted to be with you, too. I have been lonesome for so long, but...in the back of my mind I knew a relationship between us couldn't work. I could never take someone away from their family." Amy took a deep breath. "Go home to your wife. I hope she realizes what a wonderful husband she has."

If guilt could be weighed, Mark Truitt had just shed a thousand pounds of it. They said a brief goodbye and parted.

Mark headed home, deep in thought. His oldies station so far had provided little comfort, the first several tunes mostly falling on deaf ears. Then it was Morris Albert's turn on stage. The melancholy tone and sad lyrics of "Feelings" struck a chord. He almost shut it off, then weighed the futility of trying to escape your emotions. The radio played on.

Chapter 38

The sun was gliding through Virgo (or Leo, depending on one's astrological bias), when Jamie Littlebird finally came across a good lead.

A motel clerk provided Littlebird with a more complete description of a man who fit the rough outline recalled by the bar owners. He had stayed at the motel for three nights and checked out two days earlier. The motel was located in the Minneapolis suburb of Maple Grove, and so Littlebird decided to concentrate his search in that general area.

Friday night. The start of Labor Day weekend. Patrons were gathering at their favorite watering holes, and Mixer's Sports Bar was one of the more popular establishments. The festivities were in high gear when Jamie entered the bar.

Littlebird stood inside the door and scanned the scene before him. Along the outside wall to his left was a row of tables. Ahead of him and along an inside, half-high wall was another row of tables. The wall supported wooden posts which rose to the ceiling. The tables framed two sides of a large dance floor, presently in full motion with customers dancing to the music of a rock n' roll band blasting their songs from the corner opposite Jamie.

Past the dance floor were more tables spread out to the far end of the room. The half-wall ended in line with the dance floor, allowing the bar to be accessed from the far end. To Jamie's right there was an entrance to the bar area, as the half-wall ended short of the outside wall. The bar itself was in the form of a long U-shape. Tables hugged the outside walls as well as well as the half-wall in this side of the room.

Jamie took the dance floor route, making his way slowly through the crowd. No one struck him as a "person of interest" as he passed through the dancing throng.

Tom Moore sat at the bar with his two friends, a shot of Four Roses and a bottle of Dos Equis Amber. Dressed in tan slacks and a Vikings jersey, Moore fit right in the with the fall sports enthusiasts who were more than ready to begin the football wars anew. Although nothing in particular seemed threatening, Moore had an ominous feeling and gripped the jacket slung across his knees.

He looked around the room, then cast a glance between the wooden posts over to the dance floor...*the Indian!*

To Moore's seven o'clock position was a narrow hallway leading to a back parking lot. In the hallway on the left side was the ladies' restroom. On the right, the men's restroom.

Moore nonchalantly rose from his stool, setting his jacket on the seat. He turned to a patron sitting next to him. "Watch my jacket, will ya? I, uh, wull be right back. Gotta go...you know." Moore pretended to be drunk as one is less inclined to question a person who has had too much to drink.

"Sure, sure, buddy," the slightly surprised man answered as he gave Moore the once-over.

Still on the dance floor, Jamie caught something in the corner of his eye. He turned his head. Through the moving bodies and heads he saw him, the man he was looking for.

At the same time Moore reached the hallway and aimed for the exit. A woman exiting the restroom was broad-shouldered right back in by Moore. The hit, though vicious, probably saved her life.

Jamie reached the end of the half-wall.

Moore hit the exit and detonated a plastic explosive in his jacket. *...And to all a good night,* he smirked.

The last thing Jamie Littlebird remembered was a flash of light, followed by an ear-splitting noise.

And, oh yes, there were things flying.

Chapter 39

Mark Truitt heard the emergency call on his scanner. He knew Jamie had planned to visit a few night spots in the area where the blast occurred and so was rather concerned.

Flashing lights and sirens were everywhere when Mark arrived at Mixers. The scene was horrible. There was a steady stream of people being carried out of the mostly demolished building. Crying, screaming, and shouting competed with sirens and horns. He couldn't help but think to himself—*and this is commonplace in some parts of the world.*

Fortunately, what was left of the sprinkler system had succeeded in dousing the explosion- induced fire, which undoubtedly would have claimed more lives if left unchecked. The devastation exposed to Truitt as he entered the building, flashlight in hand, seemed complete. The explosive had done its handiwork. There were parts of tables, chairs, ceiling materials, along with parts of patrons strewn everywhere. Rescue personnel were working feverishly to gather up the injured.

Mark climbed over piles of debris, offering assistance as needed. He made his way toward the back of the building, shining his flashlight back and forth. Suddenly, he froze. His flashlight cast its beam on a rather portly woman, quite dead, a splinter of wood protruding from her temple. However, it was the body beneath her that made Truitt freeze. A man with a ponytail. Jamie's ponytail. Mark quickly, but humanely moved the woman and, sure enough, there was his partner. Bruised, bloody, out cold, but alive.

Jamie came to as he was being put on a stretcher.

"Looks like you found our boy." Mark smiled.

"He found me, first." Jamie grimaced.

"We'll get him."

"He's good. He's really good."

"We'll get him."

"I need a few days off."

"You got it. Come and stay at our house. Liz will fill you up with her cure-all chicken and wild rice soup. You'll be as good as new before you know it. By the way, did you get a look at him?"

"His face is etched in my memory, along with the terrible headache he left me. You know what, Mark?"

"What, Jaim?"

"This rogue business isn't as much fun as I thought it would be."

Truitt knew his partner was going to be all right.

Chapter 40

Jamie Littlebird's injuries from the explosion included a mild concussion, a rather deep gash in his left forearm, a very sore back, ringing in his ears for a few days, and several minor cuts and bruises. Following a night in the hospital, Jamie continued a brief convalescence at the Truitt residence, taking full advantage of the recuperative powers of Liz Truitt's famous chicken and wild rice soup (in September it is very nice...), then headed "up north" for an extended R&R.

The fact that Jamie Littlebird was alive after the horrendous explosion at Mixer's Sports Bar could be credited to the woman deposited on top of him. She was positioned between Jamie and the explosion and had taken the brunt of the concussion, along with absorbing a fair amount of shrapnel. Eleven other customers suffered a similar fate. Twenty-three more had injuries of various degrees.

The sports bar bombing added to the nervousness of a citizenry already on edge with more than its share of unsolved grisly murders. The tempo was quickening for the police to come up with some answers, and Laverne Hathaway, along with the rest of the department, was feeling the heat. The fact that Jamie Littlebird was among the victims of the explosion was not lost on Hathaway. This actually worked in the detectives' favor as their precinct commander, Captain John Kirgalis, congratulated Mark and Jamie on their "steadfast pursuit" of a crazed killer. Kirgalis was one hundred percent above board and Truitt had considered sharing his qualms about Hathaway with him, but that would have had implications Mark wasn't ready to address just yet.

As for Truitt this day, he had been summoned to the A.M. Pallidin estate.

"Good morning," Mark was dryly greeted by Pallidin's butler, Marvin. "Please follow me."

Mark was escorted to the now familiar study/office. There to greet him was Armondo, Brewster's wife Joan, Chelsea Pallidin, and Vincent Ponce. Actually, "greet" was a bit of a misnomer as it looked more like an inquisition. Truitt assumed that Brewster, who had posted bail, was close by.

"What can I do for you folks?" Truitt opened.

"Do?" Vincent Ponce spoke first. "I think you have done enough already. I mean, thanks to you, my future brother-in-law may soon be behind bars for the rest of his life." Chelsea grabbed his arm; Ponce took a step back. "Sorry, Joan," Vincent waved himself off and walked away.

Grandstanding, Truitt concluded.

Chelsea spoke next. "That day with the auditors. It goes through my mind again and again. I should have stayed with Brewster but he could see how upset I was and insisted I not go back in. I mean they were so hard on him; and Peter, well, he wasn't much help. I don't think he can wait till we fail." Chelsea folded her arms and joined her fiancé.

Mark had already met Joan Pallidin the day Brewster was arrested. Joan radiated a "Don't get too close to me" look. Standoffish and businesslike, she gave Truitt a steely glare. "Sergeant Truitt, be honest, does Brewster have any chance at all to prove his innocence?"

"You best talk to your lawyer about that, Mrs. Pallidin," Truitt answered. "My job is to gather evidence."

"And you seem to have done a pretty good job of that, haven't you?" It was A.M.'s turn. "The trouble is that all of the 'evidence' points towards my son being guilty, which, I assure you, he is not! Maybe Paramount has you in their pockets, too."

Truitt was looking at a broken, scared old man. What could he tell him...them? There was a message he wanted to convey to the family and maybe now was the time to play that card. He decided to hint at his belief in Brewster's innocence, but without offering them unrealistic expectations.

"You have your grievances. I have mine, also. One of the people I loved most in this world, died. He was murdered shortly after the confrontation with you, Mr. Pallidin. I almost lost my partner and my best friend a few days ago. You have lost two of your key employees. I am searching for a mass murderer. My belief is that somehow this is all connected. I'm working for the truth and, if Brewster is innocent, and I am doing my utmost to look in that direction, then I am your best hope, but I need any help you can provide. On the other hand, if Brewster is guilty and the death of Guy Lompello leads back to your family, then the good Lord have mercy on you."

A rap on the double doors brought a quick conclusion to the meeting.

Armondo opened the doors to Peter Malik.

Chapter 41

Tom Moore paced back and forth in his motel room, every so often flicking a shredded toothpick toward the garbage can. His agitation and anxiety were well-founded and he had only himself to blame. No doubt his handler would connect him to the bar bombing and probably the jerk he sliced in the parking lot. His employers weren't dumb. They knew his style. The fact that he lost his temper and then was discovered would not sit well with them. Their tolerance for error was zero.

The Labor Day Weekend had passed and no call from X. Moore figured it might be a mind game; let him sweat for a while, make him more "bendable." With that thought still in progress, Moore's cell phone rang.

"Yeah."

"Terrible about that sports bar bombing, and wouldn't you know one of our two favorite detectives was unlucky enough to have witnessed the explosion firsthand. By any chance you weren't there also, were you?"

Moore rubbed his forehead, his phone shaking slightly, its movement directed by a nervous hand. "You know I was there. Lucky I wasn't caught. I had no other choice. I don't know if he recognized me but I couldn't take the chance."

"You *had* another choice. You could have stayed out of sight like you're supposed to. You've jeopardized the whole operation."

Moore knew that backing down would show weakness. "Look, I know I screwed up, but what's done is done. Where do we go from here?"

There was a long silence on the other end—a theatrical emphasis, Moore deduced.

Finally, "Okay, let's move on. The fact is that Truitt and his partner are hunting you and from what I'm told they are only superficially cooperating for our side in the Pallidin case. So as I mentioned before, we are going to hit Mr. Mark Truitt right between the eyes, and this time he is going to get some true 'religion.' When we get done with him he will be like a baby duck walking behind his mama."

Tom Moore had been granted a reprieve, for now at least.

X continued, "You are going to take out Truitt's family. His wife and daughter are usually together. Kill them for sure. If you can get the son also, better yet. I'll send pictures of them to your box. Now, this is going to involve more players than you. We have insiders at Metro PD that are going to set up an ex-con, a cocaine addict. His lights are permanently set on dim from drugs, so he's pretty much putty in our hands. He's going to get a call from a 'Mr. Pallidin.' The actor is a fairly decent lookalike to the real Armondo Pallidin. Our Pallidin will arrange a meeting at which he will offer the con a contract on Truitt's family. I'm told, no problem, the creep would cap his own mother for a hit. 'Pallidin' will have the guy write down on a piece of paper the negotiated price for carrying out the contract and in what denominations he wants the money. Our man will take the paper and later we'll have a handwriting expert forge Pallidin's cell phone number and his initials on the paper. The fake Pallidin will also show him the gun he's going to use and let him handle it so that it's smeared with his fingerprints. 'Pallidin' will tell him he'll get the gun when the hit's ready to be carried out. Got it so far? Any questions?"

Moore didn't like the fact of others being involved but, in view of recent events, he left well enough alone. "No, sounds okay. Keep going."

"The con will get the blame for the murders. A couple of our bought-and-paid-for cops will arrest him after being 'tipped off.' The gun and note will be 'found' in his possession. Of course he'll deny it but it will be to no avail. The 'evidence' will be conclusive. It shouldn't be a problem to get him to identify Pallidin in exchange for leniency. From there on we're home free. I'll tell you where to pick up the gun. It will be wrapped in plastic so that his fingerprints are preserved, but handle it carefully just the same. When the job's done, put it back where you picked it up. Your part will be end there, and then I want you to get out of Minnesota immediately. I will contact you sometime after that as to how you want your compensation delivered. Give me about a week or so to get my end set up. There's no strict timeline; wait for a good opportunity. This *has* to be done right."

"It will. I'll wait to hear from you." *Click.*

Tom Moore had a lot of heavy thinking ahead of him. He didn't for a minute believe he was off the hook. He was certain he got a reprieve only because his services were needed. His problem was how he was going to get his money without them getting to him. He would have to work that out later...after he took care of Mark Truitt's family.

Moore decided to "drink in" tonight.

Chapter 42

Tom Moore waited for what seemed forever to next hear his handler's childlike voice. He stayed in motels in towns near the Twin Cities, moving every day. That pretty much had been the story of his life. Constantly moving around, waiting for a contract. An envious lifestyle it wasn't, but reflecting on it was pointless.

Finally, on the ninth day, Moore got the green light. Mark Truitt's family was in his sights.

Truitt had a dilemma. Thanks to Jamie, a detailed sketch of Moore was produced. The question was: should the sketch be released to the media? If it was, the killer would probably see it and bolt for sure. If he circulated it within his own department he strongly suspected that a wrong pair of eyes would see it. If he went to Captain Kirgalis he would have to try to explain his position on the Pallidins, including the "phantom" clandestine organization. He was afraid that would drive Kirgalis away from him and towards Hathaway's camp. No, the only way was to get proof of the Pallidins' claims. The question was, how? For now, the best option was to pound the pavement and hope the killer was still in the area and would be captured before he struck again.

As promised, after a week had passed, Tom Moore was ordered to carry out the contract on the Truitt family. The next several days were frustrating for Moore. The Truitt's were not making this easy for him. There had been no sign of the boy and everyone else had come and gone at different times. At night when the two women were at home together, Truitt was there, too.

However, on the seventh day his prospects brightened. Truitt had left for work. There were two other cars in the driveway. One he knew belonged to the daughter. The other one he didn't recognize. He hoped it belonged to Truitt's son.

Moore was just about to get out of his van in his "gas company" uniform when the garage door at the Truitt home opened and a minivan slowly backed out.

Now what? Moore thought. He could see three heads sticking up above the seats in the van, and, *What's this?* Suitcases and boxes were visible through the rear window.

Moore followed at a safe distance behind the van. Wherever they were going he hoped that somewhere along the line the Truitt family would provide him with the opportunity to fulfill his contract. The van traveled northwest up Interstate 94 until it turned onto the second exit going into St. Cloud, about an hour from the Twin Cities.

Liz and Maggie were enthusiastically carrying on a conversation as they entered the bustling city. Brian sat in the seat behind, mentally counting the pills he brought with him. The day was to be spent shopping, eating, and spending time with an aunt of Liz's who they hadn't seen in a long time. Their schedule would have them leave St. Cloud later in the afternoon and continue driving north to their lake cabin.

The three of them spending time together without the distractions of city life was the purpose of this "middle of the week" weekend, orchestrated by Liz. Most of all, the main distraction, their cell phones, were banned to Liz's purse. Liz had promised Mark she would check in with him later in the evening but otherwise all communication for the next two days was to be only between each other. Interaction between Mark, Liz, and Brian had been on the upswing lately and Liz hoped to capitalize on this with a one-on-one setting with Brian. Of course, Maggie's presence would provide the stability of a neutral third voice.

It was approaching evening and Mark sat at his desk, idly tapping a spoon on his coffee cup. After spending the past several days distributing the killer's sketch to several police departments and discreetly requesting that they show it to local motels and businesses, a tip came in from a motel clerk in Buffalo, about an hour west of the Twin Cities. He vaguely remembered a man resembling the sketch had been a guest a few nights before.

If it was true, then the question again was, why was he still around? Only one answer—he was not done killing yet. But who?

Murder occurs for many reasons; among those are crimes of passion, robbery, kicks, cults, revenge, to silence, to intimidate, or...to influence.

Mark didn't quite understand why but he suddenly thought of his family, and panicked. Attribute it to a cop's sixth sense, or maybe because this case had taken so many strange turns. Mark didn't stop to speculate; he instinctively knew what to do.

"Jamie, where are you?" Mark couldn't believe his partner answered his cell phone, on the second ring, no less.

"And I thought I could sneak into town," Jamie chuckled. "I'm on the west side of Lake Mille Lacs on 169. I was visiting a cousin in Grand Rapids and this is the quickest way back."

"Okay, look, without going into a lot of explanation will you stop at my cabin? Liz, Maggie, and Brian should be there. They don't have their cell phones on...and I have this strange feeling. If you could look in on them I would appreciate it. I'm going to start heading up that way myself. I just don't feel comfortable with them being alone tonight."

Jamie sensed the tension in Mark's voice. "Sure, I'll be happy to look in on them, but you know what? I think now that I'm back, *you* need to take some time off, shake some Pallidin residue off of you."

"I can't argue with that logic. Let me know when you get to the cabin."

Chapter 43

Darkness comes early in late September in Minnesota and the Truitt family had lingered long enough in St. Cloud to make it a real push to be settled in their cabin by dark.

The gravel road leading from the highway to their cabin was approximately two miles in length. The first mile was consumed with reaching the lake. The second mile twisted around the eastern side of the lake, becoming increasingly narrow as it reached its termination point. The Truitt cabin was the second from the last property, located at the bottom of a fairly steep hill. Along the way Liz glanced down driveways leading to other cabins. Only a month ago there would have been a lot of activity, vacationers enjoying a warm summer evening. This evening there was not one car, nary a person to be seen.

A cold front had swept through earlier in the afternoon and with it enough rain to make the gravel road wet and sloppy, easily revealing recent car tracks. Tom Moore took advantage of this and followed the tracks, but allowing enough distance to deny the occupants of the van ahead a chance to spot him.

Moore took notice of the narrowing road and when he neared the top of the steep hill he pulled into a driveway, not knowing how far down the road the Truitts were and not wanting to be seen. Moore got out of his van and walked to the crest. Below him, cabin lights shone through the trees and figures could be seen unloading a van.

Perfect. Now I just wait until it gets a little darker, Moore grinned. *Say goodbye to your family, cop.*

While Maggie and Brian were unloading the van, Liz put a match to their ancient gravity oil flow heater. *It's cooling down fast; we better light the fireplace too,* Liz decided. "Brian, will you bring in some firewood, please?"

"Yeah, sure, Ma, but I'm going to go down to the lake first and catch the sunset."

The overcast sky accompanying the cold front was breaking up, allowing the setting sun to spray the undersides of the rapidly departing stratus clouds with resplendent colors. Evening fall skies in Minnesota can produce brief, but spectacular shows. Such was the case this evening as brilliant red and orange brushstrokes of light surrendered to soft purple and yellow hues as the sun sank toward the horizon. The show continued until the pines on the opposite side of the lake held their arms high enough to block the last vestiges of rays. A small flock of Canada geese honked their way across the lake, signaling the end to another day in paradise.

Brian shivered as dusk gave way to darkness. The wind quickly picked up velocity from the north, ushering in cool, crisp Canadian air. He swallowed a pill and set course for the woodpile.

Tom Moore advanced on the Truitt property silently. He reached a row of thick bushes on the far side of the woodpile and froze. He saw movement to his left; it was the boy.

Brian walked up to the front of the woodpile. He knew the more seasoned wood was on that end. As he bent over to gather an armful, a hand wielding a small log came down on the back of his head. Brian slumped to the ground. Moore dragged him around the woodpile and into the bushes. He duct-taped his mouth, hands, and ankles. Target secured. He would return to finish the job. Next target.

The light was fading as Jamie Littlebird turned onto the dirt road leading to Roundstone Lake. He could clearly see two sets of tire tracks. Nothing to be alarmed about, but he noted that both sets were on the right hand side of the road. Jamie made his way to the narrow portion of the road. The tracks merged. Jamie shut off his headlights. He had been a guest at Mark's cabin many times and so knew it was on the far side of the approaching hill.

A full moon had shooed the sun away and was now in charge. Scattered clouds were racing each other across a black sky.

Jamie noticed a van parked in a driveway near the top of the hill. There were no lights on at the cabin attached to that driveway. He did not hesitate. "Mark, I'm at your cabin. I think our man is here. Get help."

"You got it!" Mark answered as he sped up Highway 169. Jamie parked his car at a right angle behind the van.

Tom Moore opened the screen door, which accessed the cabin's back porch. He purposefully allowed the door to slam shut.

"Brian, where have you been? We need to get the fire going," Liz admonished as she advanced to the porch. Before she knew what hit her, a huge paw connected with her right jaw, sending her reeling into the kitchen table.

Maggie was standing in the doorway between the living room and the kitchen. Instinctively she turned away from the opening and grabbed the first thing she could find, a diamond willow cane carved by her grandfather. In one motion she picked up the cane and swung it around, connecting dead-on with Moore's fat red nose as he came through the doorway. For Moore it was one of those "in your nose" moments when you feel like a grain truck has driven over your face.

Maggie wasted no time with her brief opportunity for escape. She bolted out the front door and ran around to the back of the cabin.

After a brief setback, Moore followed in hot pursuit.

Jamie stood at the top of the hill, looking down at the Truitt cabin, the full moon shining brightly through the clear fall air. Suddenly, he saw a figure cross the road below him. He recognized Maggie's outline, then a second figure—a hulk of a man. There was no question in Jamie's mind as to his identity.

Jamie instantly processed the situation. He started to remove his handgun, then re-holstered it. Maggie could easily get in a bullet's path; plus any attempt at a nonviolent apprehension of this monster was out of the question and would only serve to put Maggie in harm's way.

WATERFALL

Screw it; you're in my backyard now, pal. Welcome to God's Great North Woods.

Abandoning prescribed procedure, Jamie unsnapped the Paragon knife from its case. He was downwind from Moore and the gusty breezes afforded him a decided advantage. Most any noise would be drowned out and carried away.

The woods across the road from the Truitts' cabin had been cut over and replanted with Norway pine. The trees, mostly between ten and fifteen feet tall were spaced approximately ten feet apart.

Jamie bounded down the hill in a high-stepping motion, aware of the fact that either tangled grass or dead fall could easily trip him up. Pine branches flaying in the wind mimicked cheerleaders urging him on to victory. Jamie prayed to catch up with the killer before the killer caught up with Maggie. His prayers were answered.

Jamie first saw the Moore's baseball hat bobbing at a five o'clock position between two trees, quickly followed by a full view of the man. Jamie gave a final burst of speed, catching Moore just as he was about to grab Maggie. He wrapped his right arm around Moore's neck. His knife-wielding left hand swung around to the front of Moore, the blade disappearing under his ribcage. Jamie twisted his body in hope of swinging the big man around, causing him to fall.

Tom Moore never saw Littlebird coming. All he knew was that something, someone, was holding onto him. Then came the white-hot pain in his chest...and, he could feel himself slipping away. The very thing he was the most afraid of, dying, and what may lie beyond, the one fear he could never face...it was happening! The accompanying wail that came out of Tom Moore shook Jamie right down to his toes. The only thing he could compare it to was the scream of a lynx, a sound so bloodcurdling and unnerving that once heard was never forgotten.

All five feet, ten inches, and one-hundred-seventy-five pounds of Jamie Littlebird strained for all he was worth, his body taut as a bow string, trying to turn and bring down the beast. Slowly Moore turned, teetered, then toppled to the ground on his face. Jamie lay on top of him, still gripping the knife. He could smell days of accumulated sweat now being released from Moore's body, putrefying the air. That, and because he was shaking so hard from a surge of adrenalin, made it difficult to hold back a suddenly weak stomach.

"Move, and I'll pull the knife out," Jamie threatened. "If I pull the knife out, you'll bleed to death. Got it? You gonna stay put?"

Barely above a whisper, Moore managed a reply. "Yeah, I got it."

Jamie heard sirens, their intermittent wails a result of the gusty winds. Moments after, flashing red, blue, and white lights reflected off the trees.

Maggie was barely five feet away, staring wide-eyed and speechless at the grisly scene in front of her.

"Maggie. Maggie, are you all right?" Jamie asked.

"Um, yeah, I guess," Maggie ran a shaking hand through her hair.

It had been a long evening, but the night was far from over.

Chapter 44

Tom Moore was loaded into an ambulance, knife still in place. Internal bleeding was reflected in his vital signs. Moore's chances of arriving at the hospital alive was a tossup at this point.

Jamie watched as EMTs helped Liz onto a stretcher. The right side of her face was swelling badly. Maggie was sitting in a chair in the kitchen, lost in a state of shock. An EMT was attempting to comfort her. Brian had been found, separated from the duct tape, and was fully conscious. He would be diagnosed with a slight concussion.

The ambulance transporting Tom Moore hooked up with an air ambulance dispatched from North Memorial Hospital in the Twin Cities following a six-mile ride from the Truitt cabin. Mark Truitt anticipated the need for a chopper and commissioned its departure. There was no doubt in his mind that someone(s) at his cabin would either be dead or badly hurt this night. He refused to let himself think any further than that. Now with the evening's violent confrontation over, he knew what he had to do next. Getting on that chopper was essential!

Truitt was speeding North on Highway 169, several miles south of the air ambulance, which had taken flight upon receiving its patient. He radioed his location to the Minnesota Highway Patrol and requested that the northbound lanes of the four-lane road be blocked, five miles ahead of his location. He coordinated with the pilot of the air ambulance to drop down in that spot. As Moore's condition was rapidly deteriorating, the pilot didn't want to cooperate. "This isn't your decision. I'll take full responsibility. It is imperative that I board your craft. Bring it down!" Truitt spoke with all the authority that he could muster.

Shortly thereafter the air ambulance landed on Minnesota State Highway 169 to board a passenger.

Along with ordering the air ambulance, Truitt also called Dr. Sam Pernell, an excellent surgeon and trusted personal friend. Without elaborating, Mark requested that Sam go to the hospital and be prepared for an emergency. Hopefully, his services would be needed.

Mark looked down at the man being feverishly administered to by the paramedics, as saline dripped into his veins. A big man for sure, well over six feet. A reddish-purple nose sitting on a pock-marked face. Greasy black hair. A definite body odor. But most distinguishing of all were his hands. The bartender was right; they were like bear paws. Truitt wondered how many people those hands had killed.

"Blood pressure ninety over sixty-six and dropping," brought Truitt out of his mini-trance. This wasn't looking good; Moore's vital signs were deteriorating fast. He was totally unresponsive, making it impossible for Mark to attempt even minimal communication with him.

"Eighty-eight over sixty-two."

Truitt pleaded his case to the paramedics.

"Eighty-two over forty-eight. Faint, thready pulse," the paramedic radioed to Sam Pernell.

After what seemed like forever the helipad came into view. Truitt spoke briefly by phone with his physician friend as Moore was quickly transferred to the operating room where Sam Pernell and his team were scrubbed and waiting.

Truitt waited in the hallway leading to the surgical area and took the opportunity to call his children. His family was his first priority, as always. They would soon be together; that was the good news. The bad news was that Laverne Hathaway was walking towards him.

A genial but uncomfortable dialogue ensued between the two men. Thankfully, by the time their conversation was begging to be euthanized, Sam Pernell appeared from the operating room.

Looking downcast, Pernell addressed Mark and Laverne Hathaway. "The knife penetrated the liver, gall bladder, and severely damaged one of his hepatic veins. The blood loss was just too great."

"Thanks for trying, Sam. I know you did your best," Truitt put a hand on Pernell's shoulder.

Hathaway mumbled something regarding a killer being brought to justice and quickly departed. Truitt figured that he was in a hurry to make a plan to capitalize on the situation.

Truitt thanked Sam Pernell again before calling Jamie to fill him in and find out how close his family was to the hospital.

"We're pulling into the emergency room now," Littlebird reported.

"Thanks, Jaim. Thanks for saving my family."

"Glad I was close. Can we be done being rogue cops now?"

"Yes, I think we're done."

PART THREE

Say Who?

Chapter 45

A search of Tom Moore's effects revealed little of his recent activities. His wallet produced a driver's license, social security card, gun permit, a private investigator license card from the state of Texas, eighteen hundred dollars in bills, and little else. His pants pockets gave up a can of chewing tobacco, a cell phone, switchblade, plastic cylinder of toothpicks, and a post office box key. A Smith and Wesson 629 Classic revolver was holstered to his belt. A suitcase found in his van held a few changes of clothes, personal care items, spare bullets. There was one item, however, of particular interest. A handgun wrapped in plastic, found in Moore's jacket pocket.

Moore's name was traced to military records and, ultimately his roots. The only living relative to be found was a sister living in Omaha, Nebraska. When asked what her desire was for his remains, she responded, "I ain't seen or talked to him in over thirty years, and if I did want to see him, the only way would be the state he's in now, dead. I don't care what you do with him."

Liz Truitt was recovering in the hospital with a fractured jaw as well as several superficial bruises. She would be going home in a few days. Brian had sustained a slight concussion. The blow however had "knocked" a little sense into him; and while he silently felt a great deal of remorse for his drug use and the way he had been treating his family, outwardly he wasn't ready to make the full plunge to openness and honesty. He vowed to himself, however, that he would advance in that direction.

Maggie was probably in the worst shape all around. The emotional trauma left her in a high state of anxiety. Although she would receive the necessary professional help, her best comfort would continue to be Jamie Littlebird, who had lived the nightmare with her. His soft voice and low-key demeanor would eventually guide Maggie back to a normal life.

The whole ugly episode culminated in a press conference in which Captain John Kirgalis formally announced that law enforcement officials were satisfied that the man apprehended by Sergeant Jamie Littlebird was responsible for the bombing of Mixer's Sports Bar, likely responsible for the death of Donald Borchart (the bartenders confirmed Moore's presence in the Oasis bar the night of the murder), and strongly suspected in the death of Lt. Guy Lompello.

Captain Kirgalis went on to praise the efforts of Sergeants Littlebird and Truitt in their pursuit of this heinous killer. Lt. Laverne Hathaway echoed the captain's remarks, calling the investigators "two of Metro's finest." The compliment, obviously lacking sincerity because of the author, caused both Mark and Jamie to mentally stick fingers down their throats.

Following prepared statements, the floor was opened to the media. Endless questions were raised, many redundant, most addressed to Truitt and Littlebird. Hathaway stuck his two cents in whenever he could, prolonging the affair and thoroughly enjoying himself. Mercifully, Captain Kirgalis finally called an end to the session.

In contrast to the press conference there was some promising news for Truitt when he arrived back at the office. The gun found on Moore, the one wrapped in plastic, contained fingerprints. Interestingly, the prints matched an ex-con by the name of Willie Guyanne, a name Truitt recognized. Guyanne's current address was close to downtown Minneapolis.

"C'mon partner, we're going for a ride," Mark beckoned Jamie just as he finished pouring a cup of coffee.

"Where're we going?"

"To visit an old acquaintance."

Littlebird knocked on the door of the third-floor flat. No answer. Truitt tried the door knob. The door opened. The detectives went in, guns drawn.

Willie Guyanne wasn't hard to find, the reason for not answering his door, apparent. Guyanne was lying face down in front of his couch, a blanket under his head and a pillow on top. Both were bloodstained. There were two holes behind his right ear.

Truitt walked over to a window and stared out. "Looks like they replaced Tom Moore."

Chapter 46

November 10, 1975, approximately 8:00 p.m. A young Mark Truitt and his father, Alden, were at a relative's home a few miles south of Eveleth, on Minnesota's historic Iron Range, relaxing after an enjoyable but fruitless day of deer hunting.

Mark was watching a television program being transmitted from an ABC network affiliate located in Duluth when the program was interrupted by a young news anchor who came before the camera asking that all Coast Guard personnel report for duty, as contact had been lost with an ore carrier on Lake Superior.

The ore boat was the 729-foot Edmond Fitzgerald. The vessel had gone down in 530 feet of water on the east end of the big lake. The fully loaded carrier was trying to ride out a November gale. Fifteen miles, that's all they needed was fifteen more miles to reach safety. However, neither the big ship nor its twenty-nine souls were a match for Mother Nature's fury that night. For some reason an odd, insignificant fact about the tragedy stuck with Mark;

the boat was 200 feet longer than the depth into which it sank. A young, impressionable mind forever bookmarked that cold, windy night in November, and every so often Gordon Lightfoot would refresh his memory.

The Fitzgerald tragedy notwithstanding, the month was Mark's least favorite for a host of other reasons. November ushered in winter. The trees were bare, the ground froze, raindrops turned to flakes of either work or fun, depending on one's perspective. And, maybe worst of all, the sun became increasingly stingy with its light as each day passed.

As Mark drove to work this dark November morning he corralled these disconcerting thoughts and reprogrammed to the task at hand. The previous month Truitt had contacted an old friend, a retired FBI agent by the name of Blaine McGillivray, now engaged in his own consulting business. Without going into too many details, Mark asked Blaine to see what he could find out about Paramount Investment Partners.

McGillivray got back to him after a five-week interval. His report, mostly non-indicting, did contain one interesting item. "Three white, middle-aged, highly-educated men run Paramount. Two served in the military, one of them a West Pointer. The third is a Rhodes Scholar. I can't really find a blemish on any of them."

However, he did note that the prior February, the three men had flown to an island in the Grenadines, owned by a wealthy Brazilian businessman. Also rumored to be on the island was Shane Burkholz, the lumber magnate, known for his money and ultra-conservative beliefs. A freelance investigative reporter had been tailing Burkholz, attempting to get a perspective on his political activities. He somehow found out that Burkholz was headed to this island and chartered a plane to fly over it, take pictures, whatever. Somewhere near Montserrat the plane disappeared without a trace. The reporter's girlfriend swears Burkholz had the plane sabotaged. There was no evidence to back up the claim.

"Sorry, Mark. I know that's not much information but it's the best I could do."

"No problem. In fact it's typical with what I've been coming up so far in my investigation."

"How's that?"

"People who might be able to shed some light on this case have a habit of turning up dead."

Truitt thanked McGillivray for his help, catalogued the information, and set his sights ahead to the Christmas holidays.

Chapter 47

The gales of November gave way begrudgingly to, well, the gales of December. The cold blustery winds blew in the winter enthusiasts' manna, piles of snow. It was going to be a white Christmas and even though the song immortalized in that name lauds the wonders and beauty of the season, it fails to mention the side effects: sore backs, broken bones, heart attacks. *I'm dreaming of...palm trees, beach sand, sun.*

The Truitt family, along with most Minnesotans, shoveled their way through Christmas and into the New Year. Flipping the cover on a new calendar signaled a time for fresh starts, resolutions of personal improvement, hope for the future...along with another Super Bowl minus any purple, gold, and white colors, a fresh Congress eager to ensure that unresolved important issues remained preserved in that form, more bankruptcies and foreclosures...and, of course, more snow and cold. Happy New Year—keep the ice pack handy.

The overriding story in the Twin Cities as January settled in was the Brewster Pallidin murder trial. The upcoming proceedings had all the trappings of a major sporting contest. News media from far and wide came to cover what promised to be a sensational event. As a bonus for the Twin Cities' economy they would get to do it all over again when the bird flu conspiracy trial began, scheduled for early spring.

The trial promised to live up to its top billing not only because of the high-profile defendant, but also due to the dynamic legal teams. Arguing for the prosecution was Roger Arcelli, the county district attorney. A man of pencil-straight stature, slicked-back black hair, the front guard of which were clearly in their death throes, and a body on the positive side of continual attempts to keep it firmed up. Arcelli's strong points were his attention to detail and his oratorical skills. In fact, he more or less fancied himself as a modern day William Jennings Bryan—maybe not the golden-tongued orator Bryan had been, but good nonetheless.

Arcelli was hoping this would be his Scopes trial, catapulting him into the attorney general's office. The odds were in his favor, right down to the "smoking gun."

Arcelli's aggressive style usually focused on interrogating a witness with "both barrels blazing." He was sterile, calculating, precise. If Arcelli felt a witness held pertinent information, he attacked like a bulldog.

The defense was led by Arthur Lannihan, senior partner in the firm of Lannihan and Associates. A brilliant tactician, Lannihan held an impressive record of favorable decisions, including many seemingly unwinnable cases.

A first impression of Lannihan would lead one to the contrary. Tall and lanky, Arthur sported a full head of gray hair which always appeared to be a few days late for a haircut. His tie never hung quite straight and was usually a bit loose at the knot. His had a slight forward pitch to his stance, which projected a hint of vulnerability.

In contrast to Arcelli's stiff-necked approach, Lannihan presented himself as a down-home country-style lawyer. His soft, non-threatening demeanor was an excellent tool at coaxing information from witnesses. He had the habit of getting as physically close to the jurors as possible and talking to them as if they were next-door neighbors. In fact, he had often been characterized as the thirteenth juror.

The atmosphere in this trial was certain to be electric. Mark Truitt was glad the Pallidins had retained Arthur Lannihan but feared that proving Brewster Pallidin innocent might be the toughest challenge of his career.

Laverne Hathaway didn't have much contact with either Truitt or Littlebird after the Tom Moore incident. He evidently felt they had not dug up anything detrimental to the prosecution and so would have little choice but to be friendly witnesses.

Lenny Spargo was on top of the world. He couldn't wait to get on the witness stand and testify as one of the principle investigators in the case. Notoriety was certain to bring good things his way.

Charles Duchenne shunned the spotlight. He lay awake nights bemoaning the thought of testifying. Worse yet, the knowledge that Jamie Littlebird had taken down Tom Moore with a knife did nothing to allay his fear of Jamie.

On the Truitt home front, the New Year had rung in hopes of a better year to come. Liz was healing as expected. Maggie was about ninety percent back to normal.

Brian, well, Brian took a major step in the right direction. He consented to participate in a chemical dependency program. The family held their breath and prayed it would work.

Chapter 48

The Brewster Pallidin trial was called into session as scheduled on January 17. Media personalities from around the country set up on the steps to the courthouse, preparing their announcements of the start of the trial. The sentiment in most circles agreed that the dismemberment of the Pallidin family was about to begin.

The courtroom was packed and already becoming a bit stuffy even though a Polar Express was punishing the Twin Cities with below-zero temperatures. Anticipation had the gallery twitching with anxiety, suggesting a scene more reminiscent of a puck about to be dropped than a trial being called to order.

Mark Truitt found a seat in the last row. Though he wasn't scheduled to testify this early in the trial Mark was keenly interested not only in its progression but also those in attendance. He scanned the audience for expressions or body language. This strategy would intensify when testimonies began in earnest. Any type of tipoff could be helpful. Mark held to the hope that even at this late date a break in Brewster Pallidin's favor was still possible. Jamie Littlebird had a definite aversion to crowds but would attend when required.

Truitt looked around, his eyes settling on Peter Malik, a person of particular interest. Sitting on either side of Malik were two men dressed in business suits, looking very corporate. Truitt assumed they were employees of Paramount Investment Partners.

Looking further toward the front of the gallery Mark's eyes fell upon the family and friends of Brewster Pallidin. As expected they were sitting behind the defendant. Armondo Pallidin was positioned at the end of the row, looking all of his seventy-seven years, and then some. Dark circles hung under his eyes and his cheeks reflected a reddish hue. Although his life had not always been cherubic, Truitt felt a twinge of compassion for him. Mark believed the Pallidins' claim that they truly intended to present their invention to the world as a gift.

Sitting next to Armondo was Brewster's wife, Joan. She looked as though she was in church, waiting for the service to begin. She faced straight ahead, staring into the backs of the defense team, barely acknowledging any comments sent in her direction.

On Joan's opposite side was Chelsea Pallidin. She looked quite attractive but also apprehensive. She may have been thinking ahead to testimony concerning the meeting with the auditors. Hopefully, she would be able to cast a positive light of some kind.

Next to Chelsea was Vincent Ponce, Chelsea's fiancé. His facial expression and body language betrayed a meager attempt at appearing interested. Truitt couldn't get a good read on Ponce. He had checked him out and didn't find any skeletons in his past, but he definitely was on Mark's watch list.

Filling out that row and all of the next were employees of Midwest Research Labs. Some were veterans of the company, others fairly new, all there to support Brewster. It was the two women at the far end of the row that caught Truitt's eye. Sitting on the very end was Denise Carpenter. He hadn't seen her since the day of her husband's death. However, he periodically spoke to her on the phone. Through this whole mess she was the person for whom he had the most compassion. That made it even harder when he thought about his promise to get to the bottom of her husband's death. Mark still intended to keep that promise.

Sitting next to Denise Carpenter was Amy Weldon. Mark couldn't help but feel a pang of excitement when he gazed upon her. He wondered what might have happened if they had given into their weakness. Would his passion have clouded his intuition that his family was in danger that fateful day? Would he have sent Jamie to look in on them? Questions that thankfully were a non-issue and best be buried and forgotten.

Chapter 49

At 9:00 a.m. sharp the bailiff called for all in the courtroom to rise. Momentarily the presiding judge entered the courtroom. More accurately, Judge Bridgett Harper made a grand entrance. Poised and self-assured, Harper measured up perfectly at every inch of her tall, black frame. With the Minnesota state flag on her left, the United States flag to her right, and the Minnesota state emblem on the wall behind her, Judge Harper looked fairly regal.

Physical appearance aside, Harper was all business. She commanded her court with the competency of an admiral guiding his fleet. Following instructions to the jury, the court was ready for the presentation of opening statements.

Roger Arcelli was first to speak. Arcelli stood, dropped his specs on his notes, tugged at the cuffs on his suit coat, and folded his hands in front of him. He walked towards the jury, head down, as if he was pondering what to say. Of course it was all for effect. If anything, Arcelli over-prepared for his cases. He was a perfectionist. But then God loves perfectionists, too, poor souls. At times they tend to be their own worst enemies as they are not wired for failure or compromise.

"Good morning, ladies and gentlemen of the jury," Arcelli began. "Of all the cases I have prosecuted in my twenty-one years in the legal profession, I am remiss to recall any more heinous or despicable than the case before you. The defendant, Brewster Pallidin is accused of murdering two innocent men; and for what purpose? Merely because they informed him that his business was in financial chaos? And it is all the more horrific because they were employees of an institution that had invested in Mr. Pallidin's business in order to save it. What a tragedy, to be so blinded by your own unattainable ambitions that you would take the lives of others rather than admit failure."

Arcelli scanned the jurors, making eye contact with each one. "Ladies and gentlemen, you are here to weigh the facts from the evidence that is presented to you. When all is said and done I submit that your judgment will be to find Brewster Pallidin *guilty* of two counts of murder in the first degree."

Arcelli's speech was compelling, his presentation impeccable. He was articulate, though somewhat sterile, exuding an air of total confidence.

When Arcelli rejoined his team, Arthur Lannihan stood and prepared to address the jury. His warm smile silently took aim at each juror, giving the impression that he was anxious to meet his twelve new friends. Lannihan's theme was to disconnect Brewster Pallidin from "this whole unfortunate set of circumstances."

"Please remember," he told the jurors, "that you must be convinced beyond any reasonable doubt that Brewster Pallidin pulled the trigger of the gun that killed the two men of which he is accused of shooting. We will explore every avenue of possibility and, when all the testimony has been exhausted, I believe you will find my client is innocent of all accused wrongdoing. Now, the prosecution will attempt to prove otherwise. They will try to convince you that Mr. Pallidin, a well-respected businessman who oversees a large family-owned company, a man who has never so much been issued a parking ticket, unconscionably murdered two men with which he has just had a difficult meeting, a meeting attended by two other people who were witnesses to the confrontation."

Lannihan pulled in close to the jury and lowered his voice. "Under those circumstances, you would have to be insane to commit a crime of that severity and, ladies and gentlemen, I *guarantee* you that Brewster Pallidin is not insane."

And so the bayonets were fixed, the battle lines drawn.

The remainder of the first day's session was consumed with character witness testimonies and evidence presentation.

Truitt and Littlebird were scheduled to make their first appearance later in the week.

Chapter 50

The residents of the Twin Cities woke up this January morning to a dazzling display of sparkling white hoar frost, which coated everything from the tops of the trees to those shrubs that still had parts of their extremities poking above the snow pack. This gift from nature, which is created when ice crystals are deposited on any object colder than the surrounding moist air, was enhanced by the backdrop of a cloudless steel-blue sky. The panorama was so bright with sunlight reflecting off of each and every crystal that it hurt the eye if not viewed through sunglasses. The appreciation level, however, was somewhat diminished if witnessed from the great outdoors, where the thermometer had sunk to minus nine degrees Fahrenheit.

Nature's beauty was not on Mark Truitt's mind as he picked up Jamie Littlebird on the way to the courthouse. The two detectives were to testify this morning and so were scrubbing up on their facts.

"I don't see how anything we say can be of help to Brewster Pallidin," Jamie lamented.

"That's pretty much the case," Truitt agreed. "Arcelli will try to use our testimony to paint as dark a picture of the Pallidins as possible. All we can do is relate the events and facts as we remember them and not let him put words in our mouths."

Jamie gazed out the window at the majestic winter wonderland. "I'd rather eat eelpout soup than do this." It was no secret that Littlebird despised being the center of attention.

"I heard that eelpout soup is actually very tasty," Truitt retorted.

"Is that so? I'll tell you what. Next time I'm at Leech Lake I'll see if I can snag a couple for you. Now, would you please turn off that noise?"

"Wassamatter, you don't like Chris Rea?"

"I can't think with all that commotion."

"Are we getting a little testy?"

"Yesty!"

The courtroom was again crowded, everyone anticipating forthcoming revelations. Upon being seated, Judge Harper called the court into session.

Mark Truitt was the first witness to be called. Arcelli immediately began to drill Truitt about the confrontation between A.M. Pallidin and Guy Lompello.

"Detective Truitt, how would you characterize the atmosphere surrounding Armondo Pallidin and Lt. Lompello when they met face to face."

"I would say somewhat tense," Truitt answered.

"Only *somewhat* tense? Lt. Lompello was heard to reveal upon your return to precinct headquarters following the interview that it was a 'bad scene.'"

At this point Arthur Lannihan cast an objection at the line of questioning. "Your Honor, Armondo Pallidin is not on trial and his relationship with Lt. Lompello should have no bearing on this case."

Arcelli rebutted. "Your Honor, Armondo and Brewster Pallidin have a close relationship, both privately and professionally. I am attempting to establish the volatile type of environment that surrounds this family. This is but one example of several conflicts I intend to bring to light."

"Very well, Counselor. Objection overruled. You may continue." Harper nodded.

Arcelli pressed on. "Again, Detective Truitt, how do you describe their encounter?"

"I would best characterize it as two old antagonists blowing a little hot air at each other pretty much for the sake of doing it."

Arcelli was taken aback. He did not expect this answer from Truitt. He assumed Mark would be a friendly witness for the prosecution. He now sensed that Truitt had not bought into a connection between the Pallidins and Lompello's death.

Arcelli had no more questions for Truitt at this time. *The evidence will speak for itself,* he reasoned. Jamie Littlebird escaped the witness chair as Arcelli assumed that he would echo Truitt's statement.

Arthur Lannihan cross-examined Truitt, his line of questioning effectively defusing the Guy Lompello matter for good.

Over the next few days Mark and Jamie were called to testify in regard to interviews they had conducted with either the Pallidins or their employees. The mutant virus case was skirted by Arcelli with the intention of establishing that dark forces were at work inside Midwest Research Labs. Arcelli was cruising. The pendulum was certainly swinging in his favor.

By the time this portion of the trial was completed, more than a week had slipped by. And it was still cold.

Chapter 51

Mark and Jamie climbed the courthouse steps as if they were about to attend a funeral. The task ahead of them would not be pleasant, for this was the day when they would tell the story of finding the evidence linking the auditors' deaths to Brewster Pallidin. As they entered the courthouse, Truitt noticed Denise Carpenter walking ahead of them.

"I'll see you inside, Jaim. I want to talk to Mrs. Carpenter."

"Oh, Sergeant Truitt," Denise greeted Mark, slightly startled as he put his hand on her shoulder.

"How are you, Mrs. Carpenter?"

"Well, okay, I guess. But I'm finding the trial rather depressing. Other than being here to support Brewster, the only reason I come is to hopefully pick up something, anything that might give me a clue about Michael's death. So far I've had nothing to grab at." Denise forced a weak smile.

Truitt made an attempt at comforting her. "I still hold out hope that something may turn up. I did promise you I would do everything in my power to get to the bottom of your husband's death. I don't want to give you any false hope, but you can hold me to that promise."

"Thank you, Sergeant. It comforts me to know that."

They continued the remainder of the way to the courtroom. Just outside the entrance Truitt saw Amy Weldon. *Well, I can't avoid her. She's standing right there looking at me.* Truitt said goodbye to Denise and walked over to Amy.

"Hi."

"Hi, yourself," Amy smiled.

"What do you think of the trial so far?" Truitt asked, not really knowing what else to say.

"I think poor Brewster is in a lot of trouble. He's not going to be exonerated, is he?"

"It's not over yet."

"I wish him the best. Anyway, whichever way it goes I've decided to move on. A friend from college wants me to move to Rhode Island; she has a job for me. I'm kind of anxious, you know, new scenery and all that."

"New England's nice. You'll like it there. Well, we better get inside. The trial will be starting shortly. Good luck on your new adventure."

Weldon nodded and made her way into the courtroom.

Judge Harper called her courtroom to order at precisely 9:00 a.m.

Roger Arcelli's approach this morning was to concentrate on the evidence collected both at the motel and Brewster Pallidin's home with the intent of connecting him to the murdered auditors. Truitt took the stand after Lenny Spargo had his day in the sun.

"Sergeant Truitt," Arcelli began, "would you please describe for the court what you found when you inspected the vehicle in which the murder victims were found."

Truitt cleared his throat. "I found a pair of reading glasses which were subsequently determined to belong to Brewster Pallidin. What I didn't find was just as important. Missing were the victims' wallets and any documents, carrying cases, laptops, PDAs, things of that nature."

"And," Arcelli added, "as Sergeant Spargo has already testified, the victims' hotel room held nothing more than a few articles of clothing. Okay, Sergeant, please go on. Tell the court the sequence of events following the search of the car and motel room."

This was the moment Truitt was dreading. "Lt. Hathaway obtained a search warrant and directed Sergeant Littlebird and me, along with Sergeants' Spargo and Duchenne to conduct a search of Mr. Pallidin's premises."

"And what did you find, Sergeant Truitt?" Arcelli could barely contain himself.

"Sergeant Littlebird and I found the victims' wallets, along with briefcases containing laptops and financial reports concerning Midwest Research Labs. There was also a handgun in one of the briefcases."

Arcelli put a hand up. "Where did you find these items?"

"They were buried in a flower garden. Also, a shovel we found in the garage had dirt on the blade that was consistent with the dirt in the flowerbed. No fingerprints were found on the shovel."

Truitt reluctantly continued. "We also noticed a footprint in the flowerbed next to where the items were found. A search of Mr. Pallidin's bedroom closet produced a pair of size eleven jogging shoes, which were confirmed to belong to him. There was dirt stuck to the sole of the left shoe which is consistent with the dirt in the flowerbed."

"Thank you, Sergeant. Now, what can you tell us about the murder weapon?"

This was it. Arcelli's grand finale, and Mark Truitt was providing the fireworks. "The gun responsible for firing the lethal bullets was recovered from one of the briefcases. That handgun is registered to Brewster Pallidin. There were two partial fingerprints on the barrel of the gun that match Mr. Pallidin's fingerprints."

He had said it all. Truitt glanced over at the Pallidin family. Armondo looked as though he could collapse any second. Joan Pallidin appeared to be in a trance. Chelsea stared downward, a hand covering her mouth. Vincent Ponce frowned, sliding a hand over Chelsea's free hand. And Brewster? He was whispering something in Arthur Lannihan's ear. *Probably a desperate thought, poor guy.*

Arthur Lannihan made a noble effort at cross-examination. Though he did not dispute Mark's testimony, he did attempt to plant seeds of doubt surrounding the evidence, albeit they were more of the mustard variety than acorn. Brewster Pallidin had claimed that the glasses found in the victims' car had been missing for a few days. The side door on the garage was never kept locked and so someone could have easily used the shovel to which the flowerbed dirt was stuck. Pallidin's home security system had been struck by lightning the previous week and was out of service. There were at least a couple of windows that were unlocked, allowing possible access to the home. Brewster kept the handgun in the back of an unlocked drawer in his home office desk, not loaded, he claimed. *Of course* his prints would have been on it; it was his gun. The shoes? Lannihan could only plead the speculation that someone had set them up along with the gun. Finally, there were no eyewitnesses to the crime.

The problem for the defense was that the various pieces of circumstantial evidence were folding neatly into a toxic package of corroborating evidence. Their best shot was to create an atmosphere of "not beyond a reasonable doubt," and it was becoming an increasingly hard sell.

Jamie was called upon next to testify. A few additional questions were asked of him but for the most part he mirrored Truitt's testimony.

The grueling session finally came to a close. The summation phase of the trial was scheduled to proceed the following day.

Chapter 52

Mark Truitt was lying back in his recliner looking more at the ceiling than the television, replaying portions of the Pallidin murder trial. The river of evidence was quickly rising against Brewster and his life jacket was on shore. Only a miracle could save him now.

Liz was settled in her chair, scanning the *TV Guide*. She had taken the brunt of Tom Moore's aggression that terrible night at their cabin but was healing well, both inside and out. The incident had served to renew their love and loyalty to each other, a comfort that was not lost on their son Brian, still trying to overcome his addiction to drugs.

The cabin on Roundstone Lake was another matter. Liz, and even more so Maggie, could not psychologically erase the trauma of the incident and so it was decided to sell the property. In fact, Jamie Littlebird had been after Mark for some time to look at property on Lake Vermilion, a treasure tucked into the northeastern corner of the state.

For sure, the lake is a bit of heaven on earth that called out to Jamie every time he returned, as it was his birthplace. It was an option the Truitts planned on pursuing as soon as the weather turned pleasant, which in January can seem light years away.

Liz looked over at Mark. "Let's watch this program. It's something about the world water crisis." As long as it wasn't a cop show, Mark didn't protest.

As the show progressed, Mark became increasingly intrigued. The concerns expressed to him by Armondo and Brewster Pallidin were reiterated by the program's narrator. The program claimed that there probably is enough fresh water to satisfy the current demand in the United States but great quantities are being squandered by thousands of miles of antiquated, leaking pipes. Also, millions of gallons of sewage is leaking into fresh water sources because of outdated systems. Mark thought to himself, *a good stimulus money project.*

Another problem the program focused on was what and where much of the fresh water is being dispensed. The narrator gave a few examples: 1,857 gallons to produce one pound of beef, 2,900 gallons for one pair of blue jeans, 37 gallons for one cup of coffee. An imbalance, especially when compared to places where people spend hours a day to procure a few gallons.

Mark had planned to give his brain the night off and relax, but this program got him thinking. *Were the Pallidins truly close to finding a solution on water desalinization that would provide a thirsty and growing world population with affordable and abundant fresh water? Was there, in fact, a secret organization trying to steal their invention? If so, who was behind it? And was*

Midwest Research Labs still being infiltrated by one or more of their operatives?

Those were questions yet to be addressed. But not tonight. Tonight is TV night. The water program was over. *Good, now maybe we can...What? Killer bees?*

Chapter 53

The final day of the Brewster Pallidin murder trial arrived. The consensus from most everyone was that the summations would serve more as a formality than a final attempt at influencing the jury. The media, as well as public opinion had already assumed a guilty verdict. As one newspaper's interpretation stated, "The evidence presented in the Brewster Pallidin trial has the defendant rapidly cascading down a waterfall of evil created by his own misdeeds and selfish motives."

Mark Truitt walked up the steps and into the courthouse. At 8:55 a.m. he entered the courtroom and approached the defense attorneys' table. For the next two minutes he exchanged words with Arthur Lannihan. Following the conversation he walked to the back of the courtroom.

At 9:00 a.m. Judge Harper called the session to order. "I believe we are ready for the summation, Counselors?"

Arthur Lannihan stood up. "Your Honor, the defense requests testimony from one more witness."

Roger Arcelli immediately shot out of his chair. "Your Honor, I object. The prosecution has been given no prior notification and..."

Judge Harper waved him off, addressing Lannihan. "Counselor, does this witness hold crucial testimony?"

"Most certainly," Lannihan replied.

"Then will the two counselors please approach the bench?"

Arcelli's face was beet red as he and Lannihan walked to the bench. On the return trip, his complexion had made a dramatic reversal and, in fact, had taken on more the color of a parsnip.

Lannihan motioned to a guard, who opened the double doors to the courtroom.

In through the doors walked four Bureau of Indian Affairs officers, two abreast, neatly dressed in white shirts, ties, and blue sport coats. Tucked between them was Jamie Littlebird, pushing a wheelchair occupied by a man looking weak and old. Once inside the courtroom the BIA agents broke off, leaving Jamie to proceed the final steps alone with his passenger. A low murmur from the gallery accompanied quizzical glances. When Jamie had the man properly positioned he retreated to the back of the room. The man was sworn in and Arthur Lannihan rose from his chair.

"Sir, would you please state your name for the court?"

The man paused, looked around the room. As if he was prying it out of himself he reluctantly answered, "Tom Moore."

The courtroom virtually erupted. Laverne Hathaway was hosting a personal "reality check" moment. Judge Harper slammed down her gavel several times. In no uncertain terms she warned the gallery, "I will have order in this court or we will continue in closed session." The warning was heeded and order quickly restored.

As Lannihan was about to continue, Judge Harper interrupted, "In view of the circumstances, Counselor, I think it would be appropriate to enlighten the court as to why a person presumed to be deceased is sitting before us."

"Certainly, Your Honor," Lannihan responded. "Mr. Moore was seriously injured during his apprehension by Sergeant Littlebird. His survival was in doubt in the hours after the altercation; but if he did, in fact, survive the ordeal, Sergeant Truitt feared for his safety. As a consequence Sergeants' Truitt and Littlebird, with cooperation from Captain John Kirgalis, took steps to assure Mr. Moore's anonymity until this day—even from their department. After Mr. Moore received emergency surgery at North Memorial he was airlifted to St. Mary's hospital in Rochester under an assumed name. Following further surgery and convalescence he was transferred to an undisclosed location near Bemidji where he was safely kept under the watchful eye of the BIA. And to them we are extremely grateful.

Your Honor, Mr. Moore is aware of his rights and in a sworn statement has admitted to several crimes. He has agreed to share with the court pertinent facts related to these crimes that are crucial to the case before us."

"Thank you, Counselor. You may proceed."

"Mr. Moore, you have confessed to several crimes, most of which in some way touch the Pallidin family. Please start from the beginning and clarify why and how these events took place."

Moore looked defiant and a little uncomfortable, most likely a result of every eye in the courtroom being fixated on him. Following a couple of weak coughs, Moore began his testimony.

"Thurber, that research guy, made a virus of some kind that they were going to use to set up Pallidin. Make it look like it was Brewster Pallidin's idea to make money to save his business. They got Thurber to do it cuz he was in debt from gambling and was promised a lot of money. Thurber got cold feet. Called Carpenter. Told him he, Thurber, was in a lot of trouble, wanted to talk to him alone. Told Carpenter that the Pallidins' were being set up. Made him promise not to say anything to anyone until he had a chance to spill his guts. Someone, I don't know who, got wind of it. My handler had to make a quick plan to take Carpenter out."

Lannihan interrupted, "Who are the 'they' to which you are referring?"

Moore's beady, dull eyes focused directly on Lannihan. "Let me make this clear. I had one contact and one contact only, which was known to me only as X. Who X worked for I don't know and I don't want to know."

Lannihan appeared somewhat disappointed. "Okay, please continue."

"I grabbed Carpenter as he came out of Midwest Research Labs and made him drive to a motel. My handler set up a lady to help me. She pretended to be a hooker. I hired a guy to sit outside of Carpenter's home with a cell phone and wait for me to call. I made Carpenter have sex with the lady, took some pictures, and left evidence on the bedsheets. Then I called the guy and told him to take a few pictures of Carpenter's house and send them to my cell phone. It worked out perfect. His kids were playing in the front yard. Then I set some pills in front of Carpenter. I told him they were to make him forget the last twelve hours. In case he did remember, we had pictures of him and the lady. He resisted but I told him it was either the pills, or the guy who sent the pictures would take out his family. He didn't have much choice."

"What happened to the cameraman?" Lannihan asked.

Moore shrugged his shoulders. "He and his car took a one-way trip out of state."

Lannihan was starting to get a feel for Tom Moore, unsettling to say the least. "Continue on to the convenience store robbery and George Thurber."

"That was a setup, too. Thurber was supposed to look like an innocent victim. It's a shame the way it turned out."

"What do you mean?" Lannihan asked.

"I killed that kid for nothing."

"Yeah, right." Lannihan rubbed a cheek with the palm of his hand. "Let's move on to Lieutenant Lompello. Why did you murder him?"

"My handler knew about an argument he had with old man Pallidin in front of the two cops…"

Lannihan broke in, "You mean Sergeants Truitt and Littlebird?"

"Yeah, them. Anyway, capping Lompello was supposed to get the cops to take a hard look at Pallidin… Also, I guess they wanted to get one of their own in his position."

"You mean you brutally murdered a well-respected, dedicated public servant to sway opinions and also to replace him with an ally of your employers?"

"Whatever."

Lannihan was incredulous.

Judge Harper decided Moore's testimony needed to be digested. "Let's take a twenty minute recess," she declared.

Captain Kirgalis immediately put Lt. Laverne Hathaway on administrative leave, pending an internal investigation.

Chapter 54

Mark Truitt caught up with Denise Carpenter as she was leaving the courtroom. He couldn't comprehend all of the emotions that must be gripping her after listening to Moore's testimony concerning the fate of her husband and so he was somewhat tentative in his approach.

"Mrs. Carpenter, I…am so sorry."

Denise held on to Truitt's arm, her eyes glistening. "No, Sergeant Truitt, you have nothing to be sorry about. You said you would do your best to get to the bottom of my husband's death and you did. For that I am grateful. Now I have closure and can start my life again. Thank you for fulfilling your promise."

Denise Carpenter's kind words had lightened Truitt's burden somewhat. He shared her comments with Jamie as the trial again was called to order.

Lannihan proceeded with the questioning. "Mr. Moore, let's move on to the main reason for this trial. The deaths of Sidney Fulton and James Wristo, employees of Paramount Investment Partners."

Moore took a sip of water. "Pallidin didn't kill them. I did."

The courtroom once again became uncontrollable. Tears and hugs of joy were freely passed around between the Pallidin family and their supporters. Judge Harper was purposefully slow in restoring order, allowing the collective sigh of relief to settle in.

When the courtroom once again quieted down, Moore continued. "My handler told me where to pick up Pallidin's gun and glasses. I waited in the parking lot at the motel where the auditors were staying. I shot them with Pallidin's gun and left his glasses in the car. Then I brought the gun, their briefcases, and wallets to a predetermined location. That was the extent of my part."

Lannihan pressed on. "In your statement you have taken responsibility for the sports bar bombing and also for killing Donald Borchart. Why did you also seek to kill Sergeant Mark Truitt's family?"

"My handler ordered that hit. Truitt and Littlebird weren't falling in line, and the trial was getting close. It was important that they support the prosecution. Killing Truitt's family and pinning it on old man Pallidin was supposed to convince them the Pallidins were evil."

Lannihan shoved his hands in his pockets and turned towards the gallery. "Now, Mr. Moore, you have mentioned this person known as X quite frequently in your testimony." Lannihan whirled around, again facing Moore. "Do you know X's true identity?"

Up until this moment Moore had not revealed his handler, as it was his trump card, keeping the cops holding to their promises. "Yes, I do, and I can prove it. I have a tape of X's real voice safely hidden away."

"And is that person in this courtroom right now?" Lannihan asked.

"Yes."

"Will you tell the court who that person is, please?"

"Moore slowly raised an arm and pointed directly at...Amy Weldon. "It's her. She's X."

Weldon didn't move. She sat staring straight ahead, a confirmation of her guilt.

A collective gasp came from those who knew and worked with Weldon. Mark Truitt had all he could do to keep his knees from buckling. A sweat broke out on his forehead and suddenly he felt nauseas. The realization that he had been used as a pawn by a beautiful woman in order to bring down the Pallidins swept over him like a tsunami. *How much worse would it have been if I had fallen for her?*

Truitt's reality check was interrupted by Judge Harper. "I think we have heard enough from Mr. Moore." She turned her attention to Roger Arcelli. "What is the prosecution's pleasure at this point?"

Arcelli stood, still reflecting the abandonment of facial color. "Your Honor, the prosecution requests the dismissal of all charges against Brewster Pallidin."

And with that, the trial came to a dramatic end; Brewster Pallidin was a free man. Not so, Amy Weldon. Two deputies escorted her out of the courtroom. Truitt was standing at the exit as she reached that point. Weldon stopped when she saw him, her facial expression and eyes faintly pleading an impossible truth. Barely above a whisper, she whimpered, "I'm sorry."

The deputies once again moved her along, leaving Truitt alone to ponder his thoughts.

Mark knew there had been chemistry between them; that was undeniable. Was it possible that her contract on his family actually had duel purposes? Truitt knew the answer. Armondo Pallidin would have been blamed for his family's death, which would serve to drive Mark into the anti-Pallidin camp. Also, Amy would have the opportunity to spin her deadly web around a grieving husband and father. That macabre thought shook him from head to toe. Truitt was glad that chapter would never have to be written. Even though Amy's eyes bespoke remorse as she passed by Truitt, realizing the intent of her plan evoked little sympathy for her.

Goodbye, Amy Weldon. It was time to move on.

Another person moving on, and much to Truitt's dismay, was Peter Malik. As far as Mark was concerned he was as guilty as Weldon. The fact that he was walking away unscathed greatly disturbed Truitt, but there was little he could do about it.

Soon after the trial Paramount Investment Partners announced the dissolution of their partnership with Midwest Research Laboratories. So, one could reasonably conclude if there truly had been a powerful organization intent on stealing the Pallidins' invention, life should now return to normal.

Define normal.

Chapter 55

There is no need to celebrate Groundhog Day in Minnesota. In fact, if Punxsutawney Phil or Sir Walter Wally or Balzac Billy's shadows were to predict only six more weeks of winter from the February 2 date, Minnesotans, particularly the northern variety, would be turning cartwheels in the snow. Besides, the minus-five degrees the Twin Cities was enduring this bitter morning would keep any self-respecting groundhog from leaving its den and testing the elements.

Cold weather or not, Mark Truitt's spirits were higher than they had been for quite a while, and for good reason. The Brewster Pallidin murder case was finally over. Justice had been served. A vicious killer was off the streets and at least one of the masterminds behind the plot to destroy the Pallidin family was behind bars. And not talking.

Amy Weldon had not given up any information since her arrest. Moore's tape confirmed that X's voice truly belonged to Weldon. Weldon did have bargaining power had she chosen to divulge information on whom she was associated with. As far as she was concerned, that was not an option. She continued to maintain her silence as a show of loyalty in hope that she would be looked upon benevolently by her employer. Time would tell.

Truitt's suspicions regarding Laverne Hathaway had led him to keeping Hathaway in the dark concerning Moore's true condition the night he was apprehended. Dr. Sam Pernell had put on a convincing performance, just as Mark had requested. Though Hathaway had been put on administrative leave with the disclosure from Moore that Weldon had wanted one of their own in Guy Lompello's job, before Internal Affairs could properly interrogate him, Hathaway met with a most unfortunate and fatal accident. *Surprise, surprise.* He took a tumble down his basement stairs, breaking his neck in the fall. His blood alcohol level was found to be .18. Another example that drinking and stairs don't mix.

Though not directly charged with any crime, Internal Affairs did have questions for Lenny Spargo and Charles Duchenne. Being put on the spot by IA could be enough to give Charles a heart attack. And it did. Poor guy died before the paramedics could get the pads on him. As for Lenny Spargo, illusions of fame and fortune evaporated like dew on a sunny day. Although he didn't kill Willie Guyanne, the ex-con who was to be set up in the failed Truitt family murder attempt (an outside hit man took out Guyanne), Spargo was assigned the job to "plant" the murder weapon and note on Guyanne. Lenny easily danced around the IA's questions. However, following Hathaway's death, Spargo decided a change of scenery might be healthy for him and so accepted a position with a security agency in the East.

Tom Moore continued to make a slow and painful recovery. Dr. Sam Pernell really hadn't held out much hope for Moore's survival when he arrived at the hospital the night of his encounter with Jamie Littlebird. In fact, when Truitt unveiled his plan to fake Moore's death, Pernell commented, "Dead, probably; faked, unlikely." But to his amazement Moore pulled through. Truitt, Littlebird, Pernell, and Captain Kirgalis collaborated on Tom Moore's "death." They went so far as to inform his next of kin and even held a mock funeral.

Moore was correct in his assumption that he was being planned for erasure. Had he successfully left Minnesota, his chances of survival were slim to none. He was much safer languishing in prison, although the tentacles of his former employers could reach there as well.

All in all, it had been a tough run for a couple of cops who, though seasoned, had not been prepared to defend either the public or themselves against people who could harbor this much evil.

Though Mark and Jamie had been lauded by their department, the news media and, of course, the Pallidin family for a job well done, they weren't comfortable with signing off on the final chapter just yet. They were convinced there had to be more to a story that revolved around such strange, violent people and a mysterious organization that "did not exist."

PART FOUR

Double Take

Chapter 56

"Good evening, gentlemen. Please follow me," Marvin, Armondo Pallidin's butler greeted Mark Truitt and Jamie Littlebird as they stood at the front door.

The Pallidins were hosting a double celebration this night and the two detectives were among the guests of honor. Not only was the family celebrating Brewster's return to freedom but also the engagement of Chelsea Pallidin and Vincent Ponce. The festivities were in full swing as Mark and Jamie joined the gathering. Armondo and Brewster rushed over to greet them.

"Thank you for coming," greeted Brewster as handshakes were passed around.

"You *know* you guys are half the reason for this party," exclaimed Armondo.

"We were just doing our job," Jamie answered. "Glad everything turned out the way it did."

"There's even more good news," Brewster declared. "A group of the good citizens and businesses in our community have come together and provided the necessary funding for us to continue our venture. Moreover, they agree with our philosophy that any success realized in the water desalinization project should not be for personal gain but should be shared with those who desperately are in need of its benefits."

"Well, that's great," Truitt responded. "I hope it all works out for you. And thanks to my wife, I have a better understanding of how significant your invention will be in the future."

"Oh, how's that?" Armondo asked.

"Long story. By the way, I don't want to detract from your celebration, but could Jamie and I have a couple of minutes of your time alone?"

Pallidin chuckled. "Don't you guys ever relax? Sure, give me a couple of minutes to make a toast; then I'll give you all the time you need."

Armondo got the group to quiet down with a few taps on his wine glass. He offered a toast first to Brewster's return to a normal life, highlighting the two detectives who "rode in to save the day" as Armondo put it.

The attention was embarrassing for Mark and Jamie but they took it in stride.

Next he toasted Chelsea and Vincent on their engagement, to an extent that somewhat exceeded the attention span of the guests. But it was, after all, his third glass of wine and it was, after all, his party.

Following the toast, Armondo invited Mark and Jamie to his study. Jamie declined to take part as he was engrossed in a conversation with a history professor on the consequences of nineteenth century treaties imposed on the Gichi-ziibiwininiwag, otherwise known as the (upper) Mississippi Chippewa.

"So, what can I do for you?" A.M. asked as he closed the doors to his study.

Truitt rubbed his forehead. "I don't want to throw any curves into your sense of relief at putting this whole episode behind you, but I can't help but feel we're missing something. I'm thinking there may be another player or two for the other side still among us."

Pallidin bristled. "What do you mean? You think there is still a mole in my company? Now don't go spoiling my party, Truitt."

Mark plopped down onto the leather couch. "Yeah, I know. I'm sorry. I don't want to dampen your night, but this could be important. I can possibly justify the concept that Weldon, Moore, and let's say Peter Malik, accounted for the majority of the criminal activity surrounding your family. But I have this hunch that there was—is someone else that may still be in the shadows."

Armondo lit a fresh cigar. "All explainable. For instance, Brewster was with Malik among others the morning that the evidence was planted at his house. Malik could have given Weldon the green light to bury the briefcases. And how do we know, maybe they had other people working with them who packed up and left with Malik. Oh, and Brewster also remembers mentioning to Malik that his family was gone for the week."

"How about your employees in the desalinization research facility?"

"I've thought of that. I know all of those employees personally. Most of them have been with me for years. The project has so many separate facets that it would be extremely difficult to hijack all the different parts. And, the security in that section is intense. Seizing the operation in its entirety would be a much better option."

Truitt persisted. "Well, I would just as soon err on the side of caution. Do you have all your data stored in one place?"

Pallidin flicked the ashes from his cigar. "I keep an up-to-date compilation of our research on a disk in my safe."

Armondo walked over to the bookcase next to the bar. He removed a set of books, revealing the safe. "The safe has an alarm, plus only two other people know about the disk."

Truitt pursed his lips. "Chalk it up to my suspicious nature, but if there still is someone after your invention, the disk is what they would want to get their hands on."

Pallidin threw his hands in the air. "You're killing me, Truitt. I need a glass of wine."

Mark stood in front of the safe, deep in thought.

"Okay, okay, what do you want to do?" Armondo finally relented.

"I've got an idea...."

Chapter 57

The Minneapolis-St. Paul International Airport was still waking as the man entered the Lindbergh Terminal at 5:30 a.m. He carried only a briefcase, as this was to be but a day trip, one he was not at all looking forward to.

He strolled up to the ticket counter and procured his boarding pass. He proceeded to a security checkpoint where he got in line behind a family of four who were anxiously about to defeat the winter doldrums. The father had already donned a pair of shorts and was in an animated conversation with his wife. A boy who looked to be about ten years old was intently listening to his parents' conversation while the fourth member of their family, a little blonde-haired girl about six was punching at the boy, trying to get his attention.

Stepping up to the conveyor the man removed the necessary items, placed them in a basket, and sent it along with his briefcase on their journey through the x-ray machine. As he was about to pass through the metal detector, the little girl turned around and stuck out her tongue at him. He responded with a finger gesture. A TSA agent observed this exchange and gave him a dirty look, which the man likewise returned. He wasn't in the mood. Not today.

He walked behind the family for a short while after they had passed through security and into the mall area. The father was all but dragging the little girl, as she had her own agenda.

Soon they turned down one concourse and the man continued on to another. He thought about them as they traveled out of sight. They were obviously on their way to have fun in the sun. He would have loved to have joined them, bratty little girl included. He was headed for the warm sunshine also, but unfortunately not in pursuit of leisure activities.

As he stepped off the plane at the Tampa International Airport he realized just how miserable he had been in that frozen tundra the past several months. Yes, Hell actually did freeze over.

However, after just a few minutes of the warm morning Florida sun beating on his face, and the fresh, moist sea air wafting through his nostrils, road salt and ice-glazed windshields were all but forgotten. Regrettably, that was to be the highlight of his trip.

The traveler hailed a cab and directed the driver to set a course that would take him to St. Pete's Beach. The ride was consumed with thoughts of defensive strategies—okay, excuses he knew would be to no avail. In reality there was no choice but to face the music and hope for the best.

All too soon the cab stopped in front of a seven-story beachfront condo complex. The man walked through the building, taking an exit leading to the beach. Once outside he took a moment to soak in the happier side of life. How inviting it looked. White sand, cabanas, people walking and jogging up and down the beach. There were happy faces everywhere; and why not? It was a beautiful day to be a beach bum, ride a parasail, commandeer a wave runner, or…forget it. No more stalling.

The reluctant visitor found his way to the elevator. Once inside he engaged the button for the seventh floor. Soon he was at his destination. A rap on the door produced a young Hispanic man, obviously no stranger to strenuous workouts. Without saying a word he patted the visitor down and led him into a large room, which was bordered on two sides by outside building walls.

On one of the outside walls a patio door opened to a large balcony. Floor to ceiling windows occupied most of the adjacent outside wall. The room's shiny floor had Persian rugs scattered throughout. The ceiling, as well as one of the inside walls was painted white. The remaining wall sported a terra cotta color.

A brown leather couch blended in nicely with the terra cotta wall. A large, ornate mahogany desk sat in front of the white wall into which an arch was cut, allowing access to the rest of the living quarters. It was from this desk that the guest presumed his accountability would be scrutinized.

As if on cue, the "judge and jury" entered the room. "Vincent, my young friend, it's so good to see you."

Yeah, sure it is, Poagi. Cut the bull. Let's get this over with, Vincent Ponce thought to himself…and swallowed hard.

Chapter 58

Poagi Serrantat, a fairly dark-skinned man in his late forties, was a product of a Jamaican mother and French father. When he was still a young boy Poagi and his parents moved from Jamaica to the United States, the family obtaining U.S. citizenship a few years hence. Poagi served several years in the military, much of it in the type of work that doesn't get talked about. All Vincent knew about Poagi was that he was as ruthless as he was loyal to the organization to which they both swore allegiance.

Poagi was very good-looking. Thick black wavy hair, intense brown eyes, and a square jaw served to project an image of power and respect. He complemented his handsome looks with impeccable taste in clothing and jewelry. His detailed attention to personal appearance made Poagi's six-foot frame seem even taller.

Poagi took his orders directly from the top members of the organization, who simply referred to themselves as "The Council." But more about that later. Poagi was responsible and had to answer for the actions of those with whom he was charged, in this case Vincent Ponce. Vincent, in turn, had given direction to Amy Weldon. Peter Malik pledged loyalty to a separate branch of the organization, but did have interaction with Serrantat. Tom Moore was merely a contract employee and not a member of the organization. Of course, thanks to two cops who admirably served in their role as public servants, the results had been quite disappointing for all concerned on the other side. And so Vincent Ponce was now standing in front of his boss, waiting for the guillotine to fall. Of all the things Vincent disliked about Poagi, which was most everything, his condescending manner and theatrics topped the list; and he was about to get a good serving of both.

"Soooo, Vincent, how was your trip? Pleasant, I hope?" a smiling Poagi asked from the opposite side of the desk.

"It was all right. A little turbulence, but nothing too rough."

"Good. Good. I guess, well, I'm sure you know why you have been called in, don't you, Vincent?"

"Poagi, I can explain. Peter, Maria (Amy Weldon's real name was Maria Dunlop) and I...we had everything under control. I mean, look at when I stole the gun, then planted the 'evidence' at Pallidin's home. It went off without a hitch. It was Moore that..."

Serrantat waved a hand, cutting him off. "Vincent, believe me; I, of all people, understand how difficult these expeditions can be. In my former line of work there were misfires all the time. It happens. Unfortunately, Vincent there are those to whom we have to answer who don't appreciate the difficulty of these tasks." Poagi's voice took on a melodic tone, as if he were in extreme anguish.

"I pleaded our case, Vincent. I truly did what I could to soften the blow."

Of course you did.

Poagi sat behind his desk and faced both palms upward. "They are so unforgiving, Vincent. They really wanted to terminate your membership. Can you believe that?"

Yeah, and I'll bet you volunteered to be the terminator.

Poagi sat straight up in his chair, his eyes now two shining disks. "Vincent, now be prepared for what I'm about to tell you. I begged, I pleaded, I cajoled. Finally, they relented! I mean, Vincent, they are going to give us another chance! Isn't that great news?"

That was another thing Ponce hated about Poagi, how he had to plug his name into just about every sentence, like he was rubbing his face in the dirt. "Yeah, that's good, Poagi; that's good."

Serrantat stood up, drew in a long breath over an arrangement of flowers adorning his desk, then walked over to a window. "So, okay, Vincent. They have given us the green light to continue with our project. However, they want to emphasize how imperative it is that we succeed. To illustrate this, they have provided me with a present I am to impart to you. Now, what do you think about that, Vincent?"

As the word "present" could mean just about anything, Ponce barely muttered, "Ah, yeah, fine."

Serrantat returned to his desk, pulled open a drawer and removed a gift-wrapped box approximately five inches long, two inches wide, and an inch in height. "Here, this is for you, Vincent. Go ahead, open it."

Vincent picked up the small box and slowly removed the wrapping. After the paper had been discarded, shaky fingers lifted the lid. Taking a quick look at its contents he immediately cast the box on the desk.

Poagi feigned a look of disappointment. "Why, Vincent, don't you like your present? I'm sure you must recognize it. It is your Aunt Carmen's wedding ring, isn't it? Now if I remember correctly, wasn't she one of your favorite relatives? Didn't you live with her for several years after your parents divorced? Anyway, it's a shame we couldn't remove it from her finger, so the appendage had to come along. As for dear Aunt Carmen, I'm afraid she has disappeared." Poagi shook his head. "Such is life."

Ponce swore to himself that if he'd had a gun he would have shot Poagi Serrantat right then and there. There was no one in his life who meant more to him than his Aunt Carmen. She had been more of a mother to him than his own mother. *How much worse can this get?*

Vincent was about to find out.

"I think you get the message," Serrantat's eyes narrowed, all theatrics in his voice, gone. "It's all business from here on out, Vincent. We're going to complete this mission, no excuses. If you fail this time, I guarantee you'll be having a reunion with your aunt."

Serrantat eased off, his tone a bit more congenial, "Okay, enough of that. Let us discuss a new plan."

Chapter 59

The seven members of The Council were gathered together at a private lodge on the western shore of Lake Champlain, not far from historic Fort Ticonderoga. Due to winter's grip the scenery was nowhere near the caliber of the countryside in full bloom, nor the lake, sparkling and vibrant in nature's kinder seasons. The location was chosen simply and singularly for the substantial measure of the privacy required.

If not the entire Council, at least a majority of its members felt the symbolism of being in such close proximity to one of the more memorable sites of the Revolutionary War. Considering themselves modern day "revolutionaries" of sorts, they justified their agenda as necessary to restore and maintain order in an increasingly chaotic world. But were they truly the Ethan Allens of the twenty-first century…or were they the Benedict Arnolds?

The Council's insistence concerning the privacy of their gatherings was for good reason. Their agenda was secretive, their motives clandestine. Some were high profile, others less visible, all were on the upper rungs of the wealth ladder. Together they, along with their vast network of elitist sympathizers who hailed from all corners of the globe comprised a contagion with the resources to rival most governments, which they wielded with impunity when it suited their ambitions. And when needed, from which abundance did they seek to replenish and add to their resource base? The answer was easy. It was easier than easy. Those open democratic governments boasting a capitalist, free-enterprise system where laws could be changed to favor the powerful, where people of the right influence could be bought, where officials would look the other way, where promises were broken, where lies outnumbered truths, and where the populace condoned it all with their sin of apathy.

So what were their underlying ambitions? Their ultimate goals? Quite simply, to exercise unrestrained control over human activity. Why? Their "official" and self-proclaimed noble justification professed the recklessness of a burgeoning world population that ignorantly devastates the earth's resources to the point where all mankind is one day careening towards a vortex of annihilation. That official mission statement aside, the unspoken individual ambitions included the insatiable quest for more money, more power—the sin of greed hidden by the mask of justification.

The group, who informally (and most arrogantly) referred to themselves as the "Magnificent Seven," after the movie western of the same name, had been called together to discuss their latest and what they considered most strategic venture, the procurement and sole ownership of the Pallidin water desalinization process. They were well aware that this invention had worldwide implications and in their hands it would provide an important impetus to world domination. Obtaining this process was crucial and the recent failure, disappointing. In addition to that subject an update on the current and future status of the world's fresh water supply, as well as other timely matters were to be addressed at this meeting. Each member had an area of expertise and was to give a report on their subject.

Henry Raethburn, a former diplomat whose international connections and suave charisma had propelled his monetary fortune as well as his influential prominence among the world's elite to superstar status, was the facilitator for this meeting. The first order of business was the failed mission to separate the Pallidin family from their desalinization process.

"Good morning, all. I believe Arlo has our first report, concerning the unsuccessful attempt at procuring the Pallidin water desalinization process."

Arlo Vance was a retired military officer who built a private international security business as well as dealing in the arms trade (through any and all channels). He wasn't quite as prominent as the others but did provide the security blanket for a group paranoid about secrecy as well as personal safety. On a moment's notice Vance could assemble a "security" force and enough accompanying firepower to start or stoke any insurrection, or other type of conflict favorable to advancing the Council's agenda.

Vance stood, cleared his throat, and assumed a most serious posture. "As you are all aware, our initial attempt at securing ownership of Midwest Research Laboratories was unsuccessful. I apologize for the setback. A new plan has been evaluated and will soon be executed.

Though it will not now be feasible to acquire the facility itself, we will soon have all the information necessary to continue our project. At some point thereafter a most unfortunate fire will destroy the Pallidin research facility and along with it all of their good intentions." Vance hoped this would be enough to placate all in the group, but that was not to be the case.

"Why was our initial plan terminated?" demanded Neil Samuels, a bank executive. Samuels, a man molded in the image of the robber barons of yore, one who could have easily taken a seat in the House of Morgan, was the type who could not tolerate failure. For him the Pallidin caper so far had been "juvenile and amateurish."

"We had inexcusable actions committed by one of our contract people, which led to his apprehension," Vance countered. "Moreover this person obtained the identity of his handler and offered her up to the police along with details of the operation in exchange for leniency and protection. It won't help him though, I guarantee it. He will pay the price, at our convenience."

"What about his handler?" Samuels demanded.

"She's loyal. I don't think we have to worry about her right now. However, incarceration has a way of rearranging one's priorities. At some point she will have to be erased."

"Okay, let's move on," Raethburn advised. "Rosalee, are you prepared to give the Council an updated report on the current status of the world's fresh water situation?"

"I'm ready." Rosalee Taylor, a Caucasian and Asian blend of head-turning beauty, was a self-made multimillionaire, her fortune amassed in the clothing and cosmetics industry, the foundation of which was laid upon the discarded relationships of those who toiled to place her on her throne. Taylor was born into an agonizingly poor single-parent household. The lack of provisions as well as the lack of love jackhammered a survival reflex into her psyche that predicated any and all other human instincts. Tragically, Rosalee Taylor would forever be chained to the nightmare of her deprived childhood.

Taylor gave her report in the sterile, unemotional manner that typified her personality. "The latest estimates conclude that two-and-one-half percent of the world's water is fresh water. Most of that water is locked up in ice and glaciers. The majority of the available water is taken by agriculture and industry. The end result allows for a very minor percentage offered for municipal usage, including drinking. And, speaking of drinking, don't think for a minute that the United States is immune to the crisis. An estimated nineteen million citizens get sick each year from drinking polluted water, much of which contains fecal matter."

She continued, "So what are the projections for the state of the world in fifteen to twenty-five years? Most of the populated world will experience severe to moderate fresh water shortages. One of the hardest hit areas will be the Middle East. I'm afraid the current conflicts in that part of the world are only a prelude to future struggles over access to fresh water. Portions of North America, Europe, and Russia will also have issues; but for the most part they will escape the worst of the problem. Now to address the question of—why is there a crisis looming? Several reasons, not the least of which is the rapid rise of temperatures on a global scale. There has been a 1.4 degree F. rise in average temperature worldwide since 1980. The last two decades of the twentieth century have been the hottest in at least the last four hundred years, and possibly longer than that."

Samuels interrupted, this time taking issue with Taylor's climate change assessment. "And I suppose you're going to blame human activity for the 'heat wave.' God forbid if we should promote an environment that would bring prosperity and make our lives more comfortable. You know as well as I, the earth periodically goes through natural cycles that bring about huge temperature swings." Samuels sat down to scattered applause.

Taylor bristled, not one to duck a challenge. "Neil, as far as I'm concerned, you can take your self-imposed collective ignorance and shove it down the world's forest of smokestacks. Anybody smarter than a chimpanzee can see that human activity has added to climate change. Look, I'm not interested in debating the moral issues on the subject. My report reflects facts only. I will say this, natural cycles have in the past and most assuredly will continue to affect the climate; but the rate of temperature rise appears to be much faster than what would normally be expected to occur. The rise in temperature is causing ice to melt at an increased rate, particularly in the northern regions, which among other possible calamities may well affect the movement of the great ocean conveyor belt. If that conveyor stops, it could trigger a new ice age. Finally, pollution is another reason for the decrease in available fresh water. All I will say about this is that it is human-inspired and will only get worse as populations increase." Taylor completed her report and sat down, but not before casting a final glare at Samuels.

Next in line to speak was Margaret Ellingson, heiress to a vast sum of old money. Ellingson's best gift to the world would be to step into the next (world) as she was totally void of the qualities of goodness, compassion, or civility. She despised any human who could not wield a significant bankroll nor share her extravagant tastes. In other words, Margaret Ellingson hated just about everyone. She spit out her report as if she were trying to eject an infection.

"As I speak, there are 6.8 billion, ah, souls on this planet and well over one billion do not have access to fresh water. It is projected that by the year 2050 the population will have risen to 9.7 billion. Now, here's a scenario right out of the Garden of Eden: More people every year hence competing for declining food reserves grown on over-fertilized, dried out soil, and fighting over dwindling fresh water supplies. Are you starting to get the picture? Can you see the chaos that is coming? Water has been the source of conflicts throughout history. However, the only known example of interstate war over water occurred 2,500 years ago, in Samaria. Well, my friends, it could happen again, and soon." With a look of disgust, Ellingson retreated to her seat.

Henry Raethburn once again took the floor. "If your thoughts are anywhere close to mine, I'm sure you can envision future opportunities; and we will address those opportunities after lunch."

Chapter 60

Vincent Ponce watched as Poagi Serrantat poured a hefty measure of scotch over the ice cubes in his glass. "Would you like something, Vincent?" Poagi offered. "You look a little nervous."

How would you expect me to be after your "present"?

"I'll have the same."

Poagi prepared another scotch and handed it to Vincent. "Okay, so you've told me that Pallidin has a disk that contains all the information on the desalinization project. Are you certain this information is accurate?"

"It is. I overheard Chelsea talking to her brother about it."

"Well, then, you are going to get that disk, Vincent."

Ponce sipped his drink. "That won't be easy. The old man has it locked up in his safe."

Serrantat set his glass on the desk, hard. "You see, that's why you fail, Vincent. It's your attitude, your lack of self-confidence. The fact that it's not easy only provides for a greater challenge, which ultimately results in sweeter success. Now, if you're not up to it, let me know so I can regroup."

The scotch was starting to take hold. "Of course I'm up to it, Poagi. I just mean we're going to need a good plan."

"I have a good plan, which is more than I could count on you to come up with. I'll tell you how you'll get the disk and, by the way, I'm sending four contract people to help you carry this out. You will take your fiancée, Chelsea, out for an evening on the town. Set it up with our people for you two to be 'kidnapped.' They'll take you and Chelsea to an old grain milling complex just outside the city. Most of the buildings on the property are being used for storage. I had a contact rent the main building with the excuse that he needed to house a couple of tractor-trailers for a month. Of course, the transaction will be untraceable. We'll have a van large enough to transport a car, parked inside the building. The kidnappers will bring you and the girl there. They will strap explosives on you which, of course, will be defused. You will then drive to Pallidin's home. Tell him the explosives are wired to detonate if you try to remove them, and tell him they have Chelsea. Have Pallidin talk to her to verify that you're telling him the truth. One of our men will get on the phone and tell Pallidin that if he doesn't have the disk in his hands in one hour, he will never see his daughter again. Got it so far?"

"Yeah, good plan. What happens to Chelsea once we have the disk?"

Poagi poured another round of scotch, answered nonchalantly. "Why, what about her? She disappears forever. We can't afford to leave loose ends."

Vincent looked down at the floor. Poagi noted his concern. "Wait a minute. What's that look? Hey, you don't have feelings for her, do you?"

Although Vincent couldn't admit it, he had more than just feelings for Chelsea. He was truly in love with her. "No, of course not. It's just that, well,...ah, forget it. You're right. We can't leave any loose ends."

Poagi continued, "When you get to the mill, kill the girl and put her body in the car, then drive the car into the van. Two guys will take the van. You go with the other men in another car. I want you and the disk back here within twenty-four hours. The girl will disappear. No trace will be found. The cops can put her in their cold case file."

"Pretty elaborate scheme, but I can handle it."

Poagi swirled the contents in his glass, watching the ice cubes chase each other. "As the saying goes, Vincent—failure is not an option."

Maybe it was the drinks, maybe for emphasis, maybe some of both, but Poagi put his acting face back on. He walked around the desk and patted Vincent's cheek. "Now, this little assignment isn't going to be too hard for you, is it, Vincent? Because, if that's the case, I will just have to make other arrangements."

"Consider it done."

"And I'm sure you realize that our plan is to be executed to perfection, don't you, Vincent?"

"Yes, I understand perfectly."

"Good. And, Vincent, the girl. Be sure you do the right thing with the girl."

"I will, Poagi, I will."

Chapter 61

The Council reconvened after a light lunch. They would complete their business in the afternoon session and then each would discreetly go their separate ways. Henry Raethburn, the former diplomat and facilitator for the gathering, was first to speak at the afternoon session.

"I have a few more facts and figures to share with you. Although they may paint a rather grim picture in the eyes of the world, *we* understand that it is a necessary part of natural selection, and it also serves to enhance our opportunities. More than 3.5 million people die each year from water-related diseases, almost all from developing countries. Close to a billion people lack safe water supplies. Polluted water and poor sanitation claim more lives through disease than any war claims through guns. At any given time more than half of the world's hospital beds are occupied by patients suffering from water-related diseases."

Turning to look at each person present, he said, "Now, before we move on I think it might be a good idea to clarify my use of the word 'opportunity.' In no way do I, we, want the word to be misconstrued to mean that our sole purpose here is to personally profit from this looming malady that is poised to wreak havoc upon humanity. I believe it is reasonable to assume in going forward that our overwhelming interest is to promote the well-being of all mankind."

A unanimous "Here, here" was sounded throughout the room.

Raethburn held up a hand. "Now to nurture us along this moral and necessary path to which we have dedicated our lives and are willing to sacrifice our personal resources, I call upon our resident spiritual expert for further inspiration."

Bobby Sylvester was a most interesting person. Born of humble roots in the Bible Belt, Sylvester heard his calling to the ministry at an early age. Upon completing an internship in a Protestant congregation, Sylvester decided that mainstream religion was too confining and promptly proceeded to build a televangelism empire. A master of Bible prose combined with a generous and polished dose of theatrical passion, the impeccably primped and styled Bobby could woo even the most unholy of souls off the street, the transgressors soon finding themselves prostrate on the carpet of his new, multimillion-dollar cathedral, begging for forgiveness from the Almighty.

"My friends," he began, "what I have heard here today...ah, distresses me to my very soul. And however great *our* sorrow may be for the suffering of our fellow man, it is but a pittance of the anguish God must feel." Sylvester raised a palm to his forehead, subsequently placing it tight to his chest. "For all of his masterful accomplishments in creating *us*, he cannot be very happy with our stewardship. He must even now be asking himself, 'Oh *who,* but *who*, will care for my creation? Who will make my life-giving waters once again flow clean, and pure, and abundant?'"

Raising a Bible high in the air, Sylvester proudly proclaimed, "WE are those people, my friends. Make no mistake about it; *we* are the precious few who have been chosen to lead this sinful...adulterous world back from the brink of destruction. And where will our inspiration come from? Let us refer to the Holy Bible, the Book of Joshua, Chapter 6. I'm sure you are all familiar with the story of how God's servant, Joshua, brought down the walls of Jericho. His inspiration for battle came directly from the Almighty, who is quite merciless to those who do not follow his Word. Now, did Joshua attack the city in a conventional fashion, risking the lives of his soldiers? On the contrary"—Sylvester's voice softened to a whisper—"*he followed God's orders.*" Swinging his arm in an arc, a now animated Bobby could barely contain himself. "He ordered his army to march aaroooouuund the outside walls of the city for seven days in a row, and on the seventh day Joshua, one final time, directed his priests to blow trumpets. *The...walls...FELL*, my friends. The army entered the city, and save for one family, killed *everyone* in it. Then, after taking the silver and gold for the treasuries of God, they burned what was left."

Sylvester pushed out a sigh, dropped his head as though he were emotionally spent. After a short pause Bobby rebounded, finishing with gusto. "This Bible story will be our template. This is our *justification*. When necessary our actions will be swift and severe. Success will be given to *us* because we are righteous!"

With that bit of inspiration Sylvester plopped down in his chair.

The next speaker was Neil Samuels, a banking executive and central player contributing to the recent mortgage meltdown. "Unless you have been living under a rock the past few years, you are aware of the dire economic situation the world is in. Many national economies are teetering on the edge of bankruptcy." Samuels couldn't help but let out a chuckle. "Yes, our plan worked to perfection, didn't it? Capitalism without controls is a wonderful thing! Banks and the Market are our tools; wealth is our reward. We made money in the subprime mortgage crisis on the way up, and we made money on the way down. *Mortgage bonds, credit default swaps, tranches, collateralized debt obligations*—they all hold a special place in my heart. And those unfortunate souls at the bottom of this delicious transfer of wealth? Well, they, to put it bluntly, were scammed, slammed, and damned. Scammed with 'teaser' rates, slammed with 'resets,' and finally damned by losing homes they couldn't afford. The best part to all this? No one is being held accountable. God, I love this country! But enough of this giddiness. The world is ready for something new and innovative to ignite a spark of prosperity; something that will spurn a demand which will lead to job creation and a renewed strength in currencies throughout the world. I think you all know where this is heading. Manufacturing the materials and building the infrastructure needed to transport fresh water on a worldwide scale would set forces in motion, resulting in an economic boom of unprecedented proportions. Also, low-cost water would result in lower costs for food production. This, in turn, would serve to raise the standard of living throughout the world, allowing people more discretionary income. It is truly a golden apple waiting to be plucked from the tree of prosperity."

"Thank you, Neil," Raethburn smiled. "The future looks much brighter from your perspective, doesn't it? Well, on that uplifting note, I call on Ross, our final speaker of the day."

Ross Denali, a mid-thirties man with a maddening smirk semi-permanently pasted across an ordinary face was an extremely successful entrepreneur who could barely keep track of his rapidly expanding financial empire. He was unique even in this group of exclusive individuals. With an IQ topping out at 146, Denali was far superior in intelligence to any on the Council. A maverick with complete self-confidence, Denali often pushed to extremes. The group usually succeeded in holding him in check, but barely. They respected his intelligence but at the same time were a little afraid of him.

"Digesting the information I've heard here today has me thinking." Denali tugged at his shirt cuffs. "There will soon be seven billion people residing on this planet. I, for one, am a student of Thomas Malthus whom I believe will finally be proved right, in that the world's population, if left unchecked, will outstrip the means to support it. In fact, man has so altered the planet in the last one hundred years that the scientific community has embraced a name for this unfolding epoch—the Anthropocene, or 'New Man' era. Now, as much as I like Neil's economics, more fresh water means more people. Demographers predict that there will be eight billion people by 2025 and nine billion by 2045. Do you want to rub eighteen billion other elbows? I don't! A population on the order of three billion sounds much more comfortable to me; a figure to set our sights on. Don't forget, we have selflessly taken on the role as caretakers of this planet and that includes preparing for the future of mankind. What kind of world will it be if we are constantly competing for the limited resources of Mother Earth? We need to be thinking population control. Unfortunately, my friends, there is not room for everyone. A grim thought maybe, but it's reality. I believe we have been mandated to decide as to who travels into the future with us and who doesn't."

Though several frowned, no one disagreed.

Chapter 62

Vincent Ponce stared out the window of the DC10, scanning the ground below. Here and there patches of white were starting to appear, signaling a return to the winter wonderland. Depressing as it looked, Vincent was happy to be anywhere that was above ground. He had chided himself for purchasing a round-trip ticket as being unduly optimistic. But here he was, resuming his mission and hopefully returning to Poagi's good graces.

Vincent felt terrible about his Aunt Carmen. In his mind he had taken revenge for her death by releaving Poagi of several of *his* appendages. But only in his mind. And, well, Carmen *was* old and not in good health. Vincent reminded himself that he had to move on. There was a more pressing problem to consider and it had everything to do with Poagi's plan.

His feelings for Chelsea had nearly tripped him up with Poagi. Vincent genuinely *was* in love with her. He hadn't meant to be. Falling in love could get him killed but, then, love can be a stranger to danger. Chelsea was a decent and honest person and that was probably the main reason he was attracted to her. He actually felt...well, clean, when he was with her. He was living two lives and he hated it. If he had his choice he would pick life number one, the one with Chelsea in it. Of course, there was no chance of that. His destiny was to function in a murky netherworld of day-to-day survival, whereas Chelsea only knew a charmed and naïve life where helping those in need was an assumed responsibility.

The thud of the landing gear locking into place jolted Vincent back to his surroundings. Ahead he could see the orange glow of the "city of death" as he now defined the Twin Cities. Looking out at the snow as the wheels touched the tarmac wasn't exactly "chicken soup for the soul" either.

The final insult that launched Vincent's darkening mood into total nightfall was the blast of fresh Minnesota air that engulfed him as he walked out of the terminal. Although Vincent had never been a student of physics he was sure that, of anywhere in the universe, the theoretical temperature of "absolute zero" could be realized in this state.

Chapter 63

Several weeks later.

Finally, all of winter's last snowy holdouts had melted from the landscape, ushering in another infant spring. Muddy roads, open water, repaired potholes, well, some repaired potholes, and budding pussy willows orchestrated a statewide collective mood swing to the affirmative.

At precinct headquarters, Sergeants Mark Truitt and Jamie Littlebird had all but abandoned their present paperwork detail and were sneaking frequent glances into their newly promoted boss's office. Ray Lopez, a respected twenty-year veteran of the department had been everyone's choice to replace the departed Laverne Hathaway.

Lopez wasn't the object of the detectives' curiosity; it was his visitor, sitting opposite him and facing away from them. The only angle of sight was from behind, which offered a view of long, light-brown hair with caramel highlights, pulled into a shoulder-length ponytail. It wasn't long before they got to see the rest of their supervisor's guest.

Lopez opened his door and motioned to the detectives, "Mark, Jamie, step into my office, please." He didn't have to ask twice.

"Guys, I'd like you to meet Sylkie Maune. She's been with MPD for two years."

Sylkie appeared to be in her late twenties. She bounced out of her chair to greet the detectives as if she was spring-loaded. A slim woman of average height, her figure stood out as well-toned. Her hair color was complemented by skin which had been colored to just the right shade by, most likely, sessions in a tanning bed, considering the time of year. Enhancing all of that were hazel-green eyes, intense and intelligent. "Nice to meet you," Sylkie enthusiastically offered as handshakes were passed around.

"Sylkie's been working in the Special Drug Enforcement Unit," Lopez said.

"In all honesty," Sylkie added, "I was glad to be transferred. I was getting a little burned out."

"I know what you mean," Jamie remarked. "I was in that unit. After awhile it has the effect of lowering your expectations for the future of civilization."

"For Jamie and me it's been pretty much of a one-horse show lately," Truitt remarked.

Sylkie leaned against Lopez's desk. "I kept up with every bit of the trial. Exciting. Wish I could have been a part of it."

"Never know. You may get your wish," Truitt counseled. "There are a lot of unanswered questions the trial didn't speak to."

"Anyway," Lopez said, "Sylkie's here because of the loss of Spargo and Duchenne…"

Jamie couldn't help himself, "That was a loss?"

Lopez frowned, "You know what I mean."

"Sorry."

"There will be another replacement coming but, in the meantime, I would like you guys to take Sylkie under your wing. Show her around, get her familiar with the area. Aaand…only pass along the good habits." Lopez winked.

Littlebird grabbed Sylkie by the arm. "C'mon, we'll get some Twinkies and sit on the steps outside. Later on we'll have a paper airplane fight."

"I think I'm going to like it here," Sylkie laughed.

The balance of the shift was divided between introducing Sylkie to fellow cops, all of whom were jealous that they didn't get the assignment, and familiarizing her with the territory. As the shift ended, Mark and Jamie looked forward to having a day off, after which they would begin a set of evening shifts with their new apprentice in tow.

As soon as Mark entered his house, he sensed something was off kilter. The quietness was telltale.

"Liz, are you here?"

A rather weak, "Yes," drifted from the direction of the living room.

"What's the matter, honey?" Mark could see that Liz had been crying.

"Brian. He quit school today. He said he's flunking out anyway so he might as well quit. He was just, well, really sad."

"Where is he now?"

"He went over to Jimmy's apartment. Said he would call in the morning."

Mark held Liz tight, let out a deep breath. "I better try to get a hold of him. I'm worried what he might do."

Mark punched in Brian's number on his cell phone. One…two…three rings, then a connection. Mark walked into the kitchen.

A few minutes later he ambled back into the living room, a cup of coffee in hand.

"What did he say?" Liz asked.

"He said he was okay, not to worry. He wants some time to think, promised to call tomorrow. I don't know, Liz. Maybe we got our hopes up too high."

Liz folded her arms, paced slowly, looking down as if she was counting the strands in the carpet. "We don't know what he's doing much of the time."

"Well, we can't make ourselves small and live in his pocket. We can counsel, we can cajole, we can listen, we can pray, we can and will be there for him. What we can't do is cater to him if he's headed in the wrong direction."

"I know. I know," Liz disconsolately answered. "But it's so hard when your own child is hurting. You just want to hold them and make it better."

"But, that's exactly what Brian would want us to do if he is going back to drugs. He will try to play on our love and sympathy. You know, 'Poor me, the world's against me, not my fault,' all the crap we've heard before. Liz, if Brian is drifting backwards, that current will only run more swiftly if we indulge him. We cannot, and will not, be enablers."

The conversation concerning Brian ended pretty much with Maggie blowing in the front door. Maggie had erased most of the scars from the Tom Moore episode, resuming her energetic nature, which generally entailed moving in all directions at once and talking at the same time. Though short in stature, her spitfire demeanor usually catapulted her to the front of the crowd.

"Oh, oh, looks like we're not so happy, tonight, huh?" Maggie said, eyeing her parents.

Chapter 64

"You didn't partner up with 'Doctor Inspiration' last night, did you?" Jamie asked, giving Truitt a hard once over.

"No," Mark responded, "I didn't sleep well. Brian quit school and I'm worried about him."

"You think maybe he's into drugs again?"

"I don't know for sure but I have my suspicions. I talked to him yesterday. He wouldn't open up about anything of substance. Only small talk. He did promise we would talk more tonight. We'll see."

Jamie rested his hand on Mark's shoulder. "Let's hope for the best. Let me know if there's anything I can do."

"Hi, guys," Slykie greeted as she approached, ready to start the shift. "What have we got going on in the world of crime today?"

It had been a rather quiet day around the precinct and the evening was starting out the same way. Truitt set their shift's itinerary. They would complete some unfinished paperwork and review a few open files. Later they would follow up on a domestic assault that had occurred the previous day. The quiet start to the shift allowed the three of them to share some personal history.

"Are you from the area, Sylkie?" Truitt asked.

"No, actually I was raised in Oklahoma City. My dad was a high school teacher and my mom...well, my mom worked for the U.S. Marshalls Service until April 19, 1995. That's the day when Timothy McVeigh protested against the 'evil empire' by killing innocent people when he blew up the Alfred Murrah Federal Building. I was only thirteen, but I decided that very day I would spend the rest of my life trying to keep ordinary citizens, like the folks who worked in that building, safe from people like him."

"That was terrible. I'll never forget the pictures on television of the building torn apart," Jamie said. "Sorry for your loss. How did you end up in Minneapolis?"

"My dad just couldn't handle my mom's death and the entire trauma surrounding the tragedy. He died three years later. Just kind of gave up on life. All I had left was my sister. When she married and moved up here, I followed along."

Sylkie changed direction, signaling an end to discussing that dark corner of her life. She opened her arms and donned an ear to ear smile, "And here I am."

Truitt piped up, "Okay, 'here I am,' here we go. Let's call on our assault victim."

It was a beautiful April evening, warm and soothing. Winter had retreated to the confines of the Arctic Circle, the last of the melted snow transported via the great Minnesota waterways to the Atlantic Ocean, Hudson Bay, and the Gulf of Mexico.

As the threesome drove to their destination an emergency call came over their radio. "Disturbance and possible shots fired at 190 Hartford Street, Northeast."

"That's less than a block away. Let's go," Jamie said.

Approaching the two-story house, they could see a great deal of commotion going on. There were lights shining from all windows, exposing people running helter-skelter in all directions.

At the same time a male who appeared to be holding a gun, flew out of the front door and ran towards a chainlink fence that bordered the property.

Sylkie was out of the car in an instant. The man shoved the gun in his pocket, grabbed the top of the fence rail, and pulled himself over. Sylkie grabbed the rail also, heaved herself over and landed on the assailant practically in one motion. He must have thought she dropped out of the sky. He was cuffed to the fence, minus one handgun, before he knew what hit him.

"Holy smokes, did you see that?" Truitt huffed to Littlebird as they reached the fence.

"I think I found my new partner," Jamie deadpanned.

"And I want to thank you for your years of loyalty," Truitt returned the shot.

The threesome entered the house just ahead of the uniforms. The partiers, mostly college-age kids, were frantically heading in the opposite direction.

As Truitt ascended the stairs to the second floor he ran into Jimmy, his son Brian's friend. Jimmy pointed to the head of the stairwell. "He's up there. He's hurt bad."

Mark grabbed Jimmy's arm. "Who's up there?"

"Brian. He got shot!"

Truitt loosened his grip on Jimmy and took the stairs two at a time. The top of the stairs accessed a short hallway with a bedroom on either side. Straight ahead was a larger room, perhaps a family room. Brian was lying in the middle of it.

Mark rushed over to the limp form. "Brian! Brian, can you hear me?" Mark cried as he put his hands on his son's shoulders. Other than a low moan there was no response from Brian. Mark saw an entry wound on the lower right side of Brian's chest as he quickly scanned his son's body.

"I'm trained as a paramedic," Sylkie said as she knelt on the opposite side of Brian. "The ambulance is on its way." She did what she could until the ambulance crew arrived. They quickly shuttled Brian away, Mark at his side.

In the meantime Littlebird collared Jimmy and was looking for answers. "What happened to Brian? Why did he get shot?"

Jimmy barely dared to look at Littlebird. He was shaking badly. "Brian was hitting the drugs pretty hard. This guy came around selling. He and Brian were making a deal, and…and then an argument started. Brian took the stuff, but wouldn't give him all the money he demanded. The guy pulled a gun and shot him. Brian went down."

"We're going to need a formal statement from you." Jamie motioned to a couple of officers who were exiting the house.

Soon after, Sylkie reunited with Jamie. "Were you able to get any information on what happened to Brian?" she asked.

"Let's head to the hospital," Jamie answered as he hurried Sylkie to their car. "I'll fill you in on the way."

Chapter 65

What was known at this point was that Brian had been shot with a small caliber handgun at close range. There was no exit wound. Complicating matters were the drugs in his system; what kind and quantity were not known.

On the ambulance ride to the hospital Mark called his friend Dr. Sam Pernell, briefly explained the situation, and asked to meet him at the hospital. The ambulance pulled up to the emergency entrance and Mark jumped out. He immediately called Maggie's cell phone, praying she would answer. He needed Maggie's strength to support Liz.

"Hello?"

"Maggs, it's Dad."

"Dad, what's wrong?" she caught the panic in his voice.

"Brian's been shot. We're at North Memorial. Just tell Mom there's been an accident and that I'll meet you two at the hospital. Let me know when you're close. I'll catch up with you in the lobby."

"Okay, but what if Mom wants to talk to you?"

"Tell her I'm busy with paperwork, whatever, and I said I'd meet you here."

"All right, I'll get her and we'll be on our way."

"Thanks. I love you."

"Love you, too, Dad."

Mark caught up with Brian as he was being wheeled into surgery. He stopped at the entrance to the room where Brian's life or death struggle would be played out. Suddenly Mark Truitt's world went from fast-forward to slow motion. He peered into a strange world of people dressed in green, arrays of gleaming instruments designed to cut and probe, and thumping and pulsating machines devised to monitor vitals and circulate life-giving fluids. In the middle of it all lay his son, his life dependant on the deftness of those who wield the instruments.

A hand on his shoulder released Mark from the scene's grip. It was Sam Pernell. A first impression of Pernell may not be one of great comfort to a patient scheduled to go under his knife. A large man top to bottom, Pernell's pant's belt usually struggled to maintain position around his center of gravity. Boyish looks and premature gray hair combed straight forward were often cause for reservation from those who weren't aware of his skills. However, as looks are often deceiving, Pernell's competent hands operated the instruments of his trade on par with the best surgeons in the country. "We'll be starting surgery in a few minutes. I promise I'll do my best to make this a happy ending. Brian has youth on his side. That's a big plus."

"Thanks, Sam. Save my son, please."

Mark returned to the hallway, stopping in front of the family waiting room. The room was empty so he stepped in. He paced back and forth for a minute and then put his hands to his face and released the frustration, sense of helplessness, feelings of failure—all of the emotions that had been building in his relationship with Brian over the past couple of years. And now it had come to this, every parent's worst nightmare. Mark mentally beat himself up for not having done more, for not confronting Brian from the beginning when his drug use was first suspected. A little accusatory voice from within kept repeating, *Wishing won't make it go away.* Mark Truitt felt as low as he had ever been. The typically impersonal world that a cop deals with every day had suddenly become all too personal.

The ringing of Mark's cell phone re-channeled his thoughts. It was Maggie. She and Liz were almost at the hospital. He walked down the hallway to meet them as if he were walking to the gallows. His brain was pulsating with explanations of how he could ease into the gravity of the situation. Skirting the truth would only add confusion. *Just tell Liz exactly what happened,* he concluded.

Liz and Maggie arrived at the lobby in unison with Mark. He said little, directing them back to the family waiting room. When the door was closed behind them, Liz grabbed Mark's arm. "What happened? What's going on?"

Mark hesitated for a moment, then choked out, "Brian's been shot."

Liz fell back into the nearest chair. "What? Why?"

Mark put one knee down beside her, "That's not the entire story. Brian has drugs in his system. But listen, he's got the best team possible working on him."

Maggie crouched to Mark's level. The three of them embraced.

After a few minutes, the waiting room door opened. In walked Jamie and Sylkie. Sylkie was introduced to Liz and Maggie. There was instant good chemistry between them, which helped to lighten the load.

An hour went by. Then another. The third bell had almost rung when Sam Pernell appeared in the doorway, looking very tired. "We removed a bullet, which was lodged next to Brian's spine. Upon entry, the slug was deflected by a rib. If that had not been the case it most likely would have pierced his heart. However, there is a fair amount of internal damage."

Sam rubbed a hand through his hair. "To be honest with you folks, right now Brian is hovering between life and death. His youth is his best ally, but ultimately his future depends on his will to live. He will be in intensive care in about thirty minutes. You can see him there. Your presence will be his best prescription."

"Thanks, Sam. Thanks for everything," Mark said as Liz and Maggie took turns giving Pernell hugs.

Soon after, Jamie and Sylkie gave the Truitts' their well-wishes and left.

After what seemed like an eternity, the Truitt family was standing alongside Brian's bed, Mark and Liz each holding a hand. Brian looked so peaceful, so serene. If that were only the case. If only this hadn't happened. If only Brian hadn't gone back to drugs. If only they were at home now, peacefully resting their bodies and minds in preparation for the new day. *If only, if only*. A million "if onlys" wouldn't change anything. It was what it was, Brian fighting for his life.

After countless silent prayers and what seemed like forever, Mark convinced Liz and Maggie to retreat to the family room and get some rest.

Mark was now left alone with his son. Only the noise of the life support systems and monitoring machines filtered through the room. A lone courtesy light shone above Brian's bed. Mark's thoughts reverted to the day when his only son came into the world. A more proud father there never had been. What achievements would the future hold for his baby boy? For sure, his son would possess athletic abilities. He would learn to skate, play hockey. That was practically a rite of passage for Minnesota youth. If hockey was not his choice, there were plenty of other sports to participate in. And, of course, the boy would be an excellent student. Honor rolls, scholarships. No doubt, they would be a part of his future.

Then over the years, one by one, the dreams faded into the realm of wishful thinking. The end product of the boy named Brian could best be described as average. Of course, there is absolutely nothing wrong with being average. After all, that's what most of us are. That's why it's called average.

Much to ponder, little to understand. Right now all that mattered was that Brian was alive.

Mark sat at his son's bedside holding his hand, praying. Through his prayers, the old Hollies song, "He Ain't Heavy, He's My Brother," kept swimming around in his head.

No, you're not heavy, Brian; you're my son.

Chapter 66

Mark Truitt's absence to care for his son brought Jamie Littlebird and Sylkie Maune together as temporary partners.

On this day they were traveling to the Federal Medical Center in Rochester to interview Tom Moore. The slowly recovering killer had been afforded maximum protection as promised. He had now healed to the point where Littlebird felt comfortable to squeeze him a little. The hope was that Moore may yet hold information instrumental in gaining an insight into the organization he had worked for.

The trip from the Twin Cities to Rochester took a little over an hour. It was a beautiful spring day, warm and full of bright sunshine, the kind of day where Mother Nature received atonement for her temper tantrum we call winter. The open expanse of the landscape along Highway 52 provided a panoramic view of all of the vibrancy of spring. The enhanced green of the early grasses, the enriched black of the broken soil soon to be planted.

Even the delicately unfolding leaves on budding trees and shrubs were presenting their infant colors.

"I should warn you," Jamie advised as they neared their destination. "This is not a pleasant person we are going to interview. Just getting close to him physically brings on a feeling of darkness, evil. It does for me, anyway."

"You mean as in 'an evil spirit dwells within?'" Sylkie retorted, a little on the flippant side.

"Hey, I'm just saying that meeting Tom Moore is likely not to be the highlight of your day."

"I'm sorry, Jamie. I didn't mean to make light of your warning. It's just that, well, after my mother died, I have a hard time with spiritual concepts. I look at people as either good or bad; and the bad I have very little patience or sympathy for."

The interview room at the prison was basic to the bone. A table and four chairs. That was it. Jamie and Sylkie were occupying two of the chairs when the door opened and a slightly stooped over Tom Moore shuffled in, followed by a guard. Although thinner and looking somewhat older, Moore had his color back and appeared to be making a decent recovery.

As soon as Moore saw Jamie his beady eyes widened and his purple-red nose flared. Sylkie took a mental step backward.

"Whaddya want?" Moore barked as he sank into a chair on the other side of the table.

"Looks like you're making progress, Tom. Nice to see you up and about," Jamie answered with a sarcastic edge.

"You didn't come here to see how my health is. Who's this?" Moore pointed to Sylkie.

"Another one of Minnesota's 'finest.' Now I've got..."

Moore interrupted, grabbing his crotch. "Hey, cop, why don't you give me five minutes alone with her? I could use a little extracurricular activity." A guttural laugh followed.

"That's enough!" Littlebird warned.

Sylkie put up a palm. "It's all right. He can't say anything I haven't heard before."

"Maybe so, but I've got something you haven't seen before. I'd..."

Littlebird slammed his fist on the table. "That's enough, I said! We came here to ask you a few questions and when we're done you can go back to your personal Shangri-La and contemplate how long it would take for your employers to reward your service to them if we dropped the protection."

Moore glared at Jamie, said nothing. His look made the hair on the back of Sylkie's neck rise. Finally, Moore broke the silence. "Okay, cop. Let's get this over with."

"At the trial you said one of the reasons Amy Weldon ordered Guy Lompello's murder was because 'they' wanted one of their own in his place. You also said somebody heard about the argument between Lompello and Pallidin. Since the trial, has your memory improved any? Have any other names come to you, like Peter Malik, for instance? How about Paramount Investment Partners? Anything ring a bell there?"

Moore scowled. "You ain't too bright, are you? How many ways do I have to tell you that my *only* contact was Weldon. And if I wasn't smart enough to figure that out, I wouldn't even know her real identity. You can ask me these questions a hundred times and you're going to get the same answers. I'm done." Moore stood. "Hope you enjoyed the ride, cuz otherwise you wasted you're time coming here."

"Oh, not really," Jamie nonchalantly answered.

"What do you mean?"

"You got to see my smiling face."

"I'm satisfied that he's not holding anything back. I had to give it one more attempt to be sure," Jamie reflected as he and Sylkie walked to their car. "Sorry you were subjected to that outburst."

Sylkie quietly shook herself out of deep contemplation, "Remember on the way down you mentioned something about evil spirits and I said I don't believe in them?"

"Yeah, I remember."

"Well, Tom Moore just changed my whole outlook on the subject."

Chapter 67

"Why do you look so exceptionally beautiful tonight?" Vincent asked Chelsea, their eyes meeting in the reflection of the mirror in front of them.

"Could the reason be this beautiful diamond necklace that some handsome stranger presented to me in hopes that I would be swayed by his devilish charm?" Chelsea pretended to ponder.

Vincent wrapped his arms around her waist and rested his head against hers. "I guarantee you that my intentions are purely honorable, my lovely lady. And, by the way, would you consider marrying this sincere and humble pauper?"

Chelsea gave him a playful poke in the ribs and moved away from the dressing table. "Yeah, why not?" she frivolously answered. "Let's see, how about we make plans for the fall."

"I will check my schedule to see what dates I have open," Vincent countered.

"Oh, shut up," Chelsea teased back. "By the way, where is my humble admirer taking me tonight?"

"How about Sebastion's? We haven't been there in forever."

"That's so expensive. Did my dad give you a raise or did a rich relative die?"

Rich, no. Relative, yes. "No, I didn't get a raise but I don't see anything wrong with splurging a bit of my meager savings on the woman I will spend the rest of my life with. Course we could dine at Happy Burger if you prefer."

Chelsea grabbed Vincent's chin. "I will go anywhere as long as it's with you. Give me a kiss."

Go anywhere with you. That statement unleashed a gut punch on Vincent. *If you only knew!*

"How's Brian doing? Did you see him today?" Jamie asked Mark as they settled in for their shift.

"I was at the hospital this morning. Hard to believe it's been three weeks since the shooting. Pretty much of a blur to me. Sam Pernell is pleased with his physical progress. He said Brian's recovery is a testament of his will to live. You'd never know it when trying to communicate with him, though."

"Not talking much, huh?"

"Like trying to get the attention of a hibernating bear."

"I'm sure he has a lot on his mind," Jamie contemplated. "Coming that close to death is pretty traumatic."

"For sure," Mark agreed. "He'll be coming home in a few days. When he recovers enough we plan on getting him some professional help. But I think reviving his spirit will be up to us."

"How about letting me help with that," a voice came from behind Truitt. It was Sylkie. "I mean it. I've had training in drug rehabilitation. And I got a lot of firsthand experience on the dark side of the situation being on the drug unit this past year. Let me try. I'd like to help."

Truitt turned around, completely taken back. "That's a big commitment. Are you sure you want to take it on?"

Sylkie didn't bat an eye. "Absolutely. You know, there's not that much difference in our ages. Maybe he will relate to me better than someone older…you know, not that he doesn't respect you and Liz, but sometimes a person with his type of problem will open up to a third party easier than a loved one."

"That's probably true. For sure we haven't been able to bridge the gap." Mark thought for a moment. "But there is one more thing to think about."

"What's that?" Sylkie asked.

"Well, as you said, you and Brian are not that far apart in age. Trouble is you are a very nice-looking young lady. I'm afraid he, ah, may come to think of you in ways other than just wanting to help him overcome his addiction."

Sylkie laughed. "Don't worry about that. I'll make my intentions very clear. Besides, Oscar wouldn't allow another companion in my life."

"Oscar?" Truitt looked puzzled. "I didn't know you were dating someone?"

"Oscar, Sergeant Truitt, is my dog."

"Oh. By the way, you're scheduled to spend the shift at dispatch."

"Sounds like I'll be having an easy shift."

"I've cancelled all criminal activity for tonight so you won't miss out on anything."

Chapter 68

With the sun approaching the summer solstice, the sky was still lights-on when Vincent and Chelsea entered Sebastion's at 8:45 p.m. On the ride there Vincent alternated between keeping Chelsea entertained with light conversation and mentally going over a plan to make this night end with Chelsea alive and well.

Vincent knew his plan would not be easy to pull off. The goons Poagi Serrantat sent weren't amateurs, but Ponce concluded that since he had the element of surprise on his side he could handle them. Vincent ran the sequence of events through his mind: *Allow the kidnappers to overtake Chelsea and me in the parking lot. At the old mill, Chelsea gets tied up and I get strapped with the explosives. I get the disk from Pallidin. That should be no problem. Let's see, now the hard part. Once I'm back at the mill I take my Colt out of the trunk. When I get inside, I'll set the disk down in front of the "kidnappers." That should distract them; then I'll pull my gun, keep them at bay. I untie Chelsea, leave the disk for Poagi—that's really what he wants anyway. We escape in my car. When we're safely away, I tell Chelsea I'm not who I've pretended to be, but that's all I tell her. I drop her off at a safe place, then I drive to Des Moines. I'll park my car downtown and take a cab to the airport. I buy a ticket to Anchorage with my false I.D—then freedom. I will never have to do another man's bidding again.*

Vincent looked admiringly at Chelsea, a table candle the source of flickers of light reflecting from her diamond necklace. She had never looked lovelier. As Vincent pondered a life without Chelsea, a suppressed thought insisted on bobbing to the surface: *Maybe, just maybe, I could contact Chelsea in the future and she would join me.*

The evening progressed smoothly. Wine was poured liberally. Chelsea had lobster. Vincent, prime rib. They completed the meal with Irish coffee, no dessert.

Artificial lighting had replaced the sun by the time they exited the restaurant. Vincent kept Chelsea's attention centered on him as they crossed the parking lot. Vincent opened the car door on the passenger's side. Suddenly, a hand covered Chelsea's mouth and a gun was shoved in her back. Out of the corner of her eye she could see another man close to Vincent. The man holding Chelsea pulled her backward, opened the rear door, pushed her in the backseat and quickly slid in beside her. In the meantime, the other man, who also had a gun, ordered Vincent to get in the front seat and move to the driver's side.

Chelsea began to cry and talk at the same time, but a piece of duct tape quickly sealed her protestations. The man in the front seat gave directions to Vincent as he drove, promising their safe keeping if they followed orders.

Arriving at the mill, they parked their car in front of a service door, which opened to a railroad car barn accessed by huge doors on either end. The van was parked inside. The foursome entered the building and walked around the van, which straddled a set of railroad tracks. On the other side of the van an elevated floor area supported several offices. On one side of the office complex was a large, open repair bay. Silos occupied the other side, which in the mill's operational days accepted raw product from rail cars. Between the silos and offices, a set of stairs dropped one floor to the business end of the mill.

Vincent and Chelsea were directed into one of the offices. A kidnapper pulled the tape from Chelsea's mouth. He motioned her to sit in a chair, grabbed a roll of tape, and secured her hands to the arms. Two other "kidnappers" strapped the explosive pack to Vincent. Chelsea viewed the scene with a look of horror on her face. Vincent gave her a reassuring look, hoping to ease her shock at what was happening. The men instructed Vincent and sent him off.

Here we go. Showtime. Vincent said to himself as he drove away from the mill. When he neared the Pallidin estate Ponce pulled out his cell phone and dialed Armondo's number.

"Hello?"

"Armondo, it's Vincent. I'll be at your house in a couple of minutes. Let me in."

"What's going on, Vince?"

"I'll explain when I get there. Just let me in."

Soon the front door opened and Vincent hurriedly stepped inside. A very puzzled-looking and impatient

Armondo Pallidin greeted him. "Will you please tell me what this is all about?"

"We gotta go to your study," was all Vincent said as he brushed by Pallidin.

Once there, Ponce opened his jacket, exposing the explosives. "Look Armondo. Look what they did to me!" A distraught-looking Vincent blurted out. "And they've got Chelsea. You gotta give them this disk they're looking for or they're going to kill Chelsea and blow me up! Here, they want to talk to you."

Ponce pulled out a piece of paper with numbers written on it, punched them into his cell phone with shaky fingers, handed the phone to Armondo.

"Pallidin?"

"Yes, this is."

"Someone wants to talk to you."

"Dad, it's Chelsea. They want the research disk. They'll…"

The phone was pulled away from Chelsea and the first voice came back on. "Yeah, that was your daughter, Pallidin. You got one chance at this. Give Ponce the disk. He will tape your hands and feet, take a picture, and send it to me. If he gets the disk to me within an hour, we let him and your daughter go. If anything, and I mean anything, goes wrong, they're both dead. Do you understand?"

"I understand."

"And no cops!"

Armondo handed the phone to Vincent and walked over to the bookcase. Soon the disk, safely enclosed in a smoke-colored plastic case, was in Ponce's hands.

"Sorry I have to tape you up, but I'm afraid not to do what they tell me."

"Don't worry about it," a now very distraught Armondo Pallidin answered. "Just get my daughter back. And, Vincent, *you* be careful."

"I will."

Armondo Pallidin lay on the floor, his hands and feet taped. He had followed Truitt's orders. Mark told him that under *no* circumstances, such as the one in which he now found himself, was he to reveal the disk's secret. Mark had promised to stay on top of any dire situation. *Truitt better know what he's doing,* Pallidin reflected.

Chapter 69

Mark and Jamie were about to call it a night when a rapid beeping noise came from inside Truitt's jacket.

"Whoa!" Mark exclaimed. "The disk is moving."

"I thought you scheduled a quiet shift?"

"I'll have to review the procedure."

Mark made a quick call from his cell phone to the police dispatcher and confirmed that the disk was indeed moving and was being tracked by the dispatcher on a directional locator. He immediately requested a check on the Armondo Pallidin residence.

"Don't use the police band," Truitt told the dispatcher. "Someone could be monitoring it. We'll use cell phones. Keep giving me directions."

"Looks like your plan is working, weaving a sensor into the plastic case," Littlebird gave a thumb up.

"Yep, the signal starts transmitting once the case is removed from the safe."

"Too bad Sylkie's going to miss all the action," Jamie added.

"That's okay. She can listen in from the dispatch center. Besides, it might get a bit rough."

"And your point? Remember, she's a cop, like us."

"I know, I know. But she's just a young girl and... forget it."

"You never worry about me like that."

"You're not a cute young lady."

"Just drop me off at the next corner."

"Did I hurt your feelings?"

"Right here is fine."

The signal targeted Vincent on a southbound route. It was a matter of minutes before he turned off the main highway and onto a secondary road, continuing in a southerly direction. A few more minutes of travel and he turned onto yet a narrower, less used road.

"We're getting close to the Minnesota River," Truitt alerted the dispatcher. "There may be a rendezvous point nearby. Alert the local police but tell them to hold back. When the driver stops we'll give you the precise location."

Another half mile down the narrow, winding road brought Vincent to the mill. The detectives kept far enough back so as not to expose their headlights. When they got close to the area where the disk stopped moving, they shut off their lights and advised the dispatcher of their location. The dispatcher gave them a report on the Pallidin residence.

Truitt and Littlebird proceeded down the road on foot until they came to the mill. There were two cars parked outside. The detectives saw the service door but bypassed it, moving farther along the outside wall of the car barn.

Near the far end of the wall they came to a metal-framed swing window about five feet off the ground, which was partially open. Jamie peered inside. He could see a van down at the other end. He also could see lights shining through window openings on the other side of the van, but the truck obstructed a better view.

The detectives climbed in the window and made their way back along the inside wall towards the truck. Fortunately, the van also obstructed the line of sight towards their direction from those inside of the office. Once they got to the van, Truitt stepped on the running board and peered through the cab. In plain sight, through windows whose glass had long ago been broken by vandals, Mark could see Vincent Ponce aiming a gun at four men who had their hands in the air, while at the same time untying Chelsea Pallidin.

Hmm, what's he up to? Truitt thought as he watched the drama unfold. Just as he and Jamie were about to make their move, the service door opened and two uniforms burst through. Ponce immediately turned his gun on them and fired. One officer reeled backwards, taking a bullet to the forehead. The other man fell back out through the open doorway, obviously hit also. A hail of bullets aimed in the direction of the office came through the door opening. Two more cops came in low through the doorway and ducked behind the van.

Mark and Jamie drew their guns, preparing to rush the office. But by this time the four other men were wielding assault rifles and the bullets started flying. Mark reached over the hood of the van and fired. One of the men went down.

A spray of bullets shattered the windows on the van. Truitt ducked behind the truck. They were pinned down as were the cops at the back of the van.

"Have I ever asked you if there was anyone in your family history by the name of Custer?" Jamie queried as the truck was being peppered.

"You know, now that you ask, my grandfather once made mention of a relation by that name. Died up in Montana, I guess."

"You don't have anything white, do you?"

"Just my skin."

"That'll do."

Jamie went around to the front of the van in hope of getting a clear shot. At the same time an assault rifle exploded, sending bullets in his direction. Jamie didn't duck fast enough and a bullet creased the side of his head, a fair amount of blood started to drip down his face. Woozy and bleeding, Mark pulled him back behind the van, propping him against the front tire. Truitt pulled off his shirt, holding it against Jamie's head to stop the bleeding.

By this time there were shots coming from the repair area, meaning the shooters were being caught in a crossfire. Truitt peeked through the van's shattered cab window. During a slight pause in the automatic weapons fire, a single shot rang out. Vincent Ponce lurched into view, holding his back. Another shot, he stumbled forward again, the upper half of his body passing through one of the broken out windows.

What the...? "Jaim, stay put. I have to check out something."

"Yeah, go ahead. I'm fine."

Truitt poked his head around the front of the truck just in time to see Chelsea Pallidin come out of a side office door and head down the adjacent stairway leading to the floor below. Mark ran around the front of the van, jumped up on the elevated floor and was quickly at the head of the stairs. Chelsea had not quite made it to the bottom.

"Stop right there, Chelsea," Truitt ordered as he stepped down below floor level.

Chelsea whirled around, putting a hand on her chest. "Oh, gosh, Sergeant Truitt, you scared me. Thank goodness it's you. Vincent, he was one of them. I…I grabbed his gun, and shot him. I'm sorry…I was so scared."

Truitt had to think flash-fast. He did.

"You can drop the act, Chelsea. It's over. I'm placing you under arrest for, at the moment, the murder of Vincent Ponce. Other many and varied counts to follow."

Chelsea had to react flash-fast. She did.

Chelsea turned and double-stepped to the bottom of the stairway, swinging open a metal door. She quickly disappeared among the ancient array of milling machines and conveyor belts.

Until that moment, Truitt had not strongly suspected Chelsea as part of the clandestine organization. However, from the start he had harbored suspicions about Vincent Ponce. Now, the events of the past few minutes had cast uncertainty on Chelsea. His telling her to "drop the act" was a bluff. Her reaction gave him his answer.

Truitt was determined to take her alive. He had questions, lots of them. Mark reached the bottom of the stairway, crouched, and swung open the door. Chelsea fired twice from behind a conveyor table. One of the bullets caught him in his left side, passing through mostly muscle. However, he was bleeding and it hurt like everything.

"Tell me, Chelsea," Truitt called out, hoping to zero in on her position, "did Vincent even have a clue?"

At first, no response—then, "Vincent was stupid. He thought he was running the show. He had no idea about me. How did you figure it out, Truitt?"

"Your father told me that only he, Brewster, and you knew about the disk, and that he had sworn you two to secrecy. Vincent had to know about it or he wouldn't have gone after it. I'm guessing *you* leaked him the information and then set him up."

"You're in the right profession, Truitt. I pretended to be on the phone with Brewster. Talked about the disk, knowing Vincent was eavesdropping."

"Why, Chelsea. Why did you do it?"

"Ask my father that question."

The cat and mouse game continued in the dimly lit room. Truitt was losing a fair amount of blood and starting to feel weak and dizzy. They maneuvered between the rows of milling machines and conveyor decking, each trying to get an angle on the other. Suddenly, the door at the bottom of the stairs swung open, exposing Sylkie Maune.

"Sergeant Truitt, are you down here?"

Chelsea stepped out from behind a hopper, taking aim at Sylkie. At the same time Truitt stood, fired. Chelsea fired once, the bullet harmlessly hitting a wall. She then slumped to the floor in a heap.

"Chelsea, hang in there. We'll get you to a hospital," Truitt kneeled alongside her, his blood dripping on her dress, mixing with hers.

Chelsea looked up at Truitt with sad, scared eyes. "Looks like you won another round...Sergeant. They're really going to love this."

"Who are 'they' Chelsea? Please, help me. Who do you work for?"

Chelsea looked away, as if she was pondering whether or not to answer. Focusing once again on Truitt she tried to speak but coughed up blood. After a few moments she tried again. "Po...Po...P..P.," she whispered, and then nothing. Chelsea Pallidin had drawn her last breath.

"Come on, Sergeant," Sylkie urged. "We need to get you to a hospital."

Chapter 70

"I guess this isn't such a bad game, after all," Brian decided as he moved his pegs.

"Grandpa and I used to play cribbage quite often," Mark responded. "It was kind of a bonding thing for us."

"Guess that's what we're working on now, huh?"

"Speaking of bonding, how are things going with you and Sylkie?"

"She's easy to talk to. Understands drug addiction. Like she said, it's all about choices. We're making progress."

"Well, when you're ready, we're here to listen, too."

"I know."

The doorbell interrupted the father and son conversation. Liz ushered in Sylkie, Jamie, and Bernard "Binky" Shepard, Jamie and Mark's downtown informant. Jamie or Mark would sometimes take Binky for a ride, get him out of downtown, expose him to some different scenery. In return, Bernard gave them an occasional pass to a Twins baseball game through a friend in the organization.

"Good morning to the walking wounded," Sylkie greeted.

"Good morning, back at you," Mark retorted. "Well, Binky, glad to see you. Are you keeping the peace downtown?"

"I smile at everybody. It makes people happy."

"I know it does, Bink. We should all be that way."

Binky raised a finger. "It takes less muscles to smile than to frown."

"Hey, when are you guys going to be back in the saddle?" Jamie changed the subject.

"Well, I plan on returning to work in a couple of weeks, and Brian is getting stronger every day."

"With a little help from a friend," Brian added, shooting a look at Sylkie.

It was the first time Mark, Jamie, and Sylkie had been together since the mill incident. For Sylkie especially, there were a lot more questions than answers concerning the Pallidin affair.

"How about some coffee and rhubarb cake?" Liz offered. "I took it out of the oven an hour ago."

"I'll take a big piece," Jamie replied.

"Oooh, that sounds good," Sylkie added.

"I love any kind of cake," Bernard nodded.

"Let's sit on the deck. It's a beautiful morning," Mark suggested.

Liz and Sylkie distributed the cake and coffee. Brian quickly finished his piece and left the group to work on strengthening exercises.

The bright morning sun was starting to give way to high cirrus clouds, the advance guard of a front which would sweep through later in the day bringing a welcome rain to the Twin Cities.

"Do you guys feel like talking about the Pallidin affair?" Sylkie asked. "It's all a tangled mess to me."

"I have lingering questions myself," Mark confessed. "But this is how I have it figured. Paramount Investment Partners is a front for a larger, still unknown organization. Their goal was to get their hands on the desalinization facility. The initial plan was to use the microbiology lab to set up Brewster with a bogus mutant virus charge. George Thurber was their vehicle to make it happen, but he got cold feet at the last minute and wanted out. He was going to spill his guts to Michael Carpenter, but someone heard him make the call to Carpenter. It could have been a lucky break that either Malik or maybe even Chelsea Pallidin overheard the call on Carpenter's end, but I think it was Amy Weldon. She told me that the day Carpenter was killed, Thurber was acting strange. My guess is that she kept real close to him. As far as the emails sent from Brewster's computer to Wu Zhong's computer, that was most likely Malik or Chelsea. I would bet that Malik and Chelsea were conspiring together. As to who knew about Guy's argument with Armondo Pallidin—Guy did mention it at the office so Hathaway may have known, but my guess is that either Chelsea or Vincent Ponce overheard the altercation. At any rate, the information was channeled to Amy Weldon."

"Who planted the evidence at Brewster Pallidin's home?" Sylkie asked.

"It had to have been Ponce. I say that because the day of Brewster's arrest I went to Midwest Research Labs and talked to the receptionist at the main desk. Every employee from Brewster to the custodians has to wear an identification badge, all of which are kept at the main desk. I asked the receptionist if she knew which, if any, employees came in late that day. The only one of our main players to do so was Vincent Ponce. He signed in at 9:50 a.m. Only Jamie and I knew about that bit of information. For sure it kept my sights squarely on Ponce."

Liz shook her head. "And I still can't believe we were targets."

"And their reasoning behind it," Jamie added. "To set Mark and me against the Pallidins."

"And also to set up Armondo," Mark added. "With Brewster *and* Armondo out of the way, Chelsea and Paramount would have no obstacles to prevent them from taking complete control of the company."

There was one more possible reason why Mark's family was targeted that obviously could not be mentioned—Amy Weldon's personal feelings for Mark Truitt.

"Okay for that part," Sylkie said, "but what's really confusing is the mystery surrounding Chelsea and Vincent. How did you figure out that Chelsea was involved?"

Mark took a sip of coffee. "The disk was the key which led to my suspicions of her at the end. No one other than A.M., Brewster, and Chelsea should have known about the disk. The fact that Vincent retrieved it meant he knew it existed. Who would have filtered the information to him but Chelsea? When I saw him untying her and holding the four other men at bay I was, at first, a little confused, then assumed he meant to escape with her and the disk. What really threw me was when Chelsea shot Vincent and not just once, but twice. I knew there was purpose to it. At that moment her involvement, although I didn't understand the motivation, seemed possible. I took a chance and called her on it. She took the bait. But now, I believe there is a missing link, an unknown person that

Chelsea, Vincent, Malik, and possibly Weldon communicated with. However, for sure Ponce and possibly Weldon weren't aware of Chelsea's involvement, and it's anyone's guess which of them knew about Malik. Anyway, I think this person received information from the players and strategically metered it out. I believe Chelsea tried to tell us who it was when she was dying. An intricate web designed to protect the next layer."

"So Chelsea was secretly overseeing the whole operation and maybe contributing helpful hints to that person, who would then direct Vincent and Amy Weldon," Sylkie proposed.

"That's the way I have it figured."

Mark turned to Jamie. "You talked to Brewster. What were his thoughts on Chelsea's involvement?"

"Brewster did have a plausible theory. There is a dark episode in their family's past that goes back twenty-five years. According to Brewster, Armondo and his wife—her name was Victoria—were at odds with each other much of the time. She drank heavily, blaming her unhappiness on Armondo's overbearing manner. Armondo claimed that their problems stemmed from her drinking. Anyway, the family was on vacation at a lake near Detroit Lakes. Armondo and Victoria got into a heated argument in front of Chelsea. I think Brewster said she was about ten years old at the time. Victoria had been drinking. Armondo slapped her. She grabbed a bottle of vodka and took off in their pontoon boat. A couple of hours later a fisherman found the unoccupied pontoon drifting near a shoreline. Victoria's body was recovered a few days later."

Jamie went on, "Brewster clearly remembers the incident and, at the time, was mystified by Chelsea's reaction to her mother's death. He never saw her shed a tear nor did she speak a word for several weeks. Then one day she appeared to be fully recovered, completely back to her bubbly, animated self. Brewster said it was as though she had totally blocked out that time period, along with her mother's memory."

"Sounds more like she fed off of it and waited for her chance to avenge her mother's death," Mark concluded.

"In so many words, that was Brewster's analysis," Jamie confirmed.

"How is Mr. Pallidin taking it?" Sylkie asked.

"Brewster said not very well at all. Armondo confines himself to his study, smokes cigars, drinks wine, talks to no one."

"That's a heavy load to bear," Mark said.

"Brewster said Armondo has mellowed considerably over the years. He looks at their plans for the distribution of the desalinization process as his dad's atonement for his past discretions."

"I wish him well." Mark finished his coffee. "Now, there is one more person we haven't talked about, possibly the most important person." Mark pointed directly at Bernard.

"Me, Sergeant Truitt?"

"Yes, you, Binky. You gave Jamie the first clue to finding Tom Moore when you told him about Marsha Porter's missing boyfriend. We are forever grateful to you."

"I was just doing my civic duty, Sergeant Truitt," Binky proudly answered.

"Remember you telling me that your mother said you are one of God's angels on earth?" Jamie asked. "Well, Bink, your status has been raised to guardian angel as far as we're concerned. You've been promoted."

Binky donned a wide smile. "I like that."

"By the way," Jamie continued, "I went to the correctional facility at Shakopee the other day to interview Amy Weldon. She's scheduled to be moved to a Federal facility in Illinois in a few weeks and I wanted to try one more time see if she would give anything up."

Mark felt his stomach tighten a notch. "And?"

"She came into the interview room, sat down, didn't acknowledge me, didn't say a word. About what I expected, but it seemed to me that this time there was more sadness than defiance that hung over her. I mentioned that Vincent Ponce was dead, and why. There was just the slightest change in expression on her face but enough for me to confirm that she understood what I was talking about. When I told her about Chelsea, now that got her attention. She looked up and stared at me for the longest moment. I really think she was on the verge of talking."

"Did she?" Sylkie pressed.

"Not about that, but then I asked her if there *was* anything she wanted to talk about. She looked away for a second as if to gather her thoughts. Then she turned back to me and said, 'Tell Sergeant Truitt that he was wrong. I'm not going to get a third chance after all.' I don't know what she meant by it. That's all she said."

Truitt jumped up to the plate before questions could be thrown his way. "I think I know. When we were discussing Amy's father-daughter relationship with George Thurber she mentioned, and it probably was just a story, that the two men she previously cared about had been erased from her life, even if under entirely different circumstances. She said she wasn't meant to have a normal relationship with a man. I just said 'give it time, the right person will come along.' I was only being nice, ah, supportive."

Liz's eyes narrowed. "I didn't realize you practice grief counseling on the side. Kind of an intimate subject to be discussing with a near-stranger, isn't it?"

Mark's internal thermal reading was rising disproportionately to the ambient air. In situations like this the best defense is a good offense. "Exc*uuuuse* me, I was merely reacting to her statement. She brought it up, not me."

Liz cracked a smile. "Don't get defensive. Why don't we all have another piece of cake and enjoy the rest of the morning."

Mark felt a subsequent drop in temperature having avoided a direct hit, although the near-miss did put some cracks in the foundation.

PART FIVE

Twilight Zone

Chapter 71

The Council assembled for an emergency meeting several miles east of Tillamook, Oregon, deep in Oregon's Coast Range Mountains. A heavy fog draped the green-clad mountains like a thick, puffy blanket, leaving only the deepest recesses of the valleys exposed. The glum atmospheric conditions matched the mood of those attending as the main topic for this meeting would address the failed second attempt to secure the research data for the Pallidin desalinization process.

In a small office not far from the main meeting room, Poagi Serrantat stood between two muscular bookends, explaining himself to Arlo Vance, a retired military officer and Poagi's superior.

"How do you explain this, Poagi? You have never let us down, not once. Never. Now, you have failed twice in succession. I don't get it. How could this happen?"

Poagi's past profession in espionage demanded coolness, nerves of steel. Although he now portrayed that on the outside, his internal relief valves were close to the release point.

"What do you want me to say? I had all the players in place. Everything was set up perfectly. We failed because of two very persistent cops. They were one step ahead of us."

"And if they were such a problem why weren't they erased?"

"Vincent and Maria (Amy Weldon) had plans for them. They wanted to use them against the Pallidins. I admit I went along with the plan and when everything fell apart because of Moore I would have called Vincent in but I needed him to obtain the disk. Once the disk was in Chelsea's hands, Vincent was to be eliminated, which he was, but not in the intended way."

"That all really worked well, didn't it? Now in a few minutes I have to explain to my colleagues why we have failed again. Wish us luck, Poagi."

The Council gathered a short while later. Ross Denali, the highly intelligent entrepreneur, was the facilitator. "Let's get started. I know several of you have broken into busy schedules for this emergency meeting so we'll expedite our agenda. There are a few things that have to be discussed, the first of which is our failed second attempt at obtaining data crucial to our desalinization project. Arlo, would you please explain this embarrassment?"

"No excuses. My top lieutenant did not realize success from his field representatives. Good operational plans were in place. However, two detectives in cooperation with Armondo Pallidin were a step ahead of us."

Margaret Ellingson, the heiress, asked, "If your plans were as 'good' as you say they were, how could you let yourself get upstaged by two local cops and an old man? A strategic operation ground to a halt by three stumblebums who don't even have a clue who they're up against. Disgusting!"

"Okay, okay," Denali took charge. "We can't change what happened, and kicking sand at each other isn't going to help the situation. Let's address the matter at hand. We need to vote on Poagi Serrantat's membership. Now remember the crucial point that your decision should be based on—is Mr. Serrantat still an asset...or has he become a liability?"

Denali allowed a few moments for reflection, and called for the vote. "All those in favor of continuing Mr. Serrantat's membership, raise your hands, please."

Rosalee Taylor and Henry Raethburn raised their hands.

"All those in favor of terminating Mr. Serrantat's membership, raise your hands."

Arlo Vance, Margaret Ellingson, Neil Samuels, Bobby Sylvester, and Ross Denali gave thumbs down. Denali nodded to a guard standing near the exit door. He quietly opened the door and disappeared.

The bookends would leave no loose ends. Vincent Ponce would have approved.

Bobby Sylvester had to have the last word on the matter. "What a man sows, so shall he reap. My good friends, let us now beat our plowshares of mourning into a sword of vengeance against those who would deny us our destiny!"

Denali clasped his hands together. "All right, on to new business. Henry what's your take on the present political and social climate in our country. Is it still favorable to our aspirations?"

Raethburn stood. "Let's see. How does the adage go? You can fool all of the people some of the time, some of the people all of the time, and, in our case, most of the people most of the time. I'm happy to report that it's working to perfection. In fact, conditions have degenerated to the point where the pot is stirring itself. Only in America, but can you believe that one of our greatest allies is the Supreme Court of the United States? You need only look at two of their recent decisions for proof. Allowing unlimited corporate funding of independent political broadcasts in candidate elections? We couldn't have orchestrated that little gem better ourselves! And if you thought that couldn't be topped, well, their recent decision to 'protect first amendment rights' by upholding the right to protest military funerals is a truly nefarious concept, even for us. Demoralize and divide for the skewed justification of protecting a constitutional right at the expense of common sense and decency. Wouldn't our Founding Fathers be proud? I guess the 'powers that be' have yet to understand that the Constitution is but a worthless piece of paper if it will not stand against the profane affronts of a misguided few and defend the moral glue that holds its citizenry together. Let's hope it stays that way."

Raethburn looked a tad glum after spitting that out, needing a moment to collect his thoughts. "So, on what other fronts are we gaining ground? Well, we've made great strides in demonizing education and we'll continue in our efforts to pit unions against policymakers. It makes for great theatre and also draws out festering jealousies. Of course, the whole point is to reserve education for the privileged. With that said, I'll finish by reminding you all of our formula for success: when they're divided, we stand; when they're united, we fail."

"Yes, it fosters the perfect climate for us to thrive," Denali added, and called on the next speaker. "Neil, are you prepared to comment on the current economic status for us?"

Neil Samuels was the corporate banker. "Conditions could not be better for us. The current administration seems to have no stomach for pursuing indictments concerning the recent mortgage meltdown. I wonder why? Don't get me wrong; I'm not complaining. Also, we continue to profit tremendously from relocating some of our investments offshore. Likewise, our banking. I hate taxes. Now, a slight problem. The nagging high unemployment rate is exerting pressure to bring jobs back into this country." Samuels let out a sigh. "I suppose it would be prudent to bring some jobs back but, of course, with lower wages—*and no unions!* Finally, we can't expect the banks to keep up their charade forever, especially concerning the present loan modification push. We will have to make adjustments at some point. Of course, we all know what could throw a wrench into our future plans, and that is the 'R' word, regulation. But don't worry; we'll continue to beat the drums for smaller government. In due time, the 'Wild West on Wall Street' scenario will again be dominating a financial institution near you. I dream about once again betting against our own transactions."

"Dream on," Denali applauded. "I know I don't have to remind *you* of all people, but be sure to take good care of the banks. They kick in about forty percent of all political campaign contributions, furthering our cause. We don't want to disrupt the political process where it's the most sensitive, in the pocketbook. Let's see, we do need to discuss a few more items. For one, it looks as though the current war will continue indefinitely. There seems to be no great sentiment to end it. Am I right, Arlo?"

"To tell you the truth I am not all that surprised as to the apparent lack of interest in terminating the current conflict. Remember, this war is being fought by a volunteer military force, which is what separates it from past contentious conflicts. However, the fact remains that the Iraq war was started under false pretenses, and in Afghanistan the military invaded on the premise of bringing a terrorist to justice. Having succeeded at that, they now seem determined to firm up a corrupt government. The wrong wars for the wrong reasons. Go figure. I would have expected more intense dialogue among the politicians, pundits, public. Seems that people used to have stronger opinions regarding life and death. Nowadays the concerns are more like 'Let there be war but don't raise my taxes.' Don't get me wrong; it all plays into our hands."

"I doth not discern between complacency and apathy," Denali grinned. "Music to my ears. Now, how about it, Bobby? Are our religious brethren still brimming with fervor?"

"Oh, every so often we have to poke the hive. Whisper in their ear that the government is going to take over the church and dictate what and how they can worship. If they get too complacent I'll start a rumor that the president is going to initiate legislation to create a Department of Religion that will be headed by a person professing an alternative sexual orientation. That should start a stampede by 'God's Crusaders,' which, of course, will result in them joyfully following their leader off the cliff of righteousness."

"You mean put on the blinders and serve up some moral superiority?" Denali looked around the room.

"Ah, Margaret, anything new human population issues to discuss?"

Margaret Ellingson was becoming increasingly paranoid about protecting her fortune from the "filthy and vulgar" hoards of humanity. Recent news out of Africa had done nothing to allay her fears.

"I have come across a very disturbing example of humanity spinning out of control," Ellingson began. "It exemplifies the immediacy of our cause and the justification to proceed with haste.

The island of Madagascar located off the east coast of Africa is unfolding as a lesson to be heeded. Ninety percent of its plants and animals are found nowhere else in the world. It is a beautiful and unique land, which is not only being ravaged for its extremely valuable rosewood trees but is being subjected to an accelerated slash-and-burn agriculture policy. Why? The price of its main export, vanilla, has been depressed and the population is growing by three percent per year. More people mean more demand for food and increased competition for fewer dollars. Also, a new government has not only turned a blind eye to these anti-environmental practices but even encourages and profits from them. Of course, I don't have to tell you, but guess who is the number-one consumer of the extremely valuable rosewood, the sale of which is 'officially' illegal for the most part? Yes, it's China. Anyway, my point is this: once this growing population cuts down all the trees, destroys the soil, causes the extinction of many species of animals, and deprives the civilized world of the beauty and uniqueness of this island, they will spill into other overcrowded and impoverished countries, causing more problems. So where does it end? How soon before these horrid creatures are on our doorstep? I say we need to take drastic action...NOW!"

That rant was music to Ross Denali's ears. "Thank you, Margaret. I hope you all were listening. If that wasn't our marching orders I don't know what is. Now, hold that thought because I do have a possibility for your consideration. As I'm sure you all are aware, a world currency devaluation crisis may be looming. Compound that with the recent and continuing upward spiral in the price of food and energy, and you have a world teetering on the edge. Further, look what's happening in the Middle East right now. All of this instability is playing into our hands. Just a thought, but an option for us would be to exacerbate the situation, you know, give things a little push. There could be opportunities galore for us. Holding a good chunk of the world's wealth affords us great leverage."

Raethburn jumped up. "I am totally against that idea. What we need are small conflicts that we can control. You're suggesting toying with the possibility of total collapse. Remember, the sovereign debt crisis was a factor in jump-starting World War II. I, for one, don't want to be a part of anything that extreme."

Rosalee Taylor, The clothing and cosmetics mogul, echoed Raethburn's sentiment. "I strongly suggest that we put that idea on the back burner and keep it there unless the situation for us becomes otherwise untenable."

Denali put both palms out, gritting his teeth. "That's fine, starting a conflict between humans is easy...even a caveman—forget it. I only brought it up as a possibility for your consideration.

If there are no further items I call to adjourn this meeting. Good luck to all. We'll meet again when necessary."

WATERFALL

Ross Denali left the Coast Range Mountains in a rather sour mood.

Chapter 72

Plop! Mark Truitt's Rappala hit the water, sinking a foot into the tannin-colored liquid before abruptly beginning its journey back to the boat from which Mark and Jamie Littlebird were fishing. The two cohorts were enjoying a picture-perfect summer evening on beautiful Lake Vermilion, Minnesota's fourth largest lake. Spread out over nearly forty thousand acres of bays and inlets, the lake boasts an island for every day of the year. Originally named Onamuni by the Ojibwe Indians who first settled the area, the name was later translated to Vermilion by French fur traders.

Mark and Jamie weren't conversing much, as they were appreciating the sights around them. Every so often a bald eagle left its observation post high in a white pine and soared into the blue-gold evening sky through which towering but harmless cumulus clouds silently paraded. Even less often, an osprey would spot its evening meal and seemingly fall out of the sky in a less than graceful dive bombing performance, hitting the water with a *smack*.

The aerial show culminated with the bird lifting off with a perch or small bass clenched tightly in its claws.

Mark had accepted Jamie's invitation to relax in God's great north woods not only to divert his mind from lingering thoughts of the Pallidin case and his son's near-death experience, but also to consider relocating their summer cabin adventures to Vermilion. Jamie had grown up on this lake and was forever a willing captive of its hold over him. He would be proud if his friend also decided to enjoy its beauty and uniqueness on a more frequent basis.

"How many more walleyes before we reach our limit?" Truitt asked as he pondered switching from a Rappala to a leech and spinner.

"Let's see," Jamie answered, opening the cover on the live well. "We have six—so two more."

"I'm in no hurry and I wouldn't feel bad if the fish aren't."

Just as Mark finished the sentence his line went taught. "Looks like number seven's about to come aboard," he pronounced. The fish felt a little light, probably too small to keep.

Suddenly the fish stopped coming in, as if it was stuck behind a rock—but only for an instant. Abruptly the water boiled and the line stretched like a bowstring.

"Big northern or muskie," Jamie determined.

The fight went on for several minutes before fish and fisherman got within sight of each other. It was a muskie and once the big fish got a look at the boat it released its grip on the smaller fish which was hooked on Mark's line. In a flash it was gone. "Guess it decided to dine elsewhere," Mark shrugged. "How big would you say it was?"

Littlebird lifted the bill on his baseball hat a bit. "Well, I'd say maybe thirty-four, thirty-eight inches."

"Is that big for this lake?"

"Forty-two is a good size, but they come bigger than that—over fifty."

"What? Now *there's* a good selling point, especially for a family like mine that spends a lot of time in the water."

Jamie laughed. "Nothing to fear. I've never heard of anyone getting bit by one, not on this lake, anyway."

"Yeah? Well, convince my wife of that when she puts her toe in the water and a four-footer just happens to swim by. After that she'd be doing all her water sports in a diving bell."

Truitt's cell phone interrupted their conversation. The call lasted less than a minute, the caller doing most of the talking. Mark snapped the cover on his phone and turned to Jamie, his expression downcast, the blood seemingly drained from his face.

"That was Ray Lopez. Amy Weldon was to be moved from Shakopee to a maximum security facility tomorrow. This morning she apparently slipped and hit her head in the shower. She never regained consciousness."

"So much for being loyal," Jamie philosophized.

"Too bad. It didn't have to end this way," Mark half-mumbled to himself, memory flashes filling his head.

Jamie took advantage of the quiet moment. "Um, Mark, I was kind of waiting for the right time to bring this up, but I guess I might as well just spit it out."

Truitt cleared his head, looked at Jamie. He knew his friend well and could tell this wasn't one of his teasing moments. Cringing, he said, "I'm listening."

"I've decided to quit the job," Jamie looked squarely at Mark. "The BIA has a job opening I applied for a few weeks back. I got a call earlier this week informing me that the position is mine if I want it. Guess I'm going to take it." Jamie looked out over the lake.

Mark could see the gleam in Jamie's eyes as he viewed his surroundings. "I'm going to miss you, my friend. I'll always be grateful for what you did for me and my family." After a slight hesitation, Truitt lightened up. "I suppose now I'll have to buy a cabin here, muskies or not, if I ever want to see you. You're always working an angle, aren't you?"

"It's for your own good. You'll love it here. And you know what? I believe you and Sylkie will make a good team. Just don't wear her out like you did me."

"I won't worry about that at all. I think she's tougher than you...Hey, I got a bite!"

Chapter 73

The voice sounded non-threatening. He said, "If you want a true understanding of the Midwest Research Laboratories case, drive to Belle's Marina on Lake Minnetonka. Be at slip fourteen at 4:00 p.m. I will meet you there. I assure you, Sergeant Truitt, no harm will come to you. I only ask that you not share this invitation with anyone. My associate, as I'm sure you will understand, insists on privacy."

Truitt's initial interpretation of the call included the noun "setup." However, he dismissed that possibility as highly unlikely. If someone wanted him dead that act would have unfolded long before now. No, the proposed meeting seemed more puzzling than menacing. Why would any person or group that left no tracks suddenly risk exposure? It must be important to them. Whatever the reason, Truitt determined that this was his one chance to get a glimpse into the antagonists behind the Midwest Research Labs case.

The afternoon sun reflected brightly off the azure water as Truitt ambled onto one of the long docks that jutted into the lake. He stopped in front of slip 14 and waited. Soon a kindly looking gray-haired gentleman dressed in khaki slacks, white shirt, and a pull-over sweater strode toward him.

"Good afternoon, Sergeant Truitt. My associate wishes to express his appreciation at your acceptance of our invitation. Would you please step into the boat," the man pointed to a rather ordinary runabout parked in the slip.

Disarming as he appeared, Truitt eyed the man with suspicion. "Where are we going?"

"We will be rendezvousing with my associate on the opposite side of the lake. Don't be apprehensive. You will be quite safe."

Mark gave the man a quick study before climbing into the boat.

No words passed between them during the ride. Soon they were on the other side of the lake. As they approached a dock that serviced a public landing, Truitt rose out of his seat. The last thing he remembered was the driver turning around, smiling at him, then, drugged by inhalation.

When he awoke, Truitt was sitting in a chair in the middle of a room that would easily pass as a "great room." He felt for his service weapon, not really expecting to find it. His assumption proved correct. Mark surveyed his surroundings. Rough hand-hewn beams supported a vaulted ceiling. Similarly styled posts rose from the floor to meet the lower end of the beams. The ceiling was paneled in, *what? Black ash?* "Yes, definitely black ash," Truitt murmured to himself as the grogginess wore off. Windows dressed in drawn blinds lined the upper half of the outside walls, interrupted only by the vertical posts, which stood against a backdrop of sheetrock painted white. The lower halves of the walls were paneled in black ash.

A massive field stone fireplace consumed a good share of the far end of the room, complemented by a thick wood mantle of rough-sawn red pine. A narrow but bold hearth also constructed from field stone rose from a hardwood floor.

As Mark completed his scan of the room, a door opened and two men entered. Truitt immediately locked his eyes on one of the men, consternation consuming his thoughts. This was not good, not good at all.

Mark's palms began to sweat. Suddenly things, a lot of things, took on a new clarity. It was a whole different ball game from this point on. Armondo Pallidin had been right in his warnings. Mark Truitt knew he was in way over his head.

Chapter 74

The first man that entered the room gave Truitt a momentary glance, walked over to one of the windows, crossed his hands, and assumed an "at ease" stance.

The bodyguard, Mark decided. A quick scan of his bull neck and V-shaped torso fostered thoughts of—*I come in peace.*

The other man settled into a chair directly facing him.

"I'm glad you accepted my invitation, Sergeant Truitt," his host opened. "I apologize for any discomfort you may have felt during your short 'blackout' period, but I'm sure you understand our insistence on being as invisible as possible. Now, by the look on your face, I assume you recognize me."

Truitt tried not to present any perception of shock and awe. Evidently his facial muscles betrayed him. "You're Jeremy Mouldier, secretary of state in the Henessey administration. I've seen you on TV dozens of times. But, what…why would you reveal yourself to me? This doesn't make sense."

Mouldier laughed. "Sergeant, do you honestly think anyone would believe this is actually taking place—that *I'm* sitting here across from you? I don't think so. Your credibility would most likely be considerably diminished if you were to make such a bizarre claim. In fact, at this very moment I'm at a business meeting in Mexico City, which can be easily 'proven' if necessary. I guarantee you, Sergeant, the people I represent are very calculated. Of course, if you were to attempt to follow up on our meeting today in an aggressive manner, I'm afraid it would bring much anguish to you and your loved ones. Oh, and by the way, you are miles from Lake Minnetonka. The boat ride was our little way to be certain there were no unwanted visitors tagging along."

The ground rules had been set. Mark didn't know what Mouldier's interpretation of the word "anguish" might include nor did he have any interest in finding out.

"Now, let's get down to business, Mark—is it okay if I call you Mark?" It wasn't but Mouldier didn't wait for an answer. "I really am delighted to meet half of the team that so successfully has forced us into a temporary stalemate. A minor bump in the road but a setback nonetheless. Something we are not accustomed to and so I congratulate you, and—if I understand correctly—the former Sergeant Littlebird, on your success."

Truitt frowned. "I'm sure I didn't come here for the purpose of being showered with accolades. Excuse me for being blunt, but what do you want from me?"

"Okay, Mark. Fair enough. I'll be blunt back at you. There are a lot of things I want but right now there is one thing I, ah, we want more than anything: access to Midwest

Research Labs desalinization data." Mouldier stood, staring down at Truitt with steely eyes. "Understand this, Mark, we do not fail. Ultimately we realize our goals." Truitt's host turned and walked towards the fireplace.

Mark took advantage of the moment to assess the situation. Mouldier *was* transparent in declaring that his organization was not used to nor would it accept failure. That, coupled with the knowledge of his identity left Mark with a perplexity of emotions. What he was seeing and hearing weighed on him. The possible implications were hard for him to fathom. For an instant he crouched in a mental defensive mode. He didn't want to be here. He wished this wasn't happening. It was now obvious that the final chapter concerning the Pallidin family had yet to be written. These unnerving thoughts rendered him to consider the choice of being staked down on an African fire ant hill the better option to this.

Mark snapped to. So much for wishing. Being that there wasn't a star to wish upon at the moment nor was there a fairy godmother making a grand entrance, he decided to make the best of the situation and glean what information he could. "I'll ask again, what do you want from me?"

Mouldier walked slowly towards Mark, his eyes turning from ice to soft warmth. "First of all, I would like to extend an invitation to you to join our cause. A person of your tenacity and integrity, well, if channeled in the right direction could be invaluable to us and rewarding to you. Come to the winning side, Mark. Help us save the world."

"Save the world from what?" Truitt queried.

"Why, from itself, of course. I suspect you view us as greedy villains, stomping out human life at will in order to attain our selfish goals."

"That pretty much sums it up." Mark gave the man a narrow gaze.

Mark's host extended an arm in his direction, palm open. "Let me explain. If and when the Pallidins complete the work on their invention, they plan on giving it to the world as a gift. Fresh, clean, abundant water for all. You must understand, Mark, the lack of clean water is actually a blessing in that it helps to control overpopulation. Project what happens if fresh water is supplied to all people. Populations will explode, outstrip the land, deplete the soil, crowd each other out. Chaos will ultimately ensue, destroying us all. The very life-giving resources this planet has to offer will be crushed by the weight of humanity. That is a fatal scenario we cannot allow to materialize."

"And that's your motivation for wanting to get your hands on the desalinization process?" Truitt was incredulous. "I believe your thinking is way off base. Stable nations have fewer offspring. It's the poor, desperate countries that conceive more children. Fresh, clean water is certain to bring more stability, not less."

"Sorry, Mark, the logic is not there. As it is now, we are living off of natural capital, eroding soil and draining groundwater aquifers faster than they can be replenished. Because of this, the ability to grow food will soon start to deteriorate. Even if the world's population levels off between eight and nine billion, there will be mass shortages of the resources to support those numbers. Get the picture, Mark? Sometime in the next thirty years the rising population curve intersects the declining resources curve, and then…chaos. Can you envision a starving, thirsty world coexisting peacefully? C'mon, we can't accomplish that now when there's abundance. One thing about human behavior, it's predictable. When pressed, it pushes back violently. I'm afraid the weeds must be culled so that the plants can thrive."

Truitt was getting a real sinking feeling. He sensed where this was going. "In other words you want to play God," Mark said with an ample dose of disgust.

"Play God?" Mouldier cracked a wide smile. "Mark, we *are* God—at least the gods of this world. So, how do we realize our goals? One successful ploy is manipulation. Now remember, manipulation is difficult to achieve unless the manipulated desire the perceived outcome. Let's take the subprime mortgage crisis, for example— the perfect storm. This scam succeeded only as long as it did because everyone involved was greedy; they all wanted something that down deep they knew was not right. Unfortunately, the people that suffered the most could least afford it. If they had only understood mortgage lending 101. Ah, well, their loss is our gain. Ka-ching for us, ka-boom for them. But do you know what the most ironic thing of all is? The government, who by deregulating the banks and not keeping an eye on the bond rating agencies, paved the way for this fiasco, and so eloquently allowed you, as a taxpayer, to become the banks' benefactor. Too bad the lending institutions haven't shown the same benevolence for their clients. Now *that* is capitalism at its finest. Unfettered capitalism, the darling of the 'trickle up' theory— all the money trickling up to us, that is."

"You seem to take delight in the thought of people being taken advantage of," Mark pressed.

Truitt's host shrugged his shoulders. "Why should I, or you, for that matter, feel sorry for our fellow citizens? Human nature doesn't change depending where one is on the wealth ladder. Don't kid yourself, Mark. Many that are on the bottom are just as greedy and selfish as those at the top. Just as employers rape their workers when given the chance, unions, in kind, will happily bite the hand that feeds them, way past the second knuckle. The opposing bargaining sides don't compromise; it's a standoff, with each leaving the table feeling violated and hating the other. It's the American way. Look out for yourself and screw your neighbor; and the grand stage for all of this is right in Washington D.C. It's not by accident that nine out of the fourteen richest counties in the country are located near the capital of the good old U.S. of A.

Truitt's mental temperature was rising past a slow boil. "You are justifying the misdeeds of those who have inflicted a lot of pain on this country by attempting to degrade the average person to a harlot status. Deflecting blame, sign of a guilty conscience maybe?"

Mouldier set forth a hearty laugh. "Oh, and our fellow Americans are so compassionate? If my memory serves me right, aren't some of our compatriots hysterically warning about 'pulling the plug' on Grandma, then turn around and pull the plug on folks that need organ transplants, and make absurd excuses why millions of people shouldn't be insured? It's a shell game, Mark, and Mr. and Mrs. Average citizen are smack in the middle of it with their sins of greed, ignorance, apathy. You have to understand, and history bears me out, people cannot be trusted to determine their own destiny. Inherent selfishness, overindulgence of precious resources, and a lethargic vision towards the future will ultimately lead to failure. In the finality, survival requires wise and knowledgeable hands guiding the joystick. Only the group I represent has the competency to provide that guidance, and we *will* one day occupy the driver's seat, no matter how many corpses we have to climb over to get there."

Mark looked the man squarely in the eye. "How can you be a citizen of this country and believe in the subjugation of its people? Obviously, concepts like freedom, democracy, human decency, and individual rights mean nothing to you."

"Oh, no, Mark. You have it all wrong. I, ah, we, totally appreciate the United States of America. Without it we couldn't possibly exist. Everything we need to grow and thrive and expand our ideologies is sown into the fabric of this country. We can operate here with total impunity. We start, buy, or steal any enterprise that feeds our ambitions. It's no problem to buy politicians to pass laws favorable to us. We wrest free money from the taxpayers. Our group can literally steer this country in any direction at any time."

Mouldier reached in his back pocket, took out his wallet, pulled a dollar bill from it. "And we do it all with this."

The former secretary of state continued, "Money, the god of ages. In the end, when the smoke clears, when the rhetoric has played out, it's always about the money, isn't it? Take almost any situation and try to keep money out of it. Nearly everything in our lives is touched by the almighty dollar. If money doesn't buy happiness then what does the lack of it buy? Try to deny that money isn't the great motivator, the catalyst that drives human activity. In the final take, Mark, I'm afraid there are more who would follow Judas than Jesus."

Chapter 75

Truitt was getting nowhere with this man except angrier by the minute. Having really no alternative but to press on, he continued to prod his host in hope that he may slip a clue into the conversation as to who his allies were.

"So, I assume the concept of democracy isn't high on your governance list."

Mouldier squinted at Truitt, replying sarcastically, "A democracy? Really? I'll tell you what a democracy is. It is but an illusion that gives the masses the belief that they are in control of their own destiny while in reality they are slaves to the few. A diversion that keeps them occupied by giving them hope that if they work hard they can achieve wealth and live a comfortable life. A casino of expectations. Of course, a few actually do bubble to the top, leaving the rest of you poor hapless souls salivating; but do you know what the reality is, Mark?"

"I'm listening," Truitt blankly replied.

"This is the real story of America. One percent of the good citizens of this country own thirty-five percent of all privately held wealth. The next nineteen percent own another fifty percent. Add the numbers, Mark. That's twenty percent owning eighty-five percent, and counting. Flip the page over and there's you and the remaining eighty percent of your equally created brethren feasting on the fifteen percent of your rights of life, liberty, and the pursuit of happiness. So gorge yourself, pal, on the table scraps… But wait, it gets better. The top twenty percent of your compatriots have gathered in ninety-four percent of the all new financial wealth created in the American economy in the past twenty-one years. On the other hand twenty-five percent of Americans have negative net worth. Can you feel the suction? And, while the wealth avalanches in one direction, fourteen million children go to bed hungry every night in *this* wonderful democracy. Do I hear the word *prosperity?*"

"So what happens when you get it all; when there is no more left to give?"

Mouldier pressed his lips together, then gave Truitt a look so cold it sent chills right through him. "The Khmer Rouge had a saying: 'To spare you is no profit, to destroy you is no loss.'" His icy look quickly turned to a wry smile. "Now *there's* a slogan worthy of the the health care debate."

Mouldier took a breath, returned to the subject at hand. "Now, if these wealth distribution facts are unsettling to you, Mark, you may take comfort in the fact that it is by no means a recent circumstance. Already in the nineteenth century one percent of the population owned almost half of the wealth in the larger cities in this country. So you see, Mark, it's destiny."

Mouldier pulled in close, a grin pasted from ear to ear. "And one of the best things about a democracy, Mark? *You* have the privilege to vote for those who will pick your pocket and put the booty into ours."

After mentally pushing a dagger through Mouldier's heart, Truitt pressed further. "So what you're saying is that no matter how hard we try, most of us are destined to a life of mediocrity at best, failure at worst."

Mouldier eyed Truitt for an instant, then placed an open palm on each of his cheeks and pulled down on his jaw. After a long pause, he carried on. "I am going to explain this with as much sincerity as I can muster. Our organization is forced to exist largely because of the unfortunate, but undeniable truth—given most any set of circumstances, human nature tends to digress to the lowest common denominator."

Truitt surmised a more philosophical tone surfacing. "So are you saying that the human seed falls far more often among the thistles than among the grain? If so, how have great civilizations thrived for long periods? How has man been able to advance to the point where we are now?"

"I will answer your question with a question. In times of prosperity do people strive to fine tune that which makes their nation great? Or do they succumb to the enticements of the seven deadly sins? This country, though a relatively young empire, is already suffering the consequences of being founded on weak cement. Foreigners study at our colleges and universities and take their knowledge home to use against us. Our soldiers are sent on foreign crusades, draining precious resources, both human and monetary, while this country's borders are being overrun. The government allows other countries to wage unfair trade practices yet keeps open trade policies with them. China, the biggest offender with its currency manipulation and unabashed cyber crimes may soon be requiring you to speak Chinese. Has your wonderful government protected you against these outrages? *We* would."

Mouldier stood directly in front of Truitt, arms extended, shoulders slightly slumped forward as if he was pleading his case to a jury. "Mark, I'm telling you, the human condition, if left to its own devices, is self-destructive. And if you think that this is a false statement, ask yourself this: Since the dawn of recorded history has man achieved a more permanent and peaceful coexistence with his fellow earthly travelers? Has he cared for this planet so that he may survive far into the future? I think not. Even as I speak, our enlightened politicians are voting against clean air on the premise of concern for jobs. They'll be long gone when your children and grandchildren are choking on their myopic vision. So you see, that is why my organization exists, to usher in a new and peaceful dawn for all those deserving of our care and nurturing."

Truitt couldn't quite read if Mouldier was being duplicitous or if he actually believed what he was espousing. At any rate Mark had to admit there was a grain of truth in some of what he was saying. His problem was with this group's self-anointment as guardians of the world and, of course, the violent means they deployed to achieve their goals.

Though the encounter was getting long in the tooth, Mark pressed on. "So you're saying that to maintain peace and order, individual freedom must be tightly controlled. That totally contradicts the principles upon which our republic was founded. The freedoms guaranteed in our

Constitution have made this country a gathering place for souls from all corners of the earth."

This comment drew a look of irritation from Truitt's host.

"The Constitution? Written by men who very possibly were drinking beer due to the poor quality of available water at the time of its inception? Men who could not fathom where this country would be today—with the exception of, possibly, one? After the Constitution was ratified, Benjamin Franklin was asked what the founding fathers had created. 'A republic, if we can keep it' was his answer. I just wonder if he had an inkling of the future inadequacies of their brainchild—or the apathy of distant generations."

Upon saying this, Mouldier stopped talking. His eyes glazed over. Although his body was in the room, his mind seemed focused elsewhere. When he again began to speak, Truitt strongly sensed that the words were not being directed to him but to another realm, one inhabited by a throng of admirers, perhaps comprised of those allowed to survive a purge of unwanted souls.

"The well-being of a country is only as secure as the compliance of its citizens to the vision of its leaders. There must be a common purpose, universal goals. Too much emphasis on individual rights detracts from that purpose, makes the country liberal, weak. And what is a weak country? A weak country allows its lesser citizens to drain resources from the more deserved. A weak country is one that is remiss in punishing its criminals. Don't you agree that chopping off a hand is an effective deterrent to theft? It'll never happen in this 'bleeding-heart' country."

Mouldier turned his attention once again to Truitt. "All of this must change, will change. My comrades are committed to rescuing the deserved from spiraling into the vortex of destruction that is engulfing this country, this world. Sorry, but there won't be any Mayberrys in your future. That innocence is gone forever. But don't despair, Mark, it will be replaced by the comfort that order and the continuance of the human species will be maintained."

Mouldier glanced at Truitt, followed by a grin. "You look a little incredulous, Mark. I realize my convictions may sound a bit antichristal; but I assure you, my cohorts and I are mere mortals, seeking nothing more than many who have passed before us."

With that, Truitt's host turned and walked to the far end of the room, signaling that he was through making his case.

Mere mortals, right, Truitt fumed. *Like Genghis Khan, Attila the Hun, Napoleon.*

Although convinced Mouldier had jettisoned his psyche into another dimension, an exasperated Mark Truitt nonetheless fired off a last shot. "You're crazy, you know that? The human will has always rejected attempts to suppress it. Tell your organization that their time is better served chasing butterflies; because as imperfect as the rest of us are, we always have, and certainly will in the future, resolve our problems."

Mouldier stomped towards Truitt, nostrils flaring. He leaned in close, placing a hand on each arm of Mark's chair. "I really don't think you get it, Mark. The fate of the United States has already been sealed. The wealth transfer is all but complete." Mouldier stood, walked a few paces, then whirled around. "If I may quote John Adams: 'There are two ways to conquer and enslave a nation. One is by the sword. The other is by debt.' Guess which one is your reality?"

Truitt's host didn't wait for him to respond. "I want you to pick the right answer, so I'll help you. How about four hundred U.S. citizens have as much wealth as 155 million others combined. How about seventy-seven percent of Americans are basically living from paycheck to paycheck. How about one percent of wage earners make more than twenty percent of available income? How about an increase in homelessness from four to nine percent while at the same time the number of millionaires has risen by eight percent? For the last four decades your fellow citizens have demanded the American Dream, whined for their entitlements. Well, they got them—in the form of inflation and debt."

Mouldier pumped a fist in the air, then pointed a finger at his chest. "We have worked hard for the last forty years to come to this point, and this time there won't be a Roosevelt to parley for the down and out. My colleagues have expertly used the debt weapon to drive the liberal socialist jackals out of their homes and into the streets! Let them march on their state capitols until their feet are bleeding. It's too late. It's over. Bleed, baby, bleed!"

The former secretary of state pointed a finger so close to Mark's face he could bite it off. "Can I make this any clearer?—WE...OWN...YOU!"

Along with thoughts of violence on his part, Mark half-expected his host to wheel out a cart carrying strange instruments and a team of aliens to start operating on him. In fact, that may have been the better scenario than what Mouldier was proposing.

Chapter 76

Mark was certainly in one of those "where few men have gone before" moments. He had been given a glimpse of a possible dismal future for mankind from a man representing a group with the means to make it happen.

Determined to get the last word in, if not for the sake of humanity at least for his own satisfaction, Mark's internal computer connected the proper combination of zeros and ones to fire off a wife-induced viewing of a nature episode Liz had insisted they watch on one of their family nights. Mark cleared his throat.

"Are you familiar with the Asian giant hornet?"

Mouldier whirled around, a quizzical look on his face. "What?"

"The Asian giant hornet is an insect approximately five times the size of one of its favorite food sources, the honeybee. On a typical hunting expedition a single scout will approach a honeybee nest, giving off a scent which will lead the hornet's comrades to the hive's location. It doesn't take long for the hornets to dispense with the bees. A single hornet can kill as many as thirty honeybees in a minute. In a few hours a small number of hornets will exterminate a thirty-thousand-member hive, leaving a trail of severed insect heads and limbs. They then plunder the hive, eating the honey and taking the larvae."

Mouldier gave a nod of approval. This was something he could relate to.

Mark continued, "Although seemingly unstoppable, the giant hornet finally met his match when it came across the Japanese honeybee. How? Well, when the scout approaches the nest, the honeybees draw it into the hive. As the hornet enters the hive, several hundred bees surround it, completely covering the hornet. A combination of raising the hornet's internal body temperature by vibrating their wings and raising the carbon dioxide level in the hive causes the hornet to die. Although some bees perish in the process, the majority of the hives occupants have escaped a terrible end. Kind of a David and Goliath story, wouldn't you say?"

Mouldier peered at Truitt, obviously not amused with the ending. Mark braced himself, not knowing what was coming next.

Mouldier's eyes turned cold, his face expressionless. "I will ask you once more—join our cause. I guarantee you the rewards will be great. If you make the fool's choice then I must warn you, stay out of our way. Be sensible, Mark; do the right thing."

Truitt took a long moment to answer. "You know, I've always preferred honeybees to hornets."

"My associate will take you back to your car." Mouldier turned, exited the room.

"This way, please," the bodyguard walked past Truitt, motioning to the door.

That was the last thing Mark remembered. When he came to he was sitting in his car in a parking lot, but not the marina parking lot. He felt for his gun. It was holstered. The evening sun hid behind a row of elms, successful in their efforts to obstruct a majority of Sol's offering, the few survivors triumphantly flickering between leaves rustled by a summer breeze. As his mind once again cleared itself from the druggy effects, events of the past few hours were replayed.

Mark Truitt had always been the type of person to take life in stride, to keep events in perspective. This encounter, however, presented him with a view of the world that was beyond his comprehension. People this sinister existed exclusively in fiction—or did they? After all, if a president could start a war with a lie—and get away with it, why couldn't monsters like these roam freely among us, secretly designing a dark future for all but an anointed few. What could he do to stop them? How far did their tentacles reach? Who could he confide in?

The more Mark contemplated, the more melancholy he became. A somber feeling of helplessness began to engulf him. Was Jeremy Mouldier accurate in his assessment that this civilization is incapable of peacefully coexisting with its members nor sufficiently dedicated to care for a planet that provides the very sustenance of life? Was the final answer the abdication to harsh overlords charged with deciding who lived and who would be allowed to perish? Beads of sweat lined his forehead; a coating of dampness covered his body. Conversely, his mouth was dry, pasty.

Mark erased the dark thoughts and focused his attention on going home to the welcome comfort of his family. He turned the ignition key. Pulling out of the parking lot he dialed in his favorite radio station. Even the treasured tunes failed him, as Don McLean was serving up some American Pie.

Chapter 77

Mark bolted upright in bed. It was dark. A slight breeze ruffled the drawn curtains. There was something wrong. He felt cold, wet. He rubbed a hand over his pajamas. They were damp, very damp. His thoughts were running in circles. Suddenly a hand touched his shoulder.

"Mark, honey, what's the matter? You're wringing wet."

"Liz?"

"Well, I hope so. Whom did you expect?"

"No, no. I mean…I don't know…I was driving home, and now I'm in bed."

"You were dreaming, dear. You woke me up a couple of times thrashing around, talking in your sleep."

"Oh." Mark started to collect his thoughts, a vivid recollection bobbing to the surface. "Guy…is he, you know, alive?"

"Alive? I sure hope so, unless my cooking killed him. He was here for dinner last night, remember?"

That reality popped Mark's brain back into place, the knot in his stomach started to unravel. "Gee, I *must've* been dreaming."

"You poor dear, I think we need to go on a vacation. All these murders you've had to deal with this year, it's getting to be too much. Even that suicide you covered yesterday, you seemed unusually affected by it when you were describing the scene to me. His name was, ah, Carpenter wasn't it? He worked for Midwest Research Laboratories or something like that?"

Mark frowned; Carpenter's name pushed the review button on his dream. He quickly shook it off. "Yeah, I was having difficulty buying the suicide theory, especially after I talked to his wife." Mark let out a sigh. "I don't know. You're probably right. I've been dealing with too many tough cases lately. Michael Carpenter's death certainly appears to be a suicide and I'm sure that's what it is."

Liz rubbed Mark's back. "Why don't you see if you can get some time off as soon as Jamie gets back. We'll go to the cabin and relax for a week or so."

Mark gulped. "The cabin? Um, why don't we take a trip instead? We haven't gone anywhere far for quite a while. A change of scenery would be good."

Liz brightened. "You don't have to press me on that one. Just tell me when we're going and I'll have the bags packed. Now let's try to get some sleep."

"I'll relax better after a shower. And, Liz?"

"Yes?"

"Your jaw is okay and everything, right?"

"What?"

"Never mind. I'll be back in a bit…Oh, and Liz?"

"Now what?"

"You know the shows we usually watch on our family nights? The documentaries, news programs, that kind of stuff?"

"Yes, what about them?"

"How about if we watch more movies?"

"Sure, that's fine. Go take your shower."

Though morning came quickly, Mark rolled out of bed feeling refreshed, although a few of the more vivid scenes of the previous night's dream were still offering reruns. And there were points to ponder with some of the real-life scenarios that had found their way into the story. But no heavy thinking along those lines today. Today Mark was determined to keep his thoughts as upbeat as his mood. He hoped for fewer nightmares in his future and more sweet dreams.

Mark made his way to the bathroom, passing by his son Brian's door. *Sweet dreams...with the exception of Brian,* Mark thought to himself. No more putting it off, he and Liz would have to confront Brian. It appeared more and more that Brian was getting into the drug culture and the time had come for the three of them to have a serious talk.

Maggie was sitting at the table, wolfing down her second waffle as Mark pulled up a chair beside her. "Morning, Maggs. How're the waffles?"

"Excellent, as always. Mom is the best waffle maker ever."

"It's more the waffle iron than me," Liz declared. "It was Grandma's, you know. These old irons are the best."

"Well, you can throw a couple my way. I'm more than ready," Mark said.

Just then Mark's cell phone jingled in his pocket. He pulled it out and put it to his ear.

"Mark, this is Guy. On the way in would you stop at the Little Super convenience store on Broadway and 35th? There was a holdup there last night. A clerk, she was just a kid for heaven's sake, and an older man were killed. Another victim, a younger woman, was wounded but should survive. Give the scene a once-over. See if anything jumps out at you. I have the surveillance tape at the office for you to look at. See you in a bit."

Mark gingerly set the phone on the table and stared at it.

"Dad, what's the matter?" Maggie alarmingly asked. "You're white as a sheet. You look like you've seen a ghost!"

Epilogue

Chiamaka arose early, all attempts at sleep this night succumbing to pangs of excitement initiated by thoughts of the miracle about to take place. She was not alone in her anticipation as several of her fellow villagers appeared from their homes and ambled towards the only road that connected their village to the rest of the world. As a group they stood in the predawn light, gazing along the barely perceptible ribbon of dirt, saying little as their collective minds were captive to one thought: this was the day promised to bring the men and equipment that would fulfill the gift of something wonderful—fresh water.

The events responsible for liberating this little village from the effects of the lack of fresh, clean water had their origins many months previous. A group of foreigners, along with people from Chiamaka's country told the villagers of a way to get fresh water, but only if they actively participated. Committees were formed to help with design concerns, system maintenance, and to promote education on proper sanitation and hygiene practices. Construction materials were carried, in some cases, for miles on the backs of villagers. Now, finally, with all of the necessary preparation for community ownership completed, the miracle was ready to be consummated.

Acacia trees dotting the landscape were bobbing in and out of ground fog, their tops resembling giant mushrooms in the gathering light. At length, full daylight awakened the countryside, allowing a clear view to a distant rise, beyond which the road disappeared. Disparagingly, the only movement in that direction was provided by local birds and beasts. Ultimately, as the morning reached maturity, plumes of dust swirling behind the rise telegraphed an approaching convoy. Soon the originators of the dust clouds came into view—trucks carrying drilling equipment.

Chiamaka took full measure of the moment. Fresh water meant that she would no longer have to lose one of her babies to a waterborne disease. For the first time the community would have adequate sanitary facilities. And now, at long last, Chiamaka would not have to challenge a relentless sun for hours each day to find the precious liquid. Her prayers had been answered, her lottery won.

And her benefactors? Chiamaka couldn't help but wonder why people from a faraway, prosperous land where everything needed to live comfortably was within arm's reach and where surely everyone must be grateful for their abundance, would bother to help this insignificant group of villagers in a desperately poor country. She could only conclude that their prosperity must foster a sense of sharing. *Oh, what a wonderful land they must live in!*

Little did Chiamaka understand, in her naivety, the terrible price that accompanies the abuse of precious resources required to provide the abundance of which she fantasized. And little did she foresee, along with the majority of her earthly passengers, the gathering storm of events conspiring to turn the tables on humanity and provoke revenge from an angry planet. The end result? Who knows, maybe a return to the subsistence lifestyle mirrored in Chiamaka's world.

The return to an austere existence, a final option—in the Anthropocene Epoch.

Sweet dreams, Mark Truitt.

About the Author

Until recent adventures took him away from the Iron Range, Dave had the good fortune to live among, and develop an acute appreciation for, the forests and lakes so generously inhabiting the Arrowhead region of Minnesota. His respect for the sensitivity of the natural environment, a keen interest in social and political events, and his enjoyment in telling a story combined to provide the spark for this novel.